Befor There Were Rules

a trilogy by
David "Tank" Abbott

Book Two
Street Warrior

www.amazon.com

ISBN: 9781701401679

Visit Tank.Abbott on www.instagram.com for the latest *Befor There Were Rules* news and information.

Prologue

While working at a liquor store, infamous Happening Beach bar brawler and street warrior Walter Foxx steps in to stop a man from beating his girlfriend. Walter wins the fight but the man's father, who is a police detective, lies and gets him convicted of assault in a trial that has been rigged by an assistant district attorney with political ambitions. The judge on the case makes putting Walter behind bars a personal crusade due to his lengthy arrest record for fighting, even though he has never been convicted before.

With no idea of what he will do with his life, Walter, whose only passion in life is fighting, and who lives by his own personal warrior's code of conduct, is sent to jail for 180 days for assault. Walter is determined to keep his temper in check as he knows that his 180 days could easily turn into 10 years if he gets into a fight since the D.A. would like nothing better than to turn his misdemeanor conviction into a felony. But when you're a warrior and are challenged to a fight anything can happen.

As he turns himself into jail and is processed into the legal system Walter Foxx has no idea if he will ever see freedom again – and even if he does he wonders if there is any place in the modern world for a man whose mentality is more in line with the knights, Vikings, and samurai of old. Conflicted internally and beset by outside forces he has no control over, Walter finds himself on a razor's edge, walking a frayed tightrope above a bottomless pit with no end in sight and no safety net below.

Walter's only hope lies in somehow getting into the new No Holds Barred fighting show on pay-per-view – but time is running out!

Table of Contents

1. A True Warrior Stands Alone

Everything that could have gone wrong, has, in order for me to be standing in the county jail processing area getting ready to be put into the high security section. False accusations from a scumbag I got into a fight with because he was beating his girlfriend led to charges being filed against me because his dad was a Sea Lion Beach detective. Then he and his dad's cop friends lied on the stand to get me convicted. The final nail was that my regular attorney didn't represent me and I had an idiot lawyer with more knowledge of hair gel and fine clothing than he did of the law.

It didn't help that both the D.A. and the wannabe-aristocratic blueblood judge had a hard-on for me and decided to make me an example for my long arrest record for fighting, even though I had never been convicted and never smashed anyone who didn't beg for it or deserved it. I'm going to do all of my 180 days but the truth is that I'll eventually have to fight some gangbanger, skinhead, or murderer in the main lock-up and get time added to my sentence and end up doing a long stretch in state prison. I might never get out. *A true warrior stands alone.*

This sinks in like a pool cue over the head as I shuffle forward with the herd of scumbags towards the far door that leads to the main section of county jail. As I pass the castle-like booth in the center of the holding cell, the deputy inside picks up a ringing black telephone and I can hear him faintly through the glass.

"Yes, sir," he is saying. "I did call you. We got paperwork on a Walter Foxx to bus him to the minimum-security honor farm. But the duty officer ignored it and is sending him to maximum security instead. He says Foxx is too violent."

I stop in my tracks as I hear this. The duty officer with the case folders in his hands who made that decision and then cursed out the deputy who questioned him stops also; his eyes suddenly wide. The deputy on the telephone waves his arm and stops the entire line.

"Yes, sir," the deputy continues. "You're very welcome. I thought you should know. I'll give him the phone right now."

He motions the duty officer over. "Remember when you said to screw me and screw the sheriff when I asked you about changing the jail assignments? Well I thought you'd like to tell the sheriff directly." He hands him the phone.

The duty officer takes it, his face a mask of white. He is scared shitless and too shocked to even be mad at the booth deputy. He puts the phone to his ear and then moves it away a few inches as it is obvious the sheriff is yelling.

"Yes, sir," the duty officer finally says. "I just got mixed up. I'll change it back immediately and also apologize. Yes, sir, I do like my job. No sir, it won't happen again."

He hands the phone back to the booth deputy, mouths "sorry" and then takes my file from the violent offender stack. He puts it back with the drunk driving folders of the frat boy and the Mexican I was processed with, who were also assigned to the Honor Farm.

"Foxx," he says, motioning to me, "go with these two."

I feel like a prisoner who has just been taken off the gallows at the last minute and the noose removed from his neck. I can handle being at the Farm with non-violent offenders because no one there will dare fuck with me. We walk back to the cell that has our clothes and I go to the security glass window with a small hole to talk through that a deputy sits behind. I tell him I'm going to the Farm and give him my booking number. He passes over my fishnet bag and I take off the jailhouse jumpsuit and flip-flops and put on my jeans and Spooner Hawaiian shirt. Then I go over to the two cherries sitting at the end of the cell who have also changed clothes.

"I guess you're going to the Farm," the frat boy says.

"It looks that way," I answer.

"Guess your mom does have some juice."

I nod and allow myself a faint smile. It pays to be related to someone who handles the retirement accounts of the top county officials. *Thanks, Mom.*

"The screws didn't get anything over on us," the frat boy says.

I roll my eyes in amusement. The college kid is now a hardened criminal. He has been in jail for less than 10 hours and is already popping-out jailhouse slang. If he tries to call me "homie" though, I decide in advance I will knock his ass out.

Luckily for him the door slides open before he can say anything else and a deputy orders us out. We walk back past the line of holding cells we came through earlier and go out a side door to a parking lot where a bus awaits. It's an old Greyhound except there are bars on the windows and sheriff's emblems on the side. *My limo to the Farm.*

It's cold for a Southern California summer night and as we clamber aboard, I see the driver is sitting in a cage. They put me and the two DUI boys on the front seats and handcuff us to bars they've added. A few minutes later more inmates walk out and soon every seat is filled. The door flips shut, the air brakes pop, and the chain link fence topped with concertina wire slowly opens. The bus pulls forward 50 yards and passes through an identical gate and then goes onto the main road. I look back at the yellow jailhouse lights dimming behind us and promise myself I'll never go back.

The bus is old but the strong diesel motor sings a baritone melody in the cool night air. We pull onto the freeway and head towards south Orange County. After a 45-minute drive in the slow lane we pass into a commercial district with lighted warehouses on both sides. We take the off-ramp and meander along a street filled with cement tilt-up buildings, made by pouring concrete walls on the ground then "tilting" them vertically. Not the best construction method in an earthquake zone but fast and cheap. We come to a guard shack that seems out of place in the business district and go through a gate and up a two-lane road towards the foothills. We quickly leave the city lights behind and after a five-minute drive a four-building complex nestled just out of view of the city comes into sight. The bus stops at the first building, the air brakes pop, the door swings open, and a deputy gets on.

"Everybody stay seated," the deputy says needlessly, like we can move handcuffed to the metal bars.

The driver climbs out of the cage and huddles-up with the ten deputies waiting outside like they're calling a football play: *Spread right, 44-dive, crush the cons on three.* A few seconds later a deputy comes out of the huddle and gets on the bus. He has green pants, a light brown shirt with sheriff patches and big biceps with a military-style flattop haircut. His back is touching the inside of the windshield. Behind him, yellow sodium floodlights illuminate a concertina-topped chain link fence. Inside the fence are portable trailers connected together like they use for classrooms at overcrowded schools.

"Listen up," Flattop barks out. "You will do exactly as I say. I will tell you when to get up. When I do you will get off the bus. Then I will tell you to walk on the white line. When you're on the white line you will listen to the deputies and obey their every command. Let's move it!"

I arise wearily as they unlock the cuffs from the bar. I'm tired as hell and not in a good mood. I moved all morning, spent the night going through an endless succession of holding cells, and now have to deal with this Sergeant York bullshit. It would have been far easier if I just would have killed that woman-beating asshole outside the church instead of beating him up and leaving him there.

We get off the bus, walk the white line, and go through the Farm's version of the jailhouse holding cells where I get a new set of jail clothes and a bunk assignment. The trailers are arranged in a square around a volleyball court and it's 4:00 AM by the time I enter Barrack M, my new home. The two cherries have been placed together in another barrack.

The bunk beds go around the perimeter and there's a pool table in the middle with a 10-toilet bathroom open to the whole barracks. I find my assigned lower bunk, fall into it, and instantly go to sleep. The next thing I know I'm woken by a flashlight shining into my eyes.

"Wha...?" I mumble.

"Time for count," a voice beyond the light says crisply.

Holy hell. For some reason it hits me hard at that moment that I'm really in jail. Now that I've had a little sleep, I take closer stock of my surroundings as I rise to full consciousness. The light green mattress I'm on is plastic and just a few inches thick. The old blanket is scratchy wool and the cotton sheets are rough and thin. I'm rolled up inside them for warmth and feel like a caterpillar wrapped in a cocoon. It's 5:00 AM according to the clock on the wall.

"Come on, homie," the Mexican in the bunk next to me says. "Get up."

I pull myself out of bed and put my clothes on. Everyone has gotten dressed and is standing in front of their bunks. I stumble in front of mine just as a deputy walks by with a clipboard, holding the names and photos of all the scumbag inmates and comparing them with our faces.

"...Ortiz, Ruiz, Herrera, Thomas, Foxx..." he says as he passes, flipping pages as he goes.

He leaves in a couple of minutes, disappearing as fast as he appeared, and everyone takes off their clothes and goes back to their plastic mattresses and wool blankets. I go to sleep as soon as my eyes close and am once again awakened seemingly instantly.

"Get up," the Mexican from the next bunk is saying. "Time for chow."

"That's okay," I say groggily. "I need to sleep."

I pass out again only to hear the same voice waking me again.

"Get up, homie," he says. "It's count again."

I get dressed again and the deputy comes by, checking faces and names against his plastic clipboard. Once he passes me and says my name I get back in my bunk and pass out again.

"Get up, dude," I hear once more. "It's count."

I arise and go through the count again and get back in my bunk on top of the blanket, my wrinkled clothes still on. I'm more rested now but still tired. I roll over on my back and see a black guy from a few bunks down staring at me.

"Hey, brother," he says, coming over. "What's up? You okay?"

"Yeah, man," I answer. "I'm just tired. I've been up for a long time."

"Well, you can't sleep your whole sentence away," he smiles. "I'm the House Mouse, which means I'm in charge of the chores in the barracks. I'll find you something easy to do. Have a candy bar."

He hands me a Mr. Goodbar and walks away. I take off the yellow wrapper, tear off the foil and break it into little square pieces, making it last and savoring every bite. I lay around for a bit more then get up and look around and see only ten other guys inside. I walk to the bathroom area and the exposed toilets. *Oh, well. If you have to go you have to go.* I sit down on the toilet right in front of everybody but nobody even looks or notices.

I check out the pool table next then go to the front door and look out. I can see that M Barrack is in the corner of the west section of the trailer area. At the top, beyond the volleyball court, is the cafeteria building next to the watchtower. The tower is ten feet higher than the trailers and overlooks the small yard. I take a stroll around the yard to stretch my legs and go by all the other barracks, which also have assigned letters. When I get to the chow hall, I see pay phones hanging on the outside wall. I pick one up and call my former co-worker, Skip, collect at Fred's garage door office.

"How's it going in there?" Skip asks.

"Well, it could be worse," I say. "I got sent to the Farm but it still sucks. Could you call Geno, my wrestling buddy? Tell him I'm at the Farm. He used to work here. See if he can do anything for me."

"Okay, Walt," Skip says. "Will do. Call me if you need anything else."

"Thanks," I say and really mean it. I'll owe Skip one when I get out and I always pay people back for their deeds, good or bad.

I hang up and go back to M Barrack and lay down. One of the little punk inmates moves my property boxes around, turning it to face him. He's way short of 200 lbs. and only around 5'10". This little bitch is no threat at all and I have nothing in my box so I could care less what he does.

"You gotta keep the boxes pointed this way," Little Bitch says. "Don't make me get evil with you. The House Mouse always points them the other way and it drives me crazy."

I look at him and just laugh. This is what happens when morons get too much time on their hands. I'm too tired to even bother to curse at him so I close my eyes and go to sleep. I get awakened for another count then lay back down on my bunk. The little bitch who was messing with the property boxes is nowhere to be seen. The guy on the bunk above looks down on me with a friendly smile.

"What's up, homie?" he says.

"Not much," I reply.

"You don't look like the kind of guy who goes to jail," he continues. "You should call this number, Holmes." He drops a piece of paper onto my bunk.

"What is it?"

"It's the probation number to get out of here," he explains. "If you ain't got no record you can stay at a halfway house. Just call up and leave your booking number."

"Thanks, man," I say. "Worth a try."

I get up, go out to the yard, and walk by the watchtower towards the phones by the chow hall. A volleyball game is in progress and the goofy fucks can barely get the ball over the net. I stop at the bank of pay phones and dial the number on the paper. It's a recording that asks me to leave a voice message with my booking number. I read the number off my wristband and then hang up. With nothing better to do, I go back to the barrack and lie down and close my eyes. When I wake up again, I'm still at the Farm. I was hoping it was all a bad dream.

It's already been a day since I arrived and I've slept most of the time I've been here. I'm glad that I got up early and moved my stuff into storage and then stayed up all night processing because it allowed me to sleep this long to get used to the place. I get up and take another look at the quad. I'm suddenly starving but the chow hall isn't open now. After 30 minutes of hanging by the door I hear the P.A. speaker crackle to life.

"Walter Foxx to the watch."

What the hell? I must be hallucinating. I just heard the P.A. call me to the watch…or did I?

"Walter Foxx please report to the watch," I hear again.

It's real I guess but what do they want me for? I walk out of the barracks, across the yard past the pay phones, to the tall watchtower next to the chow hall. The building is shaped like a vertical "Y" with a window at the bottom of the tower. I knock on it and hear a latch click and the window releases downward from the inside.

"You Foxx?" a deputy inside asks.

"Yep."

"One second. You got a call."

He hands out a phone receiver with its coiled cord stretched to the limit.

"Hello?" I say.

"Hey, Walt," I hear Geno's voice. "How do you like the Farm?"

"Compared to what?" I ask. "It's better than jail but it still sucks."

"Listen," he says. "My boys are going to take care of you. They'll come and give you a good job. Don't take one from anyone else. Just be cool."

"Okay," I say. "Thanks."

I hand the phone to the deputy and walk back to my barrack. I go past the pool table and lay down on my bunk. The little bitch that has been messing with the property boxes is now talking to some other fools about how they are going to beat up the House Mouse because he is always ordering them around. I can tell that it's all a bunch of talk and that these twerps aren't going to do anything. This is low security lock-up. The hardest cases you'll find in here are serial jaywalkers. The House Mouse comes in an hour later and stops by my bunk.

"Your job is to keep the pool table clean," he says. "Just brush the crap off of it when it gets dusty."

"No problem," I reply.

I get up and go to the door and look out. A few deputies are outside talking to the House Mouse.

"Is everything okay with the new guy?" one of them asks him.

"Yeah," he replies. "No problems."

They talk for about five minutes then the deputies walk off. The House Mouse is more like the House Slave, I realize, doing the deputies' jobs for them. He walks back inside by the little bitch who said he was going to beat him up. I watch to see if a fight breaks out but nothing happens. All talk, just as I suspected. I look back outside as three deputies approach the barrack. I start to move aside to let them in but they stop and look at me.

"You Foxx?" one says.

"Yep," I reply.

I know some guys from Happening Beach," he continues. "They say you're a bad motherfucker."

"Okay," I say evenly.

"Well I'm thinking that you'd be a good House Mouse," he says.

My new job will be kissing ass to a bunch of deputies? I can't think of anything I'd rather do less. Geno said to not take any other jobs that didn't come from him, though, so this can't be it.

"I don't want to do that," I say. "I'll just end up getting in trouble."

"You can fuck up all you want and nothing will happen to you," he says. "You can kick ass for us."

Just as I thought: they keep their hands clean and I take the fall. I can just imagine the DA hearing about me beating someone up in here. I'd be off to the state pen in no time. This is probably his way of trying to entrap me. But even if it isn't, what joy would there be in stomping this bunch of twerps for not taking out the trash or cleaning the toilets. They never did anything to me.

"I can't do it," I say.

He nods at me and they walk away and huddle up.

"He's big but he doesn't sound that tough," I hear one of them say.

"But I was told he can kick ass," the deputy who spoke to me answers.

They keep mumbling among themselves but I walk away and go to the pool table to do my chore. I pick up the brush and sweep all the dirt to the end and then down the corner pocket. When it's clean I go back to my bunk. I decide the little bitch is going to get it if he comes and hassles me about the House Mouse again. That guy at least gave me a chocolate bar and the little bitch has done nothing but cry. He doesn't come around though and there's another count an hour later. As I lay down after getting my face checked off against the photos on the clipboard another deputy comes to the door.

"Foxx, right?" he says, not waiting for an answer. "You're Geno's friend. Roll it up. You got a job on the other side – in the East Complex."

I look over at the House Mouse who's standing up by his bunk. "What does that mean?" I ask.

"It means you're going to a better part of the Farm," he says. "You're out of here. You don't know how lucky you are."

I nod to myself and smile. It seems that Geno came though after all.

2. King of Camp Snoopy

I grab my mattress to turn it in, hold my paperwork under one arm, and then walk out of M barracks following the deputy. We go to the watchtower where I drop the mattress off then walk to the gate. The chain link gate vibrates open, causing the barbed wire at the top to rattle.

I walk the white line behind the deputy and go to another building across the asphalt. It's a two-story structure that looks like it has been there since the sixties. We walk through an alley and into a rectangle formed by four buildings including the one I first walked by. It's like where I just came from except there are real buildings on the periphery instead of trailers.

In the middle of the rectangle are a bunch of trees blocked off by a steel railing. We walk up to the front door of what looks to be the Farm's main building. Inside is another version of the watchtower office that I just came from in the West Complex. I sit down on an old wooden bench against the wall. The deputy that escorted me stops beside a big V-shaped desk with another deputy behind it that appears to be the control center for the entire Farm.

"This is Foxx," my escort says to the deputy behind the desk. "He's from the West Complex."

The deputy shuffles through some papers. "Put him in bunk 132," he says.

We get up and I follow my escort outside and walk over to a room on the end of the building. As we walk in, I recognize it as the room I was processed in the first night I came to the Farm. There's a long counter with an

15

inmate sitting behind it, and he asks for my jumpsuit and then gives me a pair of jeans and a blue long-sleeved work shirt.

"These are your work clothes," he explains. "The orange jumpsuit means you don't have a job or you don't want to work or you're a hippie scumbag that won't cut his hair."

"What's my job?" I ask, wondering what Geno hooked me up with.

"I don't know but you got one or you wouldn't be here," he answers.

He hands me a mattress and bedding and my escort leads me to the East Barracks and shows me my bunk before heading out. I make my bed and lie down to rest but before I can fall asleep, I hear a familiar pronouncement from a deputy walking into the room with a clipboard.

"Get up for count!"

Seems like I never get any sleep around here, I think. Maybe sleep deprivation is part of their security plan; inmates are just too tired to make a break for it. I stand in front of my bunk and go through the familiar drill of having my face compared to a picture on the plastic clipboard. Everybody is standing at the foot of their bunk as the deputy walks down the line. This is not a portable trailer but is like an old schoolhouse. It's long and skinny and houses 75 inmates in two rows of bunk beds with a single aisle between them. The floor is made of old, polished gray tiles, the walls are painted yellow, and the ceiling is two stories high. The deputy ends his check in our building and goes off to check the other one. I fall back into my bunk and sleep through the night.

I awake in the morning to the sound of revelry playing on the PA system.

"Everybody up!" a deputy barks out.

We roust out of bed, do a quick count, and then get dressed.

The guy in the bunk next to me looks over. "You've got the best job on the Farm."

"Yeah?" I ask. "How do you know?"

"You're in the coach's orderly's bunk," he answers. "You'll see."

We all get into single file and then walk slowly down the covered outdoor walkway towards the chow hall. It's one of the short sides of the rectangle of buildings that makes up the East Complex. As I walk in, I grab one of the trays that are stacked by the entrance door. On the right are roll-up steel doors on a long countertop that are opened just high enough to slide a tray through. Following those in front, I slide my tray through an opening and an inmate puts breakfast on it and slides it back.

I follow the line of guys to tables that are bolted to the floor on a center post. I sit on one of the round plastic seats that stick out on each side of the table. The breakfast is bacon, eggs and toast with a small carton of milk. Not good but passable. The floor is made of the same tile as the barracks and the ceilings are also high, adding weight to my guess that this used to be an old schoolhouse. With so much jail overcrowding this place got overloaded and it looks like they had to bring trailers in to make the West Complex. The jail business is apparently booming.

We only have 10 minutes to eat before we're sent back to the barracks so I eat fast and finish everything. I haven't had much to eat since I arrived a couple of days ago and I'm starving. As the last drop of milk goes down my throat we're ordered to our feet and walk out in a line, dumping our trash and leaving our trays by the door. When I get back to the barracks I lay down in bed and the guy on the top bunk next to me rolls over and looks down.

"Howdy, partner," he says to me. "I'm Barbeque Bob."

I try to decide if he's fucking with me but he looks serious so that must be his name. He's 155 lbs. with brown hair and blue eyes and is around 35 years old.

"Do you know that you've got the best job on the Farm?" he asks.

"So I've been told," I say. "Now if I only knew what the fuck it was."

"Stick with me," Barbeque Bob says, hopping off his bunk. "I'll show you the ropes."

"I'm Walt," I reply, getting to my feet.

I follow him out the door to the covered walkway. The top side of the rectangle is the chow hall where we just ate, the two long sides are barracks, one of them with a line of pay phones on the outside wall, and the last side is the Watch building and library, where we are heading now.

We walk by the fenced-off tree and grass area in the middle and through the Watch building's front door. We turn right and go into a small library with bookcases on the walls. It looks like something you'd find in an elementary school, including tables and chairs in the middle for people to read at. Through the window I see deputies walk by and it strikes me that none of them stopped us to ask where we were going.

"Hey Barbeque Bob," I say. "How come the deputies leave us alone when we're walking around?"

"Were orderlies, Walt," he answers. "They trust us."

We sit at one of the library tables and it's just a little past 5:00 AM and I'm tired. I think about closing my eyes and putting my head on the desk when a short guy in his 50s with gray hair walks in. He's dressed like a high school PE teacher and he's wearing sweats and has a sun-weathered face.

"Hi," he says. "I'm Coach."

"Walt," I reply.

"You're a big one," Coach says, looking me over. "You'll do nicely. Bob, take him down to get the newspapers."

"Sure thing, Coach," Bob replies.

We walk down to the guard shack that I passed on the bus coming in, at the end of the two-lane road. The early morning fog is floating just above the ground. A bundle of newspapers is sitting next to the shack by a handcart that's just big enough to hold them. We put them on the cart and go about distributing them all over the Farm, to the East and West Complexes.

Our first stop is the West Complex where we drop off some papers at the guard tower by the chow hall. We then pass out a few at each barracks, including Barracks M, my old home. I look around to see if the House Mouse is around but only spot Little Bitch moving the property boxes around. I laugh at the idiot when I see him and put a few papers at the door. We then follow the white line to the East Complex where we leave papers at the Watch building and then at each barracks.

"Guess that's it," I say to Barbeque Bob.

"Nope," he answers. "We have to go to the North Complex."

"Where's that?" I ask.

"It's that tent-looking thing to the north," he says, pointing. "It looks like a circus tent except its hard plastic. The pumpkins live there; you know, the guys in the orange jumpsuits. They won't work or cut their hair so they put them all in one place."

We head out to the North Complex where the pumpkins live and drop off a stack of newspapers at their watchtower. It's hot there and I don't know how the pumpkins can stand it. Plus, I'd fucking die from boredom if I didn't have something to do in here.

"Is that it?" I ask.

"One more stop," Barbeque Bob says. "We're going to the South Complex where all the girls live."

We take the cart there and pull it along the asphalt path and the wheels rattle as we move. We go south to the watch office and make our final delivery. The South Complex is also comprised of trailers around a central volleyball court area but these girls are no beach bunnies. They're trashy and beaten down with missing teeth, mostly from being hookers and drug abusers I guess – not the greatest combination in the world. They look at us appraisingly as we put the papers down but I don't say anything or make eye contact.

We head back to the East Complex past the central command post and then into the old elementary school library where Coach is waiting.

"What do you think, Barbeque?" Coach says. "Will he work out?"

"Oh, yeah," Barbeque Bob answers. "He's good."

20

"Glad to hear it," Coach says heartily, as if I just made the high school football team. "Why don't you boys go set-up a softball game at the field now."

Coach puts a big box of chocolate bars on the table and counts out enough to give to all the players on one team then gives Barbeque Bob three extra.

"Come on, Walt," Barbeque Bob says. "Batter up."

I follow him and take in my surroundings, scoping out any potential scumbags I might have to take out later. We go past the East Complex Watch, where the deputy nods to us neutrally, and then to the West Complex where a guard opens a chain link gate to let us in. Barbeque Bob walks to the volleyball court where a bunch of inmates are milling around and asks if anyone wants to play softball. Guys start raising their hands and within a few minutes we have enough for two teams and line them up at the watch tower.

A deputy comes out of the watch and escorts everyone through the gate where we turn left and go through a stand of trees to a softball field on the other side. The two teams split up and go to their separate dugouts while Barbeque Bob and I sit on a bench just outside the first base line.

"Play ball!" Barbeque yells.

The two teams grab equipment from each dugout and one group takes the field while the other bats. The game goes on for a while, with varying degrees of incompetence on both sides, until finally one team wins by being just a little bit less shitty than the other.

"Is that it?" I ask.

"Yep," Barbeque replies. "The winning team gets a Mr. Goodbar. It gives them something to play for."

The winners line up in front of us and Bob passes out the candy. In a land without stores the chocolate bar is apparently king. Some of the inmates tear off the yellow wrappers immediately and eat them there, while others trade them for unknown reasons and a few stash them away in their clothes. The inner foil shines in the summer sun like the fool's gold that it is. The deputy gathers everyone and starts to march them back to the West Complex while Barbeque and I walk at the rear. The chain link gate opens for them but we keep going straight on the white line as they peel off to the west.

"Let's go back home to East Complex," Barbeque Bob says.

We pass the watch center and go in the gate, then turn left and go back to the library, which apparently serves as the unofficial office for Coach. No one is there so Bob opens a chocolate bar for us to share.

"Why do they call you Barbeque Bob?" I ask.

"Well," he says between bites, "if you ever go down to Oldport Beach, I have a barbeque joint on the corner of Second and Admiral."

"How did you end up here?" I ask.

"DUIs, bro," he says, "same as everyone else." He sits back and pulls out three more Mr. Goodbars and fans them out like money and gives me the middle one. "Your reward for a job well done," he smiles cynically. "We're off till 1:00 PM. Meet me back here then."

I walk back to my barracks while Bob wanders off by himself. I see there aren't that many people around inside, which is a perfect time to use the can. The bathroom is different than the one in the West complex. It isn't in the barracks but rather in front of the Watch office. On the other side of the wall is the outdoor yard and then further down are the showers.

I take a seat and read a sign on the wall: Every Time You Flush, Yell Flushing!

It apparently changes the temperature in the showers when the water pressure changes and gives guys a chance to jump out of the hot spray before getting a cold blast. I finish what I have to do, yell out *Flushing* at the top of my lungs, feeling a little foolish, and then head back to my bunk to lie down.

For the next few days this becomes my regular routine. Get the newspapers, pass them out, put together a softball game, hit the can, yell *Flushing*, and then rest on my bunk until evening chow. One night about a week later I get up for dinner and line up at the chow hall.

"What's for grub tonight?" I ask a guy in front of me.

"SOS," he says. "Shit on a shingle."

SOS is easily the worst meal they serve, partly because it comes with their famous limp leaf salad. I give all my food away after sitting down and just drink the fruit punch from the carton. When I go back to the barracks, I see Barbeque Bob sitting on his bunk.

"Come on, Walt," he says when he sees me. "I gotta show you something."

We usually never go out after dinner but the guard just waves us though the gate. We walk down the pathway that separates the East and West complexes and go through the trees to the softball field. It's quiet and no one is around. In the distance I can see the orange tents of the Pumpkin Patch where all the lazy asses and hippies are housed.

"From now on you have to water the softball field every night," Barbeque Bob says. "It doesn't matter exactly when; it just has to be done every night. I'm getting out of here tomorrow so I'm giving you the job. You can get away from it all for a little bit out here and just relax."

"Thanks, Barbeque," I say.

"If you ever get out to Oldport, look me up," Barbeque Bob says. "The pork ribs are on me."

"You're on," I say. "Anything else I should know?"

"Just follow the routine," he says. "I've got this place wired now. I can go everywhere without being questioned and I get candy bars to barter for anything I need. Plus, I can get away by myself every night. Now I'm giving the keys of the kingdom to you, such as they are."

The sun is dipping now on the horizon so we roll up the hose and head back to the barracks. I crash on my bunk and sleep deeply before getting woken up by Revelry playing on the PA system. I get up for count, tuck in my shirt, and line up as the deputy with the clipboard makes his way down the line. When he passes me, I look over my shoulder and see that Barbeque Bob is gone. The King of Camp Snoopy has abdicated his throne.

I go to the chow hall for breakfast and after I eat walk to the library and sit down. After a little bit of a wait Coach walks in and looks around expectantly.

"Where's Barbeque Bob?" Coach asks.

"He rolled up," I say. "He's outta here."

"Well, okay," Coach says, disappointment in his voice, as if Barbeque Bob should make a career out of delivering newspapers, setting up softball games, and passing out chocolate bars. "Okay, Walt. Go get the newspapers and pass them out and then go set-up a softball game."

I only have a vague idea what to do since I'd just been following Barbeque Bob around and not really paying attention. I resign myself to a probable fuck-up and trudge out to the entrance shack at the end of the two-lane road. I put the newspapers in the cart, deliver them to the North, South, East, and West Complexes, then go back to coach and get some candy bars and set up a softball game. My only saving grace is that not only did I not pay attention but neither did anyone else. Any fuck-up will just be taken as the new standard operating procedure. This is institutional thinking in action.

After the softball game is finished it's break time so I go to the can, yell "Flushing", take a nap, then get up for chow. It's Terrible Taco night so I decide to work out instead while the barracks is relatively clear. I put two chairs close together by the foot of my bunk, just wide enough for my head and shoulders to fit between, then kick my legs and body up over my head, sending blood rushing to my brain as I do upside-down military presses. Each rep makes my head feel like it's going to explode but I keep going and do three sets of ten.

The inmates that didn't go to chow watch me out of the corners of their eyes like I'm crazy. I finish my sets then go into the shower area where I shadow box while I shower. I bob my head under the hot water that comes out of the nozzle, pivot on the ball of my foot, and throw a left hook to the body. I switch to the right side then throw combinations. I go hard for 10 minutes, making sure no one yells out *Flushing*, then turn off the water, go to my bunk, and relax until the scumbags start coming back in. I make it through a couple of chapters of

Toynbee's *A Study of History* that I'm reading, then put on the monkey boots that I use to water the softball field.

I walk out of the barracks and past the Watch.

"Where you going?" the guard on duty asks.

"To water the softball field," I say. "Barbeque Bob rolled out today."

"Okay," he says, letting me pass.

I go out the door and down the pathway between the complexes then through the stand of trees to the field. For the first time in a long while I'm by myself. I look up at the open sky with the red sunset reflected in the clouds and say aloud, "Thanks, Barbeque Bob." I start the sprinklers and take in the setting sun before putting away the watering gear and returning to my barracks.

I've finally got my routine set and the days fly by. I get up, eat breakfast, deliver the newspapers, set up softball, Ping-Pong, horseshoes, or chess games, then go to the bathroom, yell *Flushing*, relax on my bunk, work out, then go to water the field to get away. It took me a little while to get everything going smoothly, but now I've got my shit dialed in. I ordered my commissary account a while back and it finally came in, so I can buy candy bars and other snacks.

The best thing ever, though, is the Coke card. It's like an ATM card with a 10 Coke credit that you can use to get ice cold sodas from the machine by the chow hall. I use my candy bars and Cokes as bartering chips for new boots, clothes and all the other things you can get though the underground scumbag network.

One night as I'm walking out to water the fields, a little guy with big biceps and even bigger chips on both shoulders from the other barracks intentionally bumps into me. He'd been giving me the eye for a while because I always have extra candy bars from doing Coach's work.

"Watch it, kiss ass," he says, stopping and squaring off with me.

There is no way I can let that go or else everyone will be trying to punk me. I get right in his face so he can feel my breath. "You want something you little fuck?" I say loudly, so everyone near can hear me. "I will fucking kill you if you ever so much as look at me again!"

He stares into my eyes for just a moment then looks away, drops his head and hurries off to the other barracks, nearly breaking into a run. His bluff has been called and he doesn't want anything to do with me. I continue out to water the fields and return to my barracks and get into my bunk.

"That was scary with that guy by the chow hall," the guy above me says.

"That was nothing," I say. "Trust me. I would have blasted him right there but he wasn't worth the effort."

I get up in the morning and go through count then repeat my normal routine that I've been doing for the past couple of weeks. When the softball game is over, I return to the library. Just as I sit down at one of the little desks with a couple of other guys the wall speaker crackles into life.

"Attention Walter Foxx!" the PA blares. "Come to the Watch office for an official visit!"

3. Escape From Devil's Island

I get a bad feeling as the PA cuts off. *Why me? I didn't do anything! What the fuck does the Watch want?* I ask the scumbag sitting next to me but he's a dumbass that doesn't know anything, like all these other losers. I start thinking that maybe the DA is up there and wants to come down on me; but for what? A million thoughts race through my head in seconds.

Maybe the little bitch I punked for getting in my face turned me in. But I didn't touch him so it couldn't be that. *Fuck!* I walk out of the library, stepping on the perfectly polished floor. Like a vampire I have no reflection. I feel like I'm on my way to the principal's office in grade school to get paddled.

As I go into the East Watch office, I check it out and see a guy talking to four scumbags at a table. He's wearing a cheap Hawaiian shirt with salt-and-pepper hair and beard. He has "DA" written all over him and has to be here about the night Rolando and Poppa Chulo tuned-up La Mentiroso. They probably found somebody to lie about me being the one who did it.

I think about what Barry, my regular attorney, told me: *Don't say a word.* I sit down at the table and look at the Hawaiian shirt guy.

"You Foxx?" he asks.

"Yeah," I nod. That's the last word he's going to get out of me if he mentions La Mentiroso.

The deputy behind the main desk recognizes me as Coach's orderly and comes around to me. "Fill out this form, Walt," he says.

I look over the form he hands me and fill in my name, address, booking number, and sentence. I try to scan it as I write, thinking that they might be tricking me into signing a false confession. I finish writing, put my pen down, and then slap my hand on top of the paper. *It wasn't me*, I scream to myself in my head. *You're not going to send me upstate.* I force myself to be calm and speak in my most casual voice.

"What's this about?" I ask.

The Hawaiian shirt guy looks at me with complete indifference. "I'm with Probation. You called a few weeks ago and left your name and I'm just getting back to you."

I had forgotten all about the scumbag from the West Complex who gave me their phone number and told me to call. It actually worked. I make a mental note to give him a couple of Mr. Goodbars the next time I see him.

"You do want to be in the program, right?" he asks.

"Yeah," I say, snapping back to the present.

He pushes back from the table and puts my application with the ones from the four other guys sitting here. "If you're eligible then I'll move you to a halfway house. You just can't be in for a violent crime."

He scans through the stack one-by-one and comes to mine. "Well, Mr. Foxx, I see that you're in for assault and..." he stops for a moment and catches himself. "You're not related to Mary Foxx by any chance?"

"That's my mom," I say.

"Ah," he nods. "I thought you looked familiar." He turns to the other inmates. "You four can go but I'll need to have a few more words with Walter, here."

Hmm, I'm Walter now, I think. *I like where this is going.*

Once everyone is out of earshot, including the deputy, he turns back to me and leans forward. "Look, Walter. I know your mother and she's a very nice lady. Just hold tight for a few more days and everything will be okay. The only thing is that you need to find a job once you get into the halfway house or they'll send you back."

"No problem," I say. "Thanks for the help." I get up and go back to the library.

"What was that about?" one of the scumbags ask when I sit back down at the table.

"Probation," I say. "I applied to the halfway house the first day I got in."

"Well you can't get it because you had a violent crime," he says. "I don't even know how you got into Camp Snoopy."

"We'll see," I say.

I go back to the barracks to get in my bunk and as I walk in the door a guy comes up to me.

"Hey, bro," he says. "Keep a watch at the emergency exit." He points down to an old, steel door at the end of the building. "Give us the inside."

"What?"

"If you see the Man coming towards the barracks yell out 'Inside' before he gets here," he says.

"Yeah, yeah," I reply. "No problem."

I walk to the door while three guys light up a joint and get stoned. Afterwards I go out to the pay phone and give my friend Coby a call. He's a total stoner but his dad owns a manufacturing shop and can hook me up.

"Hey, Coby," I say when he picks up. "What's up?"

"Walt!" he slurs out, letting me know he's already on his third or fourth bowl of the day. "You out already? Let's party."

"No, man," I say. "I'm still in but I'm going to a halfway house soon. But I need a job to stay there. I don't need to get paid or anything and I want to have some time to train at the boxing gym. I thought maybe your old man could hook me up."

"If you don't need to get paid then it's a done deal," Coby says. "Just come by the shop when you get out. I'll tell my old man."

"What's the name of it?" I ask. "Swapper Manufacturing?"

"Nope," says Coby. "My dad would never use that name on the shop. It's called Decisions Medical."

"Isn't Swapper your real name?" I ask.

"Well, kinda," he says. "It used to be something different. We were a famous family from England and my grandfather came here to make the big money. He changed it from Somerset to Swapper on account he was a Duke."

"Whatever," I say before I hang up. "I'll come by in a few days."

My regular routine goes on for the next several days. It's easy time but is boring as hell. In my down time from delivering papers and setting up games I find myself out in the yard on the picnic table writing dumbass letters to Shelly. She's my one and only lifeline to the free world outside the fence and razor wire. As much as it wasn't there with her on the outside is as much as I need here on the inside. I get a crazy light-bulb moment about knowing who your real friends are but then catch myself. *Yeah, right. It'll be just the same when I get out.*

Life is a routine and I've got mine down to a science. Commissary time is the highlight of my week and all I sweat is count. The rest is easy time: chow, newspapers and softball games, chilling until dinner, working out, and then watering the field and hitting the sack. One day runs into the next because of the endless repetition and I'm surprised one morning when the PA blares and announces that I've got a Sunday visitor. I'm almost certain it isn't Shelly and know that it isn't one of my crew. I wouldn't waste my time visiting them in jail so I know they won't waste theirs.

Curious, I go past the west chow hall and out to the portable trailer that they use for visitors. I walk inside and the white linoleum floor sags under the weight of my jailhouse monkey boots. I look across the trailer and see my mom sitting at the far end and get a sick feeling in my stomach.

"What are you doing here?" I ask as I sit down. "I'm ashamed for you to see me here with all these scumbags."

"Walter," she says with a smile. "I'm your mother. You really didn't expect me not to come and make sure you're okay."

"I'm fine," I say. "It's just that you didn't raise me to be in a place like this. And I never would have if it wasn't for a bunch of lies."

"I know you tell the truth," she says. "You have ever since you were a boy; but you ended up in jail because of bad choices. Sometimes I think you're going to end up on death row if you keep it up. When does the fighting stop?"

"When the smartasses learn to keep their mouths shut," I say. "Once I started wrestling and found the weight room that was it. They act out at me and then they get it. Either they try to get me physically or try to outsmart me but either way they lose. It's not my fault they get what they beg for."

"But fighting never solves anything," my mom says.

"It solves a lot of things," I say. "I just give the bullies what they've been giving to other people their entire lives and suddenly I'm the bad guy? I don't think so. They like it when they win, but when they lose, they try to get even by using the law. They're just mad they can't measure up."

"You've explained this to me before, Walter," my mom says, "but why don't you try to make something positive out of your life and go into boxing? You could make a lot of money like Mike Tyson."

"I don't like boxing," I say. "There are too many rules. I like to street fight where nobody tells you what you can do and there's no politics. There's just a winner who walks away and a loser who doesn't. But real fighting doesn't exist in sports so I ended up here. There's nothing better than hurting someone who's trying to hurt you. That's the pot of gold at the end of the rainbow."

"I'm sorry you feel that way, Walter," she says. "But you need to calm down and learn patience and self-control."

I nod at her because I can see this is going nowhere as usual. She loves me but just doesn't understand me – few people do. "Mom, I really hate you seeing me in here," I say. "I'll see you when I get out."

"Okay, Walter," she says. "I've talked to a few people and I don't think it will be much longer."

She gets up and I give her a big hug. "Love you, Mom."

I walk out the far door and go back to my bunk in the barracks.

Three more days go by after the visit from the probation guy and I'm thinking that maybe it will be a few weeks more until I hear back from him. But then the PA blares out one afternoon calling me up to the watch.

"Roll it up, Foxx," the deputy says as I walk in the door. "You're out. You're going to probation."

It hasn't been all that long so the probation officer really must have pulled some strings to get me out. I go back to the barracks and get my stuff ready and go back to the office. As I sit with my mattress rolled up on my lap a smile comes across my face and I start to give my commissary away to the other orderlies that pass by. A big black guy who is another coach comes up to me.

"I thought you assaulted somebody," he says. "I figured you were going back to the main jail once they sorted you out."

"Nah, man," I say. "I'm going to probation. My mom has a little juice and hooked me up."

The deputies who know me pass by and give me encouraging comments, glad to see me move into something better. I don't have anything against them, not like some of the city cops who have a personal beef with me. These guys are just doing a job to make a buck. As I sit in the old school building and idly look at the tiled floor that lines the watch office the phone rings and the deputy on duty picks it up. He talks quietly and looks down, avoiding eye contact with me. I know this can't be good news. Finally, he hangs up.

"Okay, Foxx," he says. "Go back to your bunk. Somebody fucked up."

"You're kidding me, right?" I say, even though I know better.

"I wish I was," he says. He's only about 140 lbs. but he tries to look weighty as he speaks by crossing his arms on his chest. "Get another mattress and head to your bunk and go back to work." He pauses for a second and lowers his voice. "That is messed up, just between you and me. If I were you, I'd file a snivel sheet."

I go to the back room where the mattresses are and grab one then go back towards the barracks. As I walk in the door, I hear the Mexicans in the back start to yell out "Shower wino!" at me. I am fucking pissed but the sound of the laughing makes me smile despite myself. I make my bunk, go out to the quad, and walk to the line of pay phones and call my mom.

"I'm so mad," I say after she answers. "The fucking probation set me up for release and at the last moment something happened and it got canceled. Fuck!"

"Walter, calm down," my mom says evenly, not reacting to me. "I'll find out who it is and what happened."

She hangs up the phone and I slam the receiver into the cradle on the wall. I make my way around the stand of trees in the middle of the quad and walk into the library.

"What happened?" the black coach asks.

"I don't know," I say. "Somebody screwed up."

"Like that doesn't happen around here every day," he says. "Go over to the North Complex and set up some chess games. Get your mind off it."

I head north trying to relax and put out the chess games. I watch the scumbags play chess for an hour and after hearing "Checkmate" a few times I've calmed down. I pack up the boards and head back to the East Complex. Everybody is still out working so I go out to the yard and stare out at the foothills. *Fuck it. I'm going to do some pull-ups.* I head over to the basketball court and jump up and grip the V-shaped steel tubes that brace the backboard.

As I pull myself up and down in the afternoon breeze my face goes into alternating light and dark where the backboard blocks the sun. At the top of my pull my arms are fully closed and I hold the position for a few seconds, letting my biceps feel the burn and get fully pumped. I lower myself until my arms are fully extended, increasing my grip, and then pull up again for another rep. The sun disappears, my biceps pump with blood, and then I lower myself down, squinting against the blast of sunlight from over the foothills. I get into a rhythm of going up and down when I hear a shout from behind.

"Get the fuck down from there!"

I let loose entirely and land on my feet and look around. A deputy with nothing better to do than fuck with me is rushing out from the watch office between the barracks.

"What the fuck are you doing?" he asks.

I think about saying "Pull-ups, dumbass," but keep my mouth shut and just shrug.

"Get out of here before I write you up," he says.

I turn away from him, not trusting what my mouth might say and start to walk the fence that encircles the big yard. I do one lap with thoughts running through my head. *I was cool doing this easy time, then I got teased with probation only to go right back to where I started.* Now I feel that I have to get out of here. I had a taste of freedom and now that's all I can think about.

I go back to the pay phones and punch in my mom's number and she picks up. "Hello, Mom? Did you call anyone?"

"Walter, I told you I'd find out and I did," she says. "I talked to the man who came to see you. He's from the employee's union and we're both on the board. He messed up. He said it was his first time to the jail and there was a form he didn't file after he saw you. The probation officials go to the jail on Thursdays and Tuesdays so just hang out over the weekend and you'll be out on Tuesday."

I feel a glimmer of light in the dark place I was suddenly in. "Alright, Mom. I love you. I wasn't mad at you. You just don't know what a shithole this place is."

"Don't worry, Walter," she says. "It's just a few more days."

I say goodbye and place the receiver on the hook and go back to my bunk for count and then to dinner and bed. In the morning I get up for breakfast, put out the newspapers, put on a softball game, and go to the library and browse through some magazines.

"Foxx," the PA blares. "You have a visitor."

Now what? The way my last few days have been going it could be anyone. I go to the visitor's trailer by the north chow hall and see my mom sitting at the far table.

"What are you doing here?" I say as I sit down.

"I just came to say hello," she says.

"Fuck, mom," I say. "I'm almost out of here. You don't need to come and see me like this."

"I was just worried when you said this place was really bad on the phone," she says. "How is it?"

"Well, it sucks," I say, "but it could be a lot worse. At least I'm not in the main jail. They call this Camp Snoopy for a reason. I've done alright."

"Well, okay," she says. "I feel better now. You just sounded so upset on the phone. You're almost out."

We say goodbye and I thank her for coming, even though I wish she hadn't. But I know she just came to see me through this predicament. I walk out of the portable trailer, look over my right shoulder at the watch building, and then go east along the white line to my barracks and bunk. I lay back to relax and hear the wild creaking of bedsprings. I look across the aisle and see an old con, doing his fifth or sixth stretch for selling designer knock-offs downtown, bouncing on his bunk like an itchy porpoise out of water looking for the ocean.

"Hey," I say. "Calm down. You're fucking bothering everyone. Cool it."

He looks at me and nods and settles into his bunk and stops bouncing. That's how jailhouse etiquette goes. Everyone has to get along or you'll eventually get your ass beat in the middle of the night. I have dinner, water the fields, then come back and go to sleep quickly. Saturday flies by with more of the same, minus the porpoise bouncing and I get up again on Sunday for count. I usually fall back to sleep but knowing I'm getting out in a few days has given me nervous energy.

I get dressed, deliver the papers, and then go to the bathroom and shave off my mustache. I stare in the mirror as the hair falls into the sink and smile at my new reflection. The clean-shaven good boy has finally reappeared from circumstances beyond his control, ready to resume his life. It's Sunday and nobody is working so the barracks is full of inmate workers on their day off.

39

One of the guys from down the row that I've given a few extra chocolate bars to comes up.

"Hey, homie," he says. "They're looking for a new worker at the coroner's office. It's a good job. You can get food and you leave the farm every day." He makes an exaggerated pantomime like he's examining my ears. "They even have Q-tips to clean your ears and you ain't got to be dead to use 'em."

I smile. Small conveniences like Q-tips are one of the many things you never think about until you get into jail and can't get them. "No, man. Thanks for the skinny but I'm good. I don't think I'm going to be around much longer."

He walks off and I get out of my bunk, drop to the floor and put on my monkey boots. As I sit on the edge, I look over to this con man on the bottom bunk across from me. He has white shoulder length hair, is in his late 50s and is fat and short. Inexplicitly, he is doing sit-ups in his bunk and I realize that was what he was doing before when I got on his case. The old bed springs sing as the old guy moves back and forth.

"I will never be like you," I say.

"Huh?" He grunts, not stopping his exercise.

"We're not birds of a feather."

"You talking to me, son?" he pauses, looking over.

"No, just myself," I say.

Instead of telling him to chill I get up and head to the library, walking past the steel railing around the trees and grass. Out of the corner of my eye I see a butterfly float over the top of the trees and get carried away by the breeze. I walk into the library and sit down at the table in the middle of the room. It's Sunday and the library is full of scumbags. Freddy, the guy who took over Barbeque Bob's bunk, is next to me.

"What happened the other day?" he asks. "You were almost out of here."

"The probation guy fucked up the paperwork and screwed the deal," I say. "This was his first time here and he didn't know the lay of the land. He figured it out so I'll be gone in a few days."

I had gotten up and delivered the papers this morning and the remnants are in a stack for the inmates. I took out the Parade section for the deputy that got me my job because he wanted the Pogs for his kids.

"The Parade section is gone," Shorty, the little guy who tried to punk me a while back, says from across the room.

"You really think you'll get out with an assault charge?" Freddy asks, ignoring Shorty's rant.

"My mom has a little juice with Probation," I say. "I'm out on Tuesday."

"Hope it happens," says Freddy. "Just don't get your hopes up."

"I wish I was out now," I say. "Can you believe this stupid fad of Pogs?"

"All the kids want 'em," a scumbag chimes in.

"They're just stupid cardboard coins," I answer. "Who cares?"

"Well, everyone wants 'em," Freddy insists.

"Where the fuck is the Parade section?" Shorty almost yells from across the room. When nobody answers he raises his voice and this time does yell. "None of these papers have the Parade section? Where are they?" He gets up from his table and walks over to mine. All the conversation in the room stops. "You're in charge of the papers," he screams down at me. "Where is the fucking Parade section?"

I've had it with this fuck. He's yelling about the paper like it was supposed to be delivered personally to him.

"It was taken by somebody else!" I stand up suddenly and yell back at him. My sudden movement startles him and he stumbles back against the bookcase behind the table. "That's it, you little fuck! I'm going to fuck you up!" I clench my hands into fists as Shorty looks at me mesmerized, too dumb to be scared or to even run away. He's begging for it.

"Don't do it!" Freddy says, coming between us. "You're almost out of here. It's only a few days away. Don't fuck it up. You'll go to the main."

I'm on the borderline of firing away. Freddy's words hang in the air just like my life hangs in the balance. All the characters in all the books surrounding me look on, watching the battle rage inside me about whether to hurt the big mouth or to walk away. I look Shorty right in the eyes, my fists still raised like the broadside of a battleship ready to open up on a rowboat at point blank range.

"You don't know it, you little fuck," I say. "But you're in the sights of a high-powered rifle. I'm going to save your life and make sure you don't fuck things up for me."

I let my hands drop, turn away from him, and then push open the door that leads to the watch office and walk down the hallway to the desk where a young deputy sits. He's the same guy who told me to file a snivel sheet when my probation was cancelled.

"What's up?" he asks, seeing the dark look on my face.

"There's a guy in the library that needs a debriefing," I say. "He's trying to start something with me and I'm about to kill him."

"Okay," the deputy says. "Stay here. I'll go check him out."

"No," I say. "I'll go back to the library and point him out. I don't want him to fuck up my probation by lying and saying I tried to start something with him."

"It's not good for you if the other inmates see you do that," the deputy says.

"You think any of them have the balls to fuck with me?" I ask.

"Okay," the deputy says. "Let's go."

The deputy walks down the tiled hallway with his black boots dulling the reflected shine on the floor. He pushes open the door and looks around but Shorty is gone, along with everyone else.

"Let's go find him," the deputy says.

"No," I say. "Forget it. I just wanted you to know he started it in case he tried to report me." *I'll find him when the time is right*, I say to myself.

"Okay," the deputy says. "You did the right thing. You're not like all these other guys."

I guess he doesn't know that I'm violent and would kill any of these scumbags if they fucked with me. But the less I say the better. I go out to the softball field to water it, since there are no games on Sunday. It's a good way of getting away. I take my time and give the ground a good soaking. As the sun sets the water glistens on the grass blades and I roll up the hose into a tight coil.

As I walk back to the barracks, I think how one punch would put me in max lockup back in the main for the rest of my sentence. Life can turn out radically different based on the smallest things. It's a sobering thought but all the same I hope I run into Shorty in the yard so I can fuck him up. I make it to my barracks uneventfully and fall asleep.

Monday is a routine day and Shorty manages to keep completely out of my sight as I deliver papers and set up games. On Tuesday I go through count and go to the chow hall. Breakfast is my favorite meal in jail but it still consists of shitty pancakes, rubber bacon, watery eggs and toast, and a lukewarm carton of milk.

"Get up and move out!" the deputy says after our 10 minutes are up.

I walk out of the chow hall door to the quad, go past the pay phones, then go to the entrance shack and get the news of the day and deliver it to all points of the compass. Finished with that, I go sit at the library table until Coach comes in and tells me to set-up a softball game. I walk the white line past the east watch then go to the West Complex and tell the guard that I'm there to organize softball for the day. He lets me in and I gather two teams together and we go out in a line through the trees to the field, the only place that has allowed me to keep my sanity in this crazy place.

The game starts and I watch from the first base bench as the top of the first inning ends. Barracks E has scored 7 runs and it looks like they'll get the Mr. Goodbars I have in the box at my feet. As Barracks M gets up to bat, I hear a shout from the pathway that leads through the trees.

"Foxx!" An orderly is yelling. "You're wanted up front. You have five minutes to roll it up and report. You're outta here!"

4. The Job That Changed My Life

Within 10 minutes I'm in a van driving on the road that brought me here three weeks ago, wearing the same clothes I showed up in. It's a smoking hot day and I'm glad to be out of the sun as we listen to FM 88 Smooth Jazz over the tinny-sounding radio. The probation guy who came to the jail and took my application last week is driving.

"Hey, sorry about what happened," he says as the gate to the Farm closes behind us, "I screwed up the paperwork."

"Yeah, I heard," I say. "No problem. Where are we going?"

"To a halfway house in Bonita Park," he answers.

I relax in the back and take in the cool breeze blowing on me from the air conditioning vent. We get on the freeway and head north where we exit on Beach Blvd. and then turn onto a road that goes in front of the Bullerton airport. As the minivan pulls into a parking lot, I see a bunch of scumbags walking around smoking cigarettes and drinking coffee. It's like an AA meeting on break. This has to be the place.

We grab our stuff and walk into the first-floor office of this old apartment building that had to be built in the '50s. It's me, the probation guy, and two scumbags from the Farm. As we walk in the front door, I can see that the office is a converted apartment that some old desks have been stuffed into. A couple of young guys are shuffling papers and they stop and give us the once over. The probation guy gives one of them our files and he looks at mine.

"Okay," he says to me. "Your bed is in 1A, across the driveway; first door up the stairs."

I leave the two scumbags I drove in with and go upstairs and find my bed. No one is home in the one-bedroom apartment. The living room is furnished with a bed on each wall with a tattered couch between them. The kitchen is stocked full of real food with a small plastic dining set at the end. Down the only hallway is the bedroom with two more beds inside. There's a bathroom off the bedroom that's painted light blue. The shower curtain, towels, and toilet seat covers are the same color. I walk back down the hallway and fall on my bed.

I laugh aloud as I lay down. The stupid Detective Dad and his pet DA stacked me up with lies and got me 180 days from the blueblood judge. But instead of six months inside I only did 21 days and now I'm in an apartment with a stocked kitchen and an attached bathroom. It's like an all-expense paid vacation with taxpayers' money. *Oh, yeah. They really got me good.* I take my first private shower in 21 days and feel the past three weeks disappearing down the drain. I fall on the bunk and go to sleep and with no count to wake me up I'm able to rest straight until 5:00 PM. It's been a warm summer and doesn't get dark till late so I roll over and look out the window next to my bed.

The old apartment building is two stories tall and I'm at the left side of the horseshoe-shaped complex looking across at the mirror image wing of the one I'm in. The walls are painted brown and the second story walkway is framed with black, wrought iron railing. Above that is a flat tar-paper roof covered with white rocks. The parking lot is just wide enough for cars to park diagonally in front of each wing. I roll over and take a closer look inside the halfway house apartment,

There's a couch next to my bed and a coffee table between it and an old TV against the wall. It definitely isn't the Ritz Carlton but at least I'm not in jail anymore. I go to the back, where the bathroom is, and sit on the toilet and almost yell out *Flushing* before I catch myself. I go back to the front room, plop down on the couch, and turn on the TV. I flip around and only find some O.J. bullshit on the local news. I hear steps outside the front door that's pushed back like it hasn't been closed in years. One of the young guys from downstairs walks in.

"Foxx, right?" he asks.

"Yeah," I say.

"If you're rested then come to the office and I'll explain how things work here," he says.

"Let's do it," I say, getting up.

We walk down to the office and he sits down at one of the desks.

"You're going to be here for a while," he says, "so every time you come in you have to take a breathalyzer. That means no alcohol and no drugs.

"That's no problem," I say. "I know the drill."

"Do you want to call anyone to bring you some clothes?"

"Yeah. My mom."

They give me the phone and I dial home and ask for some clothes to be brought over. Then I give the receiver to a small girl behind one of the desks and she gives directions and hangs up.

"We're going to take you to the grocery store now," she says pertly. She can't be over 21 or 22 and has way too much enthusiasm for a place like this.

"I don't have any money," I say.

"Don't worry," she says. "We give you vouchers to buy food and the store accepts them. We usually only go on Sundays but since you're new we'll take you now."

Another one of the kids in his early 20s who works as a probation officer takes me out to an old, white 10 seat school bus they use to ferry residents around and drives me to the store. I take my $20 voucher from him and go inside and grab a cart. After weeks in jail it feels strange to have the freedom to push my cart where I want it to go instead of following a while line. I grab some Diet Pepsi, tortilla chips, salsa, candy and other "forbidden" stuff that I couldn't get just a day ago. In jail this stuff would make me a rich man but out here it just makes me a junk food junkie.

I get back on the bus and we chug back to the halfway house. As we pull in, I notice that the airport windsock is pointing south and hanging limp in the still evening. The bus parks in the first space in the lot and I get out and head up the stairs to my new digs. I put my food away in the kitchen and grab a diet Pepsi, a couple of chocolate chip cookies, and a handful of chips. I'm in junk food heaven. I go outside of the permanently opened front door and sit on a stone bench that would look perfectly at home in Old Mother Hubbard's garden.

I munch away happily as daylight fades to darkness. I'm just glad to not see sprinklers shooting water on a jailhouse field of dreams anymore. I used to sit at the baseball field by myself and think of freedom. Now that I'm out I wonder who took over the watering and if they're doing a good job. As my first day of semi-freedom closes, I see a guy ride up on a 10-speed bicycle. He locks it and tromps up the stairs as I walk into the living room.

"Hey," he says. "You must be the new guy. I'm Richard." He's in his forties, wearing a flowered print shirt, Ocean Pacific shorts, and white tennis shoes.

"I'm Walt," I reply.

"What are you in for?" Richard asks.

"Beating up the wrong person," I say. "How about you?"

"DUI," Richard says. "Like everyone else. Did you really assault someone?"

"I beat the fuck out of an asshole that begged for it," I say.

"No shit?" Richard says, raising his eyebrows. "Everyone else is in for a non-violent offense. How'd you swing it?"

"Good karma," I smile.

He nods unsurely and then parks in the bed across the room from me. We don't say anything more so I lay down on my bed, close my eyes, and fall into a deep sleep. A while later my two other roommates come in the open front door and I jump up like I'm getting up for count.

"Relax," one of them laughs. "We're not taking roll call."

Later, in the middle of the night, when everyone is asleep, I'm awakened by a probation officer with a flashlight who comes quietly into the room. He shines the light around the place then goes into the back room to make sure everyone is in the sack. Then he leaves silently. *Oh, well, it beats jail.*

When I wake around 11:00 AM the apartment is empty and everybody has gone off to work. They know it beats being in the 1950s apartment all day with a front door that never closes. The furniture and decor are early trailer trash but at least it's better than the Farm. I take a shower and then go downstairs to the office. My mother has already come and gone and left a plastic trash bag in the office for me. I grab it, cross the narrow parking lot with my homeless suitcase in hand, and go back upstairs. It feels good to put on a different set of clothes for the first time in a month and I walk out the front door ready to face the real world again.

Downstairs in the office, the young girl that works there gives me a bus pass so I can go look for work, which they require you to do in the halfway house. I'm due back at 7:00 PM, she tells me. I walk the half mile to Beach Blvd. and figure out the bus schedule. Then I hop on one headed south for Happening Beach and ride it for a half hour to an industrial area where my buddy Coby's dad has his manufacturing shop. I hope he remembered to tell him that I was coming by.

I get off the bus and walk down a street lined with concrete tilt-ups that all look alike. I check the addresses against the one on the scrap of paper in my pocket that I wrote down from the phone book in the halfway house. I turn down a cul-de-sac and walk to the end to a building on the right side with a sign that says "Decisions Medical". I open the mirrored glass front door and walk into the lobby where a girl is working behind the desk.

"Can I help you?" she asks.

"I need to speak to Mr. Swapper," I say.

She picks up the phone and speaks into it briefly and an older man in his fifties walks in through the back door. He's a thin 6'1" with sandy blonde hair and a small pot belly. He looks like an out-of-shape basketball player.

"Can I help you?" he asks warily.

I'm Walt," I say, "Coby's friend. He said you might have a job for me?"

"Oh, yeah," he says, his eyes glimmering in recollection. "Coby mentioned you. You just get out of jail?"

"A few days ago," I say. "I'm in a halfway house now. I just need a job for a while until my probation is over."

"Sure," he nods. "I don't mind helping you out."

"Thanks, Mr. Swapper," I say.

"Call me Mort," he replies. "Be here tomorrow morning at eight."

Relieved to find something so fast I walk back to the bus stop and climb on for the trip north past Knott's Berry Farm. I get off at my stop and walk the half-mile back to the brown flat-top halfway house and go into the office. One of the probation guys sees me and waves me over.

"Blow into this," he says, producing a Breathalyzer from his desk.

I exhale into the tube and pass it back to him and he nods and puts it away.

"You need to find a job," he says.

"Already got one," I say. "I start tomorrow."

"Really?" he says. "That's great. See you in the morning then."

I go up the stone steps and make the right turn through the permanently opened front door of my apartment. Since nobody else is there I sit on the couch and turn on the news. I watch it for a couple of minutes and then another roommate, dressed in a suit, comes in the door and goes down the hallway to the bedroom. After a few minutes he comes out.

"I hear your name is, Walt," he says. "I just got off work. I'm Robert."

"I start work tomorrow," I reply.

That's cool," he says. "They get on your case if you don't work. I'm a car salesman in Happening Beach."

"No kidding?" I say. "I run Happening Beach. Nobody fucks with me there."

"Nobody will hassle you here, either," he says, settling into the recliner. "You're in a cool room. All the cellmates in here are smart and nice."

I smile at the term "cellmates." *Yeah, you're all hard cases*. The news ends and the other roommate that shares the back bedroom with Robert comes in. He's dressed immaculately in an expensive suit and looks as queer as a three-dollar bill. He drops off his purse-like bag that he carries over his shoulder in the room he shares with Robert then walks back out.

"Who are you?" he asks. "I'm James."

"Walt," I say.

"Big Walt," he answers, "With a big W. Looks like you're all settled in."

"Been here most of the day," I say.

"You don't want to be here that much," James replies. "The later you get here the better."

"Yeah," I reply. "I figured that part out. Not exactly the Ritz."

"What do you do for a job, Walt?" James asks. "I'm a hotel manager in Laguna Beach."

Ah, ha! A light bulb goes on over my head. My previous suspicions have been confirmed, as if the purse over the shoulder wasn't giveaway enough. No big deal to me, though. At least I'm in the clean apartment. We all chat a little bit about nothing and hang out in the front room. I would never hang out with anyone I met in jail on the outside, but in the halfway house I'm pretty much stuck so I might as well be civil. I pass out with the TV on before Letterman even comes on.

The buzzing of the alarm clock wakes me at 7:00 AM and when I get up to go to the bathroom, I see that everyone else is already gone. I shower and shave and have the place to myself, which is nice, and then go down the stone steps and across the parking lot to the first-floor office.

"I need to get a driver's license today," I say.

They tell me to go ahead and give me a bus pass and I retrace my steps from yesterday and end up in the lobby of Decisions a half-hour later and the receptionist calls Mort to come to the front.

"Hey, Mort," I say.

"Right on time, Walt," he replies, pleased. "You're going to be well worth the money."

"You don't need to pay me anything, Mort," I say, "All I need is a couple of hours off in the afternoon to go to the boxing gym and train. But I do need to take off today to get a driver's license so I can stop taking the bus."

"No problem with the boxing, Walt," Mort says. "If you don't need to get paid you can train all you want. Take whatever time you need."

"Cool," I reply. "I really appreciate it."

I go back out to the bus stop and check the routes and take the next bus that comes by to the DMV, making two connections to get there. I stand in line with my expired license and get photographed for my new one. I hadn't bothered to get a current one since I lost it to a DUI a few years ago. I stop at a pay phone outside and get insurance over the phone from my old agent and then dial my house.

"Hey, Mom," I say when she picks up, "it's Walt. I need you to meet me at the halfway house with my truck. I just got my license and insurance and yes, I know it's about time."

I go back out to the bus stop and manage to get back to the halfway house with only one connection and an hour later my brother shows up driving my truck with my mother following him in her car. Now that I have my truck back, I feel like I have a lot more freedom. My brother parks my truck in a diagonal parking space in front of my apartment and gets out and flips me the keys.

"The place isn't half bad," he says, looking around.

"Definitely a step up from where I came from," I reply. He has no idea what jail is like so he doesn't know how much better it really is.

My mom doesn't get out but smiles and waves to me from her car. She is obviously in a rush to get back to work. As they drive off my spirits are lifted knowing that I now have my truck, a driver's license, and a job. I'm almost a real person again. I go into the office and let them know what's going on and then blow into the machine.

"We need to send someone to check out your job," one of the probation kids says.

"No problem," I reply. "I gave you the address so they can come by tomorrow."

I go upstairs and watch TV for the rest of the day and evening, eat some junk food, and then go to sleep early. I'm up at six the next morning, beating Richard into the bathroom but not James, who has a longer trip to Laguna, and am out the door by 6:30 AM. I get to Mort's place by 7:00 AM and sit in the truck while I wait for him to open up shop. When Mort shows up driving a newish Mercedes sedan I get out and meet him at the front door.

"Hey, Walt," he says. "You're here early. How long you been waiting?"

"Oh, it doesn't matter," I say. "Not like I got anything else to do. You mind if I go to the doctor this morning to get checked out?"

"Nope," Mort says. "Not a problem. See ya in a while."

I get in my truck and drive over to the Mercy Hospital Emergency Room. Shelly has been pumping me over the phone the last few times I talked to her that she might have gotten scabies at a hospital when she was working on her masters and that I should get checked out. I would have just ignored her but my skin has been itching lately at night so I might as well see what's up. I get to the clinic and get in to see a doctor quickly and tell him the story in an examination room. He pokes and prods me for a while and takes some samples and then goes out for 15 minutes and comes back in.

"Everything looks fine, Mr. Foxx," he says. "Your skin is itching because you're in new surroundings not because of any previous contact with anyone."

I thank the doctor and go back out to my truck. I had a feeling that I was fine. This is just another waste of my time because I listened to someone else. I'm fed up with it all. *Fuck listening to everyone's bullshit! Get up. Stand in line for count. Blow into this machine. Go to the doctor.* Fuck probation checking on me today. I didn't get prior permission but I'm going to do something that I want to do today. I'm going to get a heavy bag.

I remember seeing a martial arts supply store on the way to Mort's when I was riding the bus, halfway between Bonita Park and Happening Beach and I drive there. I pull up in front in my little white truck and see Japanese characters stenciled in white on the front window. I wonder what they say. *Kick ass on the round-eyed devils*, probably.

I go in and the first thing I see is a big, black Musashi heavy bag screaming out to me, *Take me! I'm yours!* I'm like a kid seeing a doggie in the window. This heavy bag is my new pet and I must have it now.

"That's mine," I say to the Asian clerk behind the counter.

"What, sir?" he asks.

"That bag," I tilt my head. "I need it." I'm like a heroin junkie telling a dealer that he needs a fix and won't take no for an answer.

"That's just a display model," he says. "I can order a new one for you."

"I want that one now," I say. "Do you take Visa?"

"If you want to pay full price for a display model, you're welcome to it," he says, in a fake oriental accent.

I look at him closely and now see that he looks more Mexican than Asian. *Whatever floats your boat*, I think. I nod greedily and he rings up the card then unchains the bag from the steel post it's hanging from.

"Do you want me to wrap it with something?" the clerk asks, opening the door and following me out as I grab the bag and put it in the truck bed.

"Nope, I like it just the way it is," I say, like I'm talking about a new girlfriend. "Best money I ever spent."

I take off down Beach Blvd., the bag bouncing up and down in back at every intersection I go through and every bump I hit. When I get to Mort's shop I pull up, go inside the lobby where the receptionist waves me though the back door to the warehouse, and then follow a sign to Mort's upstairs office. I'm right on time as usual, and as the door closes behind me the noise of the warehouse falls silent. Coby, my friend who hooked me up with the job, is sitting in the back of the office. Mort is standing by his desk talking to a guy dressed in slacks, a button-down collar shirt, and patent leather shoes.

"How was the doctor?" Mort asks.

"Nothing wrong," I say. "False alarm."

"Good to hear," says Mort. "This is Mike from the probation office. I told him you were at the doctors."

"Mike Swapperinski," says the probation officer.

"What a small world," says Mort. "Swapperinski was our family name. Then my grandfather changed it to Swapper when they moved here from eastern Europe."

"My name is actually Polish," says the probation officer. "But nearly everyone from back there has an 'inski' on the back of their name."

"I can never keep that family stuff straight," Coby breaks in. "But I think our family was royalty that was related to the Czar."

"That's very interesting," I say. "Especially since you always told me your family were hillbillies from Tennessee."

"I've never heard about this royal family either," Mort says, throwing Coby a questioning look like he's some kind of an idiot.

Coby's face turns red and he starts to sputter out a reply but I give him a quick "shut up or you're dead" look that he's seen before. His face goes blank and he goes quiet.

I wish Coby would just keep his mouth shut. He's a good friend but he's always stoned out of his mind and talking wild shit he can't remember later. He usually just ends up getting me into trouble and I can tell this probation officer is getting ready to walk out. I give Mort a nudge.

"Walt here is a boxer," Mort says quickly, "and I'm sponsoring him. I need to have him go to the gym two hours a day at lunchtime to train. If you come by and he isn't here that's why."

Mike ignores Coby, and nods like he's satisfied by Mort's explanation. At least Mort remembered what I told him, even if Coby didn't.

"I don't see a problem with that," says Mike, "just as long as he keeps regular hours and shows up when he's supposed to. I'll just make a note in his file."

I shake hands with Mike and Mort walks him out towards the door. Coby makes like he's going to walk down with them but I grab his arm. No telling what kind of shit he would say about me. I don't need him to fuck this up for me. I'm out of jail and I have a job that lets me train during the day. It finally looks like things are coming together for me. This is the job that's going to change my life.

5. Blue Collar Blues

With the probation guy gone, I walk out of the air-
conditioned office into the hot sweaty warehouse.
Everyone wears nice clothes in the front office but in the
warehouse the workers dress in hand-me-downs.
Mexican music is blaring on the cheap radio as I walk
back to the receiving desk, which is next to an opened
roll-up door at the rear of the building along an alley. The
shipping desk clerk is a little Mexican guy who has
familiar looks and mannerisms to me for some reason.
He's sending out bundles of medical uniforms with
handwritten notes stuffed in each one.

"What's up?" he asks when he sees me.

"Just chillin', bro," I say.

"What are you doing here?" he asks.

"Just doing time," I say. "I'm on work release. My
friend's dad owns the company."

"Mort?" he questions.

"Yeah," I nod.

"What's your deal?" he says. "DUI?"

"I beat up a detective's son," I say.

"That'll do it," he answers, putting out his hand so I
can high-five it. "My name's Juan, Holmes. "I just got
out of the joint myself."

"County?" I ask.

"No," Juan says. "I did nine years in Donovan State
Prison. I shot a guy in the face but he didn't die so I got
attempted murder. I been here two months on parole."

"Guy deserve it?"

"Yeah, he was an asshole. A fat-ass *pendejo* who liked to throw his weight around at a bar I worked at," Juan says. "I can't take it here much longer, though. I've got to run."

I look at him through different eyes now. He's a hardcore gangbanger. That's why he seemed familiar. He's short and squat and doesn't care what he says. As he walks to put some papers in the trash, he has that undeniable swagger. I can't believe I didn't key in on him from the get go. It must be the bullshit of that doctor's visit, which I now figure was a lie so Shelly could get some attention. Only homeless people get scabies, you don't get them from being a social worker in a hospital. That was a big scare for nothing. I have no beef with people who respect my space, regardless of where they come from, and I figure Juan and I will get along just fine.

I walk out through the back-roll-up door and pull my truck around. In the bed is my newly purchased Musashi heavy bag. I called Skip when I was driving here and he brought a garage door spring over and left it in the back of the warehouse. I carry the big bag into the warehouse and the hot and sweaty workers look over their shoulders at me. The Mexican workers stop the industrial knives they are using to cut patterns into fabric that will be sewn into medical scrubs that thousands will wear. This Musashi is something they've never seen and they're curious.

When I drop the bag on the cold cement the knives fire up again, cutting the thick stacks of fabric into blanks for sewing. I feel like I'm in another kind of jail, because I have to be here. The mariachi music blares on as I screw the garage spring into a wooden joist over my head and clip my bag in. It swings back and forth between the cutting tables saying, "Hit me!"

I admire my construction for a few seconds then walk back to the shipping desk. Juan is sitting at the table packing a box with uniforms and I sit down beside him and shoot the shit with him. This beats jail because there are no deputies coming by to fuck with me. We continue talking as we stare out the roll-up door until 6:00 PM, when it's time to go.

I do the 40-minute drive north to the '50s flat-top apartment and pull into the narrow driveway, which has just enough space for me to park. I cross over the blacktop to the office and walk in.

"I'm Walter Foxx," I say to the probation guy behind the desk.

"Blow into this," he says, producing the Breathalyzer.

I exhale hard and he checks the reading on the side of the unit.

"Okay, you're good," he says.

I walk out the door and go up the stone steps to my apartment where I grab some food from the kitchen and then turn on the TV to a football game. I sit on the couch next to my bed and stare at the set but I don't see a thing. I lose interest in no time and walk outside and look around. The parking lot below is full of cheap cars parked diagonally, with barely enough room to back out. At the far end of the lot is a freestanding basketball hoop and a picnic table in a shady spot. The last ground floor apartment is kitty corner to my apartment and the apartment above it has been turned into a workout room. The equipment is old and cheap but better than nothing.

I'm bored so I go back in and put on my running shoes and then tuck my yellow plastic Sport Walkman into the back support belt around my waist. I put a rubber band around my head to hold the headphones on my beaten-up ears, which are slightly cauliflowered from my years of wrestling. I push the play button and *Nirvana* comes alive in my head. I jog down the stairs and run the length of the apartment complex, past the basketball hoop, across the parking lot, then back towards the main office. I then cut back across the parking lot, pass the stone steps that lead upstairs, then run on the asphalt to the basketball hoop. One of these tight laps takes only 30 seconds, so I've got 59 minutes and 30 seconds left to go. Since I've got nothing better to do I don't mind.

As I do my laps, I see all the DUI boozers come out onto the second-floor walkway drinking coffee and smoking. They lean on the wrought iron railing and look down on me like they're watching a track meet. To me they look like a group on recess at an AA meeting, because everyone is here for a DUI but me. As Nirvana blares in my ears I think how I am not like them at all, but I can pretend to fit in just to get through this.

After a while the course gets monotonous so I switch directions with a figure-eight and go the other way. This could get monotonous if I let it, so I focus on the music and go a million miles away into the zone. More drunk drivers come out and the cassette flips from side A to side B then back to side A. The hour passes and I finish by walking twice around the course to cool down before going up the stone stairs and jumping in the shower. When I get out and dressed, Richard comes in from a job he told me he had at Knott's Berry Farm.

"What's up, Walt?" he asks.

"Nothing much," I answer. "Just tired."

I lie on my bed with the football game on and drift off to sleep and don't awake until 6:00 AM. I take a shower to wake up and then climb into my truck and head south on Beach Blvd. Even though it's early in the morning the road is packed. *Where are all these people going? What do they do?* I'm only on the road because I'm in jail and have to be. It's the crack of dawn and I'm sitting with the idiots riding on a conveyor belt deep into the salt mines. I finally get to the forest of tilt-ups and drive down the cul-de-sac to the parking lot and then walk in through the mirrored front door where Mort is chatting with the receptionist.

"Hey, Walt," Mort says, looking up. "Why don't you go work with Juan in back. He says you two hit it off."

Yep, I think. *Us criminals like to hang out together.* Juan is nothing like me but he's easy to get along with unless you're a fat-ass bully, so I guess we have that in common. I nod at Mort and go into the back where Juan is sitting at the desk, staring glumly at the roll-up door like a zombie.

"Hey, Juan," I say.

This snaps him out of his trance and he looks up at me. "What's up, Holmes? Glad you're back. Least I got some person to talk to."

From 7:00 AM to noon it's just me and Juan, packing boxes in choreographed rhythm to our Mexican mariachi back-up music and the hum of the electric knives. When lunchtime comes around, I go over and admire the heavy bag hanging from the ceiling in the middle of the warehouse. It's not supposed to be here, in the middle of the workers, and looks like some strange altar to the workout gods. I look at the omnipresent and all-powerful clock hanging on the wall behind the bag. The hands have only moved a small distance on the face in objective time, but in subjective time the five hours I've been here have been an eternity. It's noon and I'm more than ready to head to the boxing gym for a while.

I haven't been to the gym for a long time, of course, but my white truck seems to find its way there like a horse returning to the barn after a hard ride. I walk in the familiar door and it's less crowded than at night because only the pros train at noon. Noe sees me and walks over.

"Hey, Walt," he says. "Haven't seen you in a while."

"Yeah," I say. "I've been in jail and I'm in a halfway house now on work release. I can come train at lunch six times a week."

"Oh, okay," he nods. Me being in jail doesn't faze him in the slightest, which I guess says a lot about boxing in general. "Let's get training then," he says.

Noe has got to be in his 70s. I'm glad he wants to train me because he knows the sweet science better than most. He taught me how to sit down on my punches a while back to increase my power. I wrap my hands and the cloth bindings are like old friends I haven't seen in a long time. Noe ties my gloves and points me over to the crazy bag in the corner of the gym. It's a small bag the size of a human head stretched between elastic cords that are anchored to the floor and ceiling. I do three rounds circling the bag, throwing left hook, right uppercut combinations. As the first round goes by and my shoulders loosen-up they start to pop, which translates into more power. The three-inch loose motion gives me the added power to knock out a horse. After I loosen up, I enter the ring for three rounds of punch mitts. After that I go three rounds on the heavy bag.

Noe's assistant, Bernie, is helping to perfect my left hook on the heavy bag. Noe gets on the opposite side of the heavy bag, face-to-face with me, while Bernie swings the old leather bag on its thick chain. I sit down on my back leg and as the bag falls back from its swing up, I turn through and crack the bag with a loud boom, putting a huge indentation into it. The rafter that the chain is wrapped around rattles and I fantasize about it being the DA, the judge, La Mentiroso's detective dad, his fat girlfriend, and every other fuck that was involved in putting me here. I could hit them like this and kill them with my hands balled up. The other trainers can't help but notice how I'm popping the bag but pretend not to because they're not coaching me.

When the buzzer sounds for the end of the final round, I pull off my gloves and go to my gym bag and unwrap my hands. I feel like I got somewhere today and moved forward with my life. For the first time since I got stuck in this situation, I feel like I'm not going down the drain anymore. I say goodbye to Noe and Bernie and then leave the gym and head back to the warehouse. When I walk into the rear roll-up door in the alley, I see Juan sitting behind the wooden tables that make up the shipping and receiving department. He has his feet up on the table with his legs crossed.

"What's up, Holmes?" he says.

"I had a good day at the gym," I say. "I hooked up with a good trainer. It sucks that I still have to deal with this jail bullshit."

"Yeah, Holmes," Juan says, "I hear you. You've got it easy so play it cool. How many days did you do in county?"

"Only twenty-one," I say.

"Yeah, I can tell," Juan replies. "You ain't beat down. That fuck that put you here got the short end of the stick."

"How long did you get, Juan?"

"They gave me fifteen-to-twenty but I did a little over nine," he says. "Once you get to state prison it gets easier. I did my nine years three months at a time. I got boneyard visits every three months. My wife would come and we'd stay in a trailer for two days."

"Oh, yeah," I say with a nod.

Juan points out the roll-up door. On the other side of the alley's chain link fence is a white building with roll-up doors every 10 yards.

"You see that building?" he says. "That looks like the joint. We would get out of our cells then go to workshops that all had doors like that. I used to make furniture. Now I'm out and I'm sitting here looking at the same thing. I can't be good, Holmes! I can't do this bullshit."

"I hear you, bro," I say.

"I need to see my homies," Juan replies. "I can't do nine to five for the rest of my life, doing bullshit to make money for others and walking around a warehouse."

Juan goes silent, lost in his own world. I go up to the office to see if Mort has anything he wants me to do. Everything is cool with him and after a long day it's 6:00 PM and time to go back to the halfway house. I drive through the tilt-up jungle and get on Beach Blvd. going north, then turn right on the airport road to the converted apartment building with its drab brown paint and flat-top roof. I park and go into the office and blow into the Breathalyzer. The young girl who works in the office sees me and walks over as I'm about to leave.

"You look depressed," she says. "Do you want to talk about anything?"

"No," I say. "I'm fine. Maybe I'm just a little mentally challenged."

"Oh, don't say that," she replies, taking me seriously. "You're doing great."

"Well, I'm glad you think that," I say.

I walk out of the office and climb the shaky stone stairs to my apartment. I put on my running shoes and waist support belt to hold my Sport Walkman. The rubber band I use to hold on the headphones stings my head as I let go of it and it snaps down. I go down the steps and push "play" to fire up *Nirvana*. I make my first couple of laps and look up. All the DUI losers are out on the second story walkway drinking coffee and smoking, looking down at me as though I was here to perform for them. The smoky poison bellows out of their mouths as I do my best to suck in fresh air with mine.

I get in my zone and keep up a good pace. I still feel good after my workout in the boxing gym. I do a figure eight and go back the other way. I switch directions a couple more times and before I know it, I'm done. I walk around the small parking lot a few times to cool down and see the boozer club looking down pointing at me as if to say, *Wow! That guy just ran for an hour in this little parking lot. Let's have another cigarette.*

I go back upstairs, grab a box of Wheaties that I bought at the grocery store, walk out of the always-open front door, and sit on the stone bench. *This bench should really be in a garden*, I think. *Like me, it doesn't belong here.* I stuff my hand in the box, grab a handful of flakes, and put them into my mouth as I look at the drunks and druggies on the second story walkway. After I while I go back into the living room and lay down on my bed. The TV is on but since I'm too tired to turn it off I go to sleep with it playing in the background.

I wake up to the beeping of the alarm clock and am disoriented for just a second by my surroundings. *Fuck! I'm in jail!* I realize. I'm back to caring about waking up again. It took a while because I was so happy to not be wakened by count. But now the alarm clock is back with its mindless message to get up and go to work. *Fuck that.* I hate being told what to do. I peel the covers back and am hit by the unfriendly morning cold. Even though its summer, the perpetual opened-door keeps the temperature down.

I tromp down the hall to the blue bathroom, take a wake-up shower, then go downstairs to the probation office to check out. The probation kid on duty checks me off in his log and I get in my truck and make the now-familiar drive with the rest of the slaves down to Mort's warehouse. I get there and go to the back to hang out with Juan. When lunch rolls around I go train at the gym with Noe, then go back to the warehouse until 6:00 PM, then head home to the halfway house. I check in, blow into the machine, change clothes, do my run, then go into the workout room.

I do some sit-ups on the creaky ab board hanging precariously from the side of the universal weight machine that was state-of-art 30 years ago. Then I stack all the stations to max weight and pump out sets of 20 reps. I get into a daily schedule and this is my entire life for the next month with very little variation.

One morning, after five weeks have passed, I get up to the hated alarm clock, do my morning routine, and get on Beach Blvd with the idiots to do the drive to the tilt-up jungle where Mort's warehouse is. The tilt-ups are starting to look a lot like prisons to me because, like Juan, I now feel like I'm locked away in one myself. I park in front and then walk through the mirrored door to the warehouse in back.

I open the roll-up door and stare out of it by myself, with no one to talk to. Juan is long gone by now. He walked out the door that was shrouded with his prison memories, never to see the nine-to-five life here again. He left at lunch a couple of weeks back and never returned, much to Mort's amazement.

"Why did he leave, Walt?" Mort asked me. "He was doing great here."

"Don't think about it, Mort," I said. "He won't be back."

6. Bimbo Connection

As I stare out the rollout door by myself a semi-truck stops in the alley in front of me. On the open trailer in back is a giant sewing-machine looking thing except 10 times as large. The air brakes pop and Mort goes out the door to speak with the driver.

"C'mon, Walt," he yells back inside at me, "check out the new embroidery machine. You're going to operate it. A guy is coming over to train you later."

"Cool," I say. "A new toy." I've been bored as hell at work so anything different is more than welcome.

We spend the rest of the morning taking the machine off the truck and wheeling it into the warehouse and plugging it in. Around 11:00 AM in walks a short fat Mexican guy in his late 30s who seems to be pretty cool.

"I'm Jesus," the guy says after Mort introduces me. "Give me one week and I'll have you operating this machine like an expert."

"Sounds good," I say. "Let's get started."

The next week goes by quickly as I learn how to set up and operate the new piece of machinery. I take off for two hours every day at noon for the gym, and Jesus doesn't complain about the long lunches. He takes off even longer and comes back to work with beer on his breath and a pocketful of one-dollar bills. Once I'm trained, I get into a new routine of operating the machine and Jesus regretfully ends our training, undoubtedly sad to give up going to the strip club on company time.

I operate the machine for the first time by myself the morning after Jesus stops coming by and then take off for the gym as normal. I get there and get changed and go off in the corner to hit the crazy bag. After a while Noe comes over to me.

"You want to spar with that big heavyweight over there?" he asks.

"Sure," I say automatically.

Noe tells me that he's from a communist-bloc country. He has a big frame, is at least 6'4" tall and weighs well over 250 lbs. His brown hair is cropped in a Three Stooges bowl haircut that makes him look a little bit like Moe. He looks very Russian to me with lots of hair on his body like a bear. His workout clothes are ill-fitting and faded and have weird lettering on them. He looks like he jumped ship off a Moscow freighter a week ago, but Noe tells me he's been around for a while and has a bad reputation of trying to hurt people who are just sparring with him in the gym.

As I get into the ring and size him up, I can see that he's big, but not wrestling big, and that it doesn't look like he's lifted a weight in his life. I'm not exactly huge myself, though, as I'm down in size by 40 or 50 lbs. to 210. I can't get to a good lifting gym and have just been doing reps on the universal machine and running in the halfway house parking lot. The guy has 50 lbs. and three inches on me easy. *Fuck it,* I think. *I don't care.* I know I'm still stronger than this Eastern European bastard.

He's standing at the far end of the ring as the bell sounds, and as he puts his hands up and moves forward, I can see he has a slow twitch movement to his style. I move forward to meet him in the center of the ring and we square up. Before I can even throw a punch, he feints left and then whacks me in the face with a left-right combination. My face vibrates from the impact of his gloves. He looks like an amateur but this guy is a skilled professional while I'm just a journeyman cutting my teeth and learning the trade.

I look at him eye to eye and throw a right. This guy is easy to hit so I blast him again. He's right there in front of me ready to go down.

"Just work your moves," Noe calls out. "Don't brawl with him."

I back off and don't hit the throttle and make it through the round and go back to my corner. Noe is waiting for me and takes out my mouthpiece and pours water on my head. It seeps under the leather headgear and wets my skull.

"How you doing?" Noe asks.

"I'm fine," I say. "Just getting some work in."

The bell chimes for round two and I go back out to the center of the ring. The big Russian hits me with a quick three-punch combo from long range that I can't block. He's not hurting me but I can feel my eye closing. I fire back but he keeps away from my power and starts to peck at me from long range. This fuck is taking advantage of the size, reach and experience difference. I'm smaller and can't close the distance with him without getting hit.

I wish I could shoot in on this fucker and turn it into a real fight, one without rules. With boxing gloves on and the rules that go with them my arms are getting tired. I slide a punch and then fire back with a combo of my own. He rolls with the punches like the veteran he is and plods forward. He is non-athletic and lumbering but he can predict exactly what I will do due to his years of experience. It's like he can read my mind. I eat another left and can taste blood coming from inside my mouth.

That's it! I'm going to shoot a double and take this big oaf down to my world. I'm going to climb the rope and smash his head into the ring floor and kick it back to Europe like a soccer ball. The thought of hurting this fuck dominates my consciousness, but this is boxing and I can't do that. These are the rules I signed up for and my favorite moves and holds are barred. This isn't the no-holds-barred fighting I do in my world. I know I'm tougher and a better athlete but he's just more experienced and his tactics are a lot better. He pulls me out of position with a left hook feint and then punishes me with a right cross when I take the bait. I'll get experience like this naturally in time.

I rifle a left-right combo and hit him but he's a professional and shrugs it off. I'm really just killing time. He is nothing special except that he has more experience and knows how to bait and counter me. But that's enough for him to repeatedly sting me. Besides my balls I don't belong in the ring with this guy. Noe thought that he was just going to get in a little work in the ring but instead he's really coming at me. Noe was dead wrong and I should have KO'd this fucker early in round one while I still had energy.

He hits me with a hard body shot and the air flutters across my tongue in the wrong direction as it flees my body. I try to take a breath but gasp like a hooked fish and can't suck anything in. I go down to one knee and struggle for air, which finally comes when I bend over at the waist. *Fuck all these rules!* This eastern European nine-ball would be dead in two seconds if we played it my way. He can put all his weight on his front leg because there are no takedowns allowed in boxing. In the street I'd kill him.

I glance over at Noe in the corner and he looks like an old, weathered cigar store Indian in front of a frontier general store. He skin is wrinkled but his eyes are full of the light you get from traveling life's road with passion and having the courage to go your own way. I get to my feet and walk back to him in the corner.

"Let's go some more," I say.

"No, Walt," Noe says. "You're not ready for this yet. You have to learn the game."

"I'm alright," I insist. I'd like to get back in and land a big shot and put this fucker on his ass.

"Let's wait a few months," Noe says. "He's too big and experienced for you right now."

"Okay," I say. "You're in charge, Noe."

I nod at the Russian fucker and then go over to the heavy bag and finish my workout. I make it back to Mort's shop and go straight to the embroidery machine and finish my last run in plenty of time to leave by 6 pm. Winter is closing in and it's already getting dark as I wind through the tilt-ups and head north on Beach Blvd. I park my car and walk into the converted office to blow into the machine. The young girl who wanted to talk about my depression glances up and her face turns into a mask of horror.

"Oh, my God!" she says. "What happened to you?"

I had forgotten all about my face being puffed up by the Russian and getting one of my eyes closed. He must have really tattooed me good because she's seen me with a black eye or two from my other workouts. I must look like I just got into a car wreck for her to freak out like that.

"I'm fine," I say, trying to calm her down and make light of it. "We did some hard sparring at lunch. Just another day at the office."

"Well, I'm glad it's your office and not mine," she says with a nervous laugh.

I blow and pass and then go upstairs and get into my running gear with my Walkman tucked into my waist belt. I run, eat and sleep in this robotic routine I have. Then I'm up early for the drive to Mort's to ply my new craft of embroidery. The newness of the job has worn off and the punching of the needles into fabric makes me fall asleep as it makes patterns in the fabric that the Mexican laborers have just cut. My only break from monotony is when a run is done and I set up for the next logo. "Central Valley Medical," "Coast Dental," and "North Canyon Surgical Center" go by in a blur. They mean nothing to me. I've got my own shit to embroider. I'll call my logo "Get Your Ass Kicked If You Fuck With Me" and put it on all my shirts.

Morning break time comes around and the factory comes to a stop. The laborers all rush outside to the roach coach and I get in line behind them and order my usual fare of O.J. with a cup of ice, a bag of Funyuns, and some chocolate chip cookies. As I sit on the curb and eat, I look at the Mexican laborers, the new cowboys of the southland, in their blue jeans and old ranch-style long-sleeved shirts. Their sleeves are rolled up and they've gone from raising chickens on their farms in Mexico to sitting around a converted motorhome eating home-cooked burritos in the middle of one of the biggest cities in the world.

The fifteen minutes tick by like jail time. I suck on the ice when I finish the O.J. and the Styrofoam cup feels like it is going fall apart before the ice melts. When breaktime ends I follow the crowd back into the warehouse and go to my workstation. The embroidery machine is still hot as I fire it up against the far wall of the warehouse nearest the alley. I run a new set of logos on the pocket panel of a physical therapy company then stop to set-up for a different run. I'm constantly changing hoops and feeding the machine because each run only lasts around 10 minutes. As I put a new stack of fabric into a hoop Coby comes out of the office and walks over to me.

"Fuck, Coby," I say. "I'm getting pissed off at this bullshit. Don't get me wrong, this beats jail, but if I didn't have to do it I wouldn't."

"I hear that," says Coby. "What is up with your face?"

"I sparred with a big Russian fuck who took me to school," I say.

"Really?" Coby asks. He's not used to seeing me get bashed up.

"No big deal," I say. "I would fuck him up if we were playing by my rules and didn't wear gloves and could fight on the ground."

"Oh, shit," says Coby. "That reminds me. You know that No Holds Barred fighting show?"

"Yeah," I say. "I watched the first one with my dad a year ago."

"Well, Bimbo fought in the last show," Coby explains.

"Who's that?" I ask.

"You know him," Coby insists. "He's from Happening Beach."

"No, I don't." I know all the streetfighters in my town and this Bimbo is not one of them.

"Yeah, you do," Coby continues. "He's the big Samoan bouncer at Bar 2095."

"Never met the guy," I say honestly. I'm drawing a complete blank. I would have known if someone from Happening Beach fought in that show.

"It happened while you were in jail," Coby says. "He's the bouncer that has the huge arms and always wears the denim vest. He always gets you a table and is very respectful; calls you 'Mr. Foxx.'"

A light goes on and the guy's face pops up in front of me. "Oh, yeah. I know. The dude from Hawaii."

"Well, if he did it then why can't you?" Coby says.

I think back to the show I watched and how the little PJ guy beat everyone. "I think it's an inside deal," I say. "They aren't just letting anyone in, just the people the PJ guy can beat. It isn't on the complete up and up."

"Do you think it's real fighting?" Coby asks.

"Yeah," I say, "but they match people up like in boxing so certain people have an advantage. What about Bimbo? Did he win?"

"No, "Coby says. "He lost his first fight."

"Well there ya go," I say.

"But if you could fight in it would you do it?" Coby asks.

"Absolutely," I nod. "They wouldn't even have to pay me."

"I met somebody," Coby says. "I think I can get you in."

7. Short Timing

I look at Coby hard, trying to see if he's been getting more stoned than usual. How could he get me into that fighting show on TV? He sees the doubt on my face and smiles.

"Look, Walt," he continues. "I know you're thinking that I don't know shit. The whole reason I brought this up is because I took some tee shirts over to a place to get them screen printed yesterday and this guy in front of me was making No Holds Barred shirts."

"Yeah?" I say, suddenly getting interested.

"Yep," Coby says. "I started talking to him and then mentioned you and he said he would give me an application. He even gave me the number of the guy who runs the show."

I'm actually listening now, because with Coby and his big mouth hooking up with a total stranger is not only possible but probable. The guy will talk to anyone.

"The person to talk to is Bart Shady," Coby continues. "He calls himself Big Bart."

"I thought the little Mexican guys in PJs run it," I say.

"Nope," Coby replies. "Big Bart is telling everyone that he's the man."

"If you think you can get me in then do it," I say. "I don't think you can. It has to be harder than that. But if you do then I'll fight, no problem."

"Okay, Walt," Coby says. "Let me make some more calls and ask around. Have a good workout at the gym."

"Yeah, okay," I say.

I walk over with him to get a drink out of the water cooler by the door and the blast of cold air coming from the office feels so good. The door shuts and the cold air disappears and I go back to the embroidery machine that has taken over my life and put in the next set of hoops. Mort has been out hustling all kinds of stitching jobs for the machine. I don't even look at the logo, just another start-up company that's doomed to fail, yet here I am putting a logo on the pocket of their trendy jeans.

Lunch comes around and I head over to the gym and my endless routine. I lose track of the calendar as the weeks fly by and my life stays stuck in one place. The days get shorter and Fall is just around the corner and my hour runs in the parking lot are now done in complete darkness. We get a constant stream of new inmates and there is a new one from another room who came in a few days ago who hasn't learned to leave me alone yet.

He looks like a fat hillbilly and is barrel-chested with a big forehead and stringy blond hair. He's only been here for a couple days and acts like he runs the place, like this dump is worth running. It doesn't bother me because I'm only here at night for a few hours to eat, run, and then sleep. The fact that I work out seems to bother this fuck, though, and he makes a point of coming down and getting in my way when I jog. Sure enough, as I go around my makeshift track, he comes down pretending to go to the office and steps in front of me and slows down almost to a stop. I swerve to avoid him and almost trip on the asphalt.

Despite my best efforts to ignore this scumbag, my frustration is catching up with me. Each lap on this little patch of asphalt is getting tighter and for some reason this idiot keeps crossing my path and making me run around him. He finally steps in front of me one time too many and I don't change course and run into him, sending him flying a couple of feet. I take off my headphones and walk up to him. Above me, the gallery of watchers on the second floor have gone silent.

"Watch out where you're going, you dumb fuck," I say. "I will take you out if you keep bothering me. You don't know who you're fucking with."

"Oh, no," he laughs, looking up and playing to the gallery of DUI boys. "I'm so scared." Nevertheless, he moves out of my way.

I continue on my run but I can't get too far away from him because the parking lot is really tight. He stands off to the side and I can tell he's thinking about it, but he keeps his distance and I just ignore him and finish my run. After taking my cool-down walk, I go into the second-floor apartment that has been changed into a workout room. The doors and windows are open and I can see the DUI boys looking at me with the Hillbilly fuck.

I go up to the old shaky bench and stack weights on bar. A few weeks ago, I brought over some more 45 lb. plates to have enough weight to work out with in this place. They're tilted up against the arms that hold the cold iron bench in place. I warm up with 225 lb. reps then load up the bar to 405 lbs. That's as high as I ever go because I have no training partners and there's no lift-off or spotter if anything goes wrong. I weigh less than 215 lbs. right now, which is light for me, and I'm not at my strongest by a long shot. I settle under the bar, take a sharp intake of breath, and start pumping out sets of three reps at 405 lbs. From across the walkway I hear a rebel yell split the night.

"Woohee!" the Hillbilly is screaming. "Did you see that? What the hell were you assholes doing telling me to mess with him? Was that some kind of joke on the new guy? He's unbelievable. He's not from this world. Did you see how much weight he's lifting? I'm an idiot to listen to you losers. He could kill me with one hand!"

I hear laughter erupt around him from the coffee-drinking cigarette-smoking DUIers. *I still might kill you*, I think. I finish my lift and go back to my apartment and fall into bed. I'm getting angrier and angrier as the weeks go by and I stick to my forced routine. The halfway house and the job are really getting on my nerves. I go to sleep and get up and make it to work at my normal time. I'm early to the warehouse, as usual, and I fire up the radio and turn it to KROQ for some alternative rock then turn on my machine and start my embroidery runs.

Within an hour the Mexican laborers come in to start their shift and the fabric knives come alive as they start on their patterns. Paco, the *jefe* of the crew, comes in. He walks across the warehouse, reaches up to the shelf that holds the radio, and turns it down to a lower frequency, sending mariachi music blasting into the warehouse. *Oh, fuck no. That is not going to happen.*

I walk over to the shelf and twist the radio dial back to alternative music. "I was here first," I say.

He walks back around his table where he cuts patterns for a living. "Fuck you, *ese*," he mumbles under his breath.

"No, fuck you!" I say loudly. He has crossed the line with me.

He takes a step back into his table. He's a skinny 175 lbs. and around 40 years old with black hair brushed straight back. I move close to him until I'm a foot away.

His eyes dart from side to side like a trapped animal and I can tell he's scared. He glances down at the tools on his table.

There's a metal ruler, a paper pattern, and big fabric scissors. His eyes get larger as the scissors register on his brain. His hand reaches down as slowly as his thoughts and he touches it. The scissors are open and the blades are sharp and gleaming. He makes a sudden move to grab them and I blast him in the chest with a straight right body shot, not wanting to leave a mark.

The warehouse echoes from the force of the blow and he crumbles to the floor with a gasp as the air leaves his body. I move on top of him with my knees on his collar bone and hold my fist six inches above his face. The whites of his eyes are filled with tears now.

"Don't even think of trying to stab me, Paco," I say, "or I will fucking kill you. I'm not here for much longer so you better stay away from me. I'm not like you and you have no fucking idea what I can do."

I leave him on the floor and walk back to my machine, which is still punching holes in the denim fabric. I keep watch on Paco out of the corner of my eye to make sure he doesn't rush me from behind. He may run the warehouse but he doesn't run me. The embroidery run finishes and I pull the hoops out and push the trendy blue jean fabric onto the round plastic holders. I push the start button and the needles start to jump again.

Paco finally pulls himself off the floor as the other workers gather around him. There is a look of fury on his face and he's in kill mode. I turn to face him and cross my arms across my chest. Our eyes meet and he suddenly bursts into tears. That's it. I've taken control. I won't have to worry about him again. I take my eyes off him and concentrate on my machine. A few minutes later Mort comes out and walks over to me.

"Walt," he says. "What is going on here?"

I'm not a snitch, like Paco is apparently, and don't want to give away too much information. "Just a squabble about the radio," I say, leaving out the part about Paco and the scissors. There's no blood because I didn't hit him in the face, so there's nothing anyone can do to me.

"You guys come into the office," Mort says.

We walk up the stairs to the office and it's like the first day I was there, when the probation officer was sitting at the desk.

"Paco," Mort says, "Walt is only going to be here for a little while more so lay off him."

"Walt," Mort says, "Will you please apologize to Paco."

"Sure, Mort," I say. Because I've already won, it isn't worth my time to make a big deal out of this. "Sorry about the misunderstanding, Paco."

The tears clear up from his watery eyes and he nods and wipes his face and we shake hands. He's back to being the man in charge and his self-respect has been restored because the boss man has sided with him. In his simple mind the status quo has been restored. As he walks by me to go out the door I whisper, "Fuck with me and I'll kill you."

The look of doubt returns to his eyes and his head goes down and he slides past me.

"Did Walt say anything just now, Paco?" Mort asks sharply.

Paco pauses, shakes his head, and leaves the room. I follow him down and go back to my machine. This work bullshit is getting to me and I'm about to explode. I know it's better than jail and I'm short timing, but I'm not sure I can make it without going off on somebody. Back in the warehouse I start another run. Nobody has changed to radio back to mariachi music so one good thing came out of this at least.

The halfway house routine continues night after night. Sunday rolls around and I sit in the apartment watching football. My only day off is my only day in this place and it sucks being here. I get a sudden urge and go downstairs where the bus is loading up to go to the grocery store. There are two groups going and I hop on with the first load. As I get in almost all of the seats are taken so I sit up front near the door.

"Shit, man," says a Mexican voice behind me, "I can't see no more."

I ignore the comment and keep staring ahead as we are driven to the store. As I get down off the bus, I see a border brother get up out of the seat behind me and follow me. *What the fuck?* He is short, fat and has a dark complexion. He's wearing the old south-of-the-border ranch clothes that I know all too well from Mort's warehouse. I walk ahead of him and into the store and grab the first cart I come to. As I stop between the snack and drink aisles, deciding which one to go down first, he comes up behind me and grabs the front handle of the cart and tries to wheel it away. His elbow pushes into my arm as he tries to take my shopping cart. I reach across the cart and grab the tops of his fingers and squeeze them together. I feel his bony fingers crack as I bend them back.

"Listen, fucker," I say. "Let go of my basket before I kill you."

He glares at me like he wants to do something but I just squeeze his fingers even harder and his glare of defiance turns into a grimace of pain. He sees the seriousness in my eyes and releases the handle. He backs off and I turn and go down the snack aisle. *I can't believe this little fuck. I'm short timing and he wants to give me grief.* I force myself to forget it and go up and down the store aisles. I start at one end and end up at the far side where the fruit section is. I grab some bananas and head towards check-out. Ahead of me, pushing his cart along an intersecting aisle is the border brother.

I change course and follow him into the produce section where the vegetables are. I conceal myself behind a pile of corn and wait patiently until my target comes out from behind the other side of the corn display. I start to push quietly and the wheels on my cart begin to vibrate. I make a sudden burst and T-bone his cart, causing the cart handle to vibrate in my hands and making him lose his balance and fall flat on his ass. As I stand silently over him, he gets up and pushes his cart towards the safety of frozen foods to get away.

I check out at the register then get on the bus to wait for the short ride back to the halfway house. As I sit quietly in the back, the border brother comes out of the store with the black guy who works for probation and is escorting us. They talk for a minute by the door and then the probation guy turns and walks up the bus stairs and down the aisle between the bench seats.

"What happened, Walt?" he asks.

"Nothing happened," I say calmly.

"I know you're almost out of here," he says. "Your papers came in and you're gone tomorrow. Just don't fuck up on your last night."

I try to stay calm and tell myself its almost over when he tells me I'm getting out tomorrow. "I'm cool," I say. "Just keep that fucker at the front of the bus."

The probation guy raises an eyebrow at me and nods. He walks out and brings the border brother into the bus and puts him in the front row. Traffic has built up while we were inside and the drive back takes a while. When we finally pull up, I grab my plastic bags and the weight of the groceries makes the handles cut into my hands. I walk up the stone stairs one more time and pack my food into the cupboards. I watch some TV and eat some cookies and chips and then finally lay down in bed. *I'm out of here in the morning*, I think over and over. I don't fall asleep until late.

I awake in the morning to the alarm clock, a little tired but more than happy to be out of here. I shower, dress, and pack my few belongings and walk down the stairs for the last time. I walk across the small parking lot and go into the office with my garbage bag of clothes under my arm. The probation kid on duty hands me some papers and I sign them and give them back.

"That's it," he says, filing the papers away. "You've done 120 of your 180 days and are free to go."

I walk to my truck, throw my clothes in the back, and open the driver's door and get in. It seems like any other day except I'm not going to Mort's anymore and I'm never coming back here. I shift into reverse and back out of my diagonal space. As I pull forward and go past the office window, I see the girl who had asked me if I was depressed. I look at her, smile, and wave goodbye.

8. Dog Daze

I can hardly believe it but I'm free. It's getting close to
Thanksgiving and I'm just thankful that my ass isn't in
jail anymore. I head down Beach Blvd. past the freeway
going south, and almost turn towards Mort's warehouse
from force of habit. I make a couple of familiar turns, and
pull up in my parent's driveway. I use my keys to get in
and as the door opens, I hear Adolf's paws on the
hallway tile.

"There's my boy," I say, bending down and slapping
my hands together. "Daddy's back!"

He runs to my arms and I give him a hard squeeze.
When I let him go, he backs away from me and circles
twice. He moves off, stops, looks over his shoulder, and
then walks away from me, obviously pissed that I left
him for so long. When I went in, he weighed 70 lbs. and
now that I'm back he is at least 100 lbs. I surmise that
every time my dad ate, so did he. *Fuck it*. That's just the
way it is. One hundred and twenty days and everything
has changed, yet at the same time nothing has changed.

As I walk further into the house I grew up in, Adolf
turns to the right, into the hallway, and lumbers back to
my old bedroom. The kitchen, on the left, is always
stocked with food, and the small dining room is clean and
tidy. With no other real options, I guess I'm staying here
for a while. I moved out three-and-a-half years ago and
now that I'm back my dog doesn't even like me. I go
down the hallway into my old room and Adolf is laying
on what is now apparently the guest bed.

All traces of me have been obliterated and the walls are covered with pastel wallpaper, and flowery sheets and a pink bedspread on the bed. *Oh, fuck no,* I think. *I can't stay here.* I go out to the garage to look at the stuff I stored there when I went to jail and it hasn't been touched. I look and see that there is a lot of room since my parents don't park their cars in it. *Problem solved!* I spend the rest of the morning moving things against the walls and then assembling my bed. Once it's set up, I block it off with big 8' x 4' plywood panels for privacy so my mom can do the laundry without bothering me. I'm out with the rodents but the decor is much more to my liking.

Noon is approaching quickly so I consider heading out to the boxing gym. I've been literally running in circles for 99 days in the halfway house parking lot, and with nothing else to do besides jog I'm now under 215 lbs. The last thing I need to do on my first day out is to work out even more. *Fuck it,* I decide. *I'm not going to the gym today.* I'm free from my nine-to-five routine and I'm calling the shots again.

Now that I've gotten my bed ready for a late-night landing I jump into my truck and take the residential highway to the grocery store following my old marching path to get supplies. Inside nothing has changed as I go up an aisle to the red cups, down a few rows to where the cranberry juice is, across to grab the Stoli handle, then make a quick left for ice on my way to the checkout to cool everything down. The steps in and out of the store haven't gotten any shorter or longer. As I walk out my heart pounds harder; it's good to be free. I go across the asphalt parking lot, get in my truck, and mix a drink over the ice sitting on the bottom of the red plastic cup. The mixture circles to the right as I slosh it around and the siren comes alive. I put my mouth on the rim, feel the ice bang against my fake teeth and slam it down. I'm finally free to chase another adventure.

I pull out of the parking lot with The Doors playing on the dashboard CD deck. I hit a bump and it skips to the end of the track: *Do you remember when we were in Africa?* Listening to a song about another place makes me wonder what is going on with everyone. I already know what those fucking nobodies have been up to, though, fucking nothing. Park me in jail, make me miss 120 days of life, and when I get out no one has done anything.

My truck bounces as I turn onto Beach Blvd., just like my life is bouncing back now that I'm out and freedom has landed on me. My first rooster goes down smoothly. *It's been a long time, friend.* My life has been pure boredom since I went in. Jail, or any kind of incarceration, mainly consists of being bored as hell all the time. It's not the life I chose but that was where the story led me. I pull into the driveway, park next to my dad's boat, and get out and go in the front door. Adolf is laying on the couch in the living room.

"I'm back, boy," I say.

He lifts his head up but doesn't move, as if to say, *Really?*

"Come on, Adolf," I say. "Let's go."

His tail beats on the sofa and he starts to stretch but then loses his balance because he's so heavy and falls off the couch. He gets up sheepishly and walks in my direction.

"Come on, boy," I encourage him. "We're going out. Don't worry. I'm here to stay. What happened to you? We traded places. You're fat now and I'm skinny."

I plant a big wet kiss on his big black snout just like I used to and he gets all excited and jumps around playfully. I go towards the open front door and he follows me out to the truck where he climbs into his usual place, on the shotgun side of the cloth bench seat. I roll the window down and pull out onto the street and just start to cruise the residential highway. As the sun disappears and the miles climb higher on the odometer so does the level of my buzz. Soon it's completely dark and I stop at a red light and look over to my happy passenger.

"I fucking love you, crazy dog," I laugh.

He looks back at me over his shoulder and his far black eyeball shines over the top of his black snout. His mouth is open from panting against the blast of air from the open window. He barks at me once then turns back to the canine big screen TV that starts to play for him again as the light turns green.

"Quit barking," I say. "I'm here to stay."

I've got a good buzz on and mix another freshy as I drive. After a while an idea pops into my head.

"Let's go to Sea Lion Beach," I say to Adolf, who doesn't turn around this time. "Let's look for the fuck who did this to us. You can bite out his throat and I'll club him to death."

We drive by Jerome's house slowly. The curtains are open and a light is on but I can see it's empty inside with no furniture at all. It's obvious no one is living there. I look at the clock on the dash and see that its 2:00 AM. I've been running hard with Adolf all day, for at least 12 hours, and it's time to go home while I can still stand up.

I drive home, park on the street and stumble in the front door with Adolf waddling after me. It's my first day out in 120 days and I spent it with my best friend.

I go through the kitchen and out to the unfinished garage where my plywood castle is. I fall back into the huge bed named after a king and stare up at the rafters. I close my eyes and see light shutters in my eyelids. My head starts to swim and the bed begins to move under me. I haven't bought a ticket on this ride in four months and I laugh at the intensity of the flashes. I pull some pillows under my legs and get them higher than my head and the flashes stop and the ride ends. I close my eyes and pass out with Adolf's head on my stomach.

The next thing I know I'm waking up to the sound of the gardener's lawnmower in the front yard. It quits after a little while and then I hear the equipment being loaded into his truck parked just outside the swing up garage door. The sun is waking my hung-over ass up as it streams in the green stained-glass window on the side of the garage. I roll over and my old friend is just where I left him, sleeping happily under my wing. I squeeze the fur on top of his head and get a low growl in return.

"That's right, Adolf," I laugh. "Daddy's back."

I roll out of bed and walk into the kitchen through the door off the garage and eat some white bread to settle my stomach. Then I go down the hallway and shower and dress. By the time I'm back in the kitchen drinking juice it's 11:00 AM and time to go to the boxing gym. It's my second day home and Adolf is looking at me with his tail down and a sad look on his face. *Fuck it.* A little time off from training is not going to kill me.

"Come on, boy," I say, which starts his tail wagging. "Let's go have some fun."

We head outside to the truck and go to the grocery store where I take my measured march through the aisles, then check out and mix a rooster in the parking lot. I do a slow cruise down the residential highway and get one down the hatch. I pull over and let Adolf out and mix a freshy while he checks out the nearest fire hydrant. When he's had a good sniff, I head down the familiar path to Mort's warehouse among the valley of tilt-ups and park in the driveway. Now that I don't work there, the front office doesn't seem so ominous when I open it. I walk to the front desk where a new Mexican girl is working, and ask for Coby. She speaks into a phone intercom on her desk and Coby comes out of the back a moment later. He is so stoned he can barely keep his bug eyes open and walks right past me.

"Hey, Coby," I say, grabbing his arm. "It's noon. Let's go get some lunch."

He notices me for the first time and looks over to the receptionist. "Tell whoever it was that wanted to see me that I'll be out for lunch."

I leave Adolf in the truck with the window cracked open and we go to a local burger joint in Coby's truck and sit down at a free table. Coby has smoked so much over the years that he is frozen into a permanent adolescent state. He orders a teriyaki bowl and is surprised when it shows up because he doesn't even like rice. I want to talk to him but he is oblivious to the world. His face is two inches from the bowl as he picks out the chicken and eats it separately. He has no idea what is going on.

"Hey, Coby," I say.

"Hey, what?" He answers slowly.

"Never mind, dude," I answer.

I grab the paper and read the news of the day as I eat my burger in silence. We finish lunch and go back to his office and I climb out of his white dually one-ton truck that he uses to tow his racing powerboats. Mort makes good money at the warehouse and so Coby has all the toys a boy could ask for. I leave Coby sitting in stoned silence in the driver's seat and as I walk past his open window to get to my truck, he asks me if I want to go to lunch again.

"No, bro," I say. "I'm not hungry."

It's early and I'm looking for fun so I drop off Adolf at home and cruise down PCH. I head north towards LA with no real destination in mind and go past Wong Beach State. I see a seedy place off to the right that is calling my name and pull into the parking lot. I've been here more than once in a blackout of drink-induced amnesia that I always seem to remember the next day. It's a bikini bar where a hot chick who used to come into the liquor store works at. Just the sight of her would inspire me to work out. I haven't seen her in a couple of years and wonder if she's still employed there.

I park the truck and walk to the front entrance where I pay the big thug who's working the door a five-dollar cover and go in. The last time I was here I was with all the boys and this stripper was smashing her tits into everybody's face for a dollar. As my eyes adjust to the dim light, I look at the stage and can see the place has changed. It's not a bikini bar anymore but rather a topless bar. I sit down at a table near the front and order a drink.

Three girls come out and dance and I finish my drink and order another. The music starts up again with a floor pounding bass beat and a girl that looks very familiar to me comes out wearing go-go boots and starts to dance.

After a while her top comes off and she comes closer to the side I'm on and I get a better look at her face. Wow! I do know her. She was my friend Marcus' girlfriend from high school and used to work in a clothes store at the mall. I wonder if he ever thought she would become a stripper. He probably wouldn't want to date her if he did. She doesn't see me and I don't say anything to let her know I'm here.

She finishes her set and goes off and the hot chick that used to come into the liquor store comes up behind me.

"Hi, Walter," she says. "I didn't know it was you at first. You've lost a lot of weight."

"Been doing a lot of running," I say.

"I could tell," she answers.

The speakers start to play another song and she looks up at the DJ who motions at her to get onstage.

"I've got to dance," she says. "I'll talk to you later."

She goes onto the stage and under the lights I can see her long brown hair, olive skin, and beautiful green eyes. She dances her two-song set and then turns towards the silver curtained back wall, the stage lights showing her perfect ass in all its glory. Her coming into the liquor store is what motivated me to start working out again. Her hand reaches up on her spine to the string that holds her top on. She slowly unties the knot and she throws her top to the floor, revealing herself to the audience.

Oh, man, I think. She had a kid or two since I last saw her a couple of years ago and her tits have been sucked off.

All of a sudden, I want to be out of here and I make my move to the bar. So much has changed in the time since I last saw her. I don't even want to know who she married or who the father is. As the DJ cues up another song for the next dancer, she finds me at the bar with a rooster in hand.

"Pretty sad, huh?" she says.

"Huh?" I grunt, wondering if she can read my mind.

"How they turned this into a strip club," she says. "It was a lot more fun as a bikini bar but I needed the money when they switched it so I just stayed on."

"You were hot," I say, seeing a way out. "You knocked 'em dead as always."

The D.J. motions her over and she puts her hand on my shoulder. "Hold on, Walter, I'll be right back."

As soon as she walks off, I slip out the door and jump on the freeway to get back home to my garage. The residential highway is safer but it's slow and I don't want to have too much time to think about what became of my fantasy girl. I make it back in a few minutes then fall into bed with Adolf curled up happily beside me.

I awake in the morning with the red LED alarm clock showing 11 AM. I've only been out a few days and already my internal clock has changed back to normal. No way could I have slept this long in jail even without an alarm clock. My mom has turned on the dryer and it's rumbling away behind the thin plywood walls I constructed. I stare up into the rafters at the crap my dad has stashed everywhere. There's junk like a 20-year-old toaster he refuses to throw out, because he claims he'll fix it one day. *Yeah, right, Pops.*

I can feel the November chill in the unheated garage but I'm warm under the covers with Adolf on top acting like my own personal space heater. I decide that life is good sleeping in a garage. At least nobody messes with me out here and I can do what I want. The rats and the cockroaches damn sure don't care if I make my bed or not. I get up and take a shower and the hot water on my cold feet feels just right. After a quick bite I grab Adolf and we head to the boxing gym in my truck.

I open the door to the silent gym and Adolf walks in beside me and plops down near the door on the cold cement. Noe sees me from across the room and comes over.

"Hey, Walt," he says. "Where ya been?"

"You know how it goes," I say. "The call of the wild."

"I know about that all too well," Noe laughs. "But Walt, you're in your prime now and you only have a little time to learn the game and take advantage of what you can do."

Noe means well but I'm done with living a structured life for somebody else. I'll come back but on my own terms. "I'm finished with jail," I say. "I just came in to tell you I'm going to take a week off for myself and then I'll be back."

"Okay, Walt, "Noe cackles in his 70-year-old voice. "Go find yourself some fun and do what you do."

He pulls his glasses down and I look into his wrinkled face. It shows every regret and loss he ever had. His brown eyes, though, still have a look of youthful bad attitude and unapologetic truthfulness. I look down at his equally battered hands that have alternated over the years from roofer to boxer. *I'll be back. There's no doubt.*

"If jail couldn't keep me away then freedom sure as hell won't," I say. "You know me. I gotta have somebody to hit."

Noe laughs again and slaps my shoulder. "Okay, street warrior, do your thing."

He walks away and I take Adolf and go out the door of the silent boxing gym that slams shut behind us and back to my truck. I decide to make another run back to see Coby at the warehouse. Traffic is light today, for some reason, and I pull in back to the roll-up door and walk into the warehouse. I walk the length of the cutting tables, past the embroidery machine that is being operated by one of *El Jefe's* boys, and walk up the stairs to the office where I know Coby will be sitting.

"Hey, let's go to lunch," I say as I open the door.

Coby looks up and his eyes are less red than yesterday. He's still stoned but maybe we'll be able to have a conversation today.

"Okay, let's go," he says. "I'll drive. Maybe you'll eat something today."

Adolf is in the truck," I say, giving Coby's dumbass comment a free pass. "I parked in the shade and left the window open. He'll be fine."

We cross the asphalt of the front parking lot, squinting against the noon sun, and get into his dually. He hits his crazy stereo that I swear can crack asphalt and break concrete. We make it to the hamburger joint in forced silence and Coby hits the salad bar so he doesn't have to try to talk to the person at the counter. I get a cheeseburger and fries and sit down. Coby comes back to the table with his salad stacked high with two big red tomatoes on the top and ranch dressing spilling down over the lettuce and overflowing the plate. He grabs the salt container and shakes it for a good 30 seconds, covering the salad. I didn't know that you put salt on a salad, but Coby is stoned stupid with the emphasis on stupid. After he gets done chewing for a few minutes he looks up at me.

"You know that guy who does the tee-shirts for the NHB?" Coby says. "I talked to him and he wants you to go to his dojo and fill out an application."

9. Invitation to a Brawl

"Would you fight in the NHB pay-per-view?" Coby asks.

"Yeah, sure," I say.

"If I can get you in, you're down?" Coby says. "You won't back out?"

"Yes, Coby," I say. "I'm always down for a brawl."

"Well, you just can't fill out an application and then fight," Coby says.

"Why not?" I ask. "That's what I do at the boxing gym."

"It doesn't work that way," Coby says, suddenly an expert on the fight game. "You have to meet people and shit like that."

"Okay," I say, not feeling like arguing with him. "Just let me know."

We drive back to the warehouse and I walk him up to the mirrored front door. For the first time I notice that "Decisions" is written on it.

Coby opens the door and looks back. "Come back around 4:30," he says.

I drive back home and go into the garage through the kitchen. Adolf follows me in and I hit the opener on the wall to crack the garage door a third of the way up. I lay down on the bed but Adolf is so fat he can barely get up so I drag him by his collar next to me. As we lay there for a while the sun comes in and I doze off. When I awake the sun has started to go down and is shining through the partially opened garage door. It's time for me to do some running around. Adolf looks at me worriedly from the shady part of the bed. His untrusting face tells me he expects me to leave him there.

"Okay, you can go with me," I say, feeling guilty.

We pile into the truck and drive over to Fred's new garage door office. He moved out of his old place when I was in jail and now has a warehouse and office in the tilt-ups, like the ones across from Decisions that Juan used to talk about. I find it without any problem and walk in. It reminds me of Mort's warehouse a little and is nice compared to the office he had at his house. I press a bell on the empty front desk and Fred walks out from the back.

"Hey, Walt," Fred says. "What's up? You like my new office?"

"This place is pretty cool," I say. "Just wanted to come by and let you know that I'm out."

"Ok, cool," Fred says. "This business has really opened *doors* for me." He waits for me to laugh but when I don't, he continues on a little miffed. "It's definitely a step up, anyway. You want some work?"

"Sure," I say. "If you need a hand then I'm around."

"I've been going out and taking bids myself since you went in," Fred says. "I have some call-ins for you to cover as soon as you're ready."

"I'm chilling the rest of the week," I say. "Getting all my shit done."

"Next week then?" Fred asks.

"Yeah," I answer. "Monday will give me some time to get settled."

"Sounds good," Fred says. "What are you doing now?"

"Just drinking and thinking," I say.

"Well, you definitely got the first one down," Fred laughs. "See you Monday."

I get in the truck and Adolf is a little too happy to see me. This is a dog with deep-seated trust issues. "Well, at least I have money coming in," I say aloud. That seems to make Adolf happy as his tail wags, but I could have said "nuclear waste" and gotten the same response. Oh well, you take what you can get.

It's getting close to 4:30 PM so I take Adolf home and head towards Decisions to see Coby. I get on and off the freeway and take the same track down the cul-de-sac that I used to take when I was in jail just a few days ago. The difference is that now I don't have to be at Decisions unless I want to. I don't need to come here six days a week and I can come and go as I please. Being in jail really makes you appreciate even the smallest things. I park in front when I get there and make my way to Coby's office. I shut the door but can still hear my old embroidery machine running through the walls.

Coby is sitting at his desk with his phone in his ear and waves me into a chair. He is pie-eyed, which is his usual look, and I wonder how he can carry on a conversation. Talking stoned is a gift I suppose. He hangs up the phone just as the door opens again and his friend Trey comes in. He's a surfer dude with the full-on Moon Doggie look of tank top, flip-flops and long brown hair parted in the middle. Unlike Moon Doggie, though, he's stoned out of his mind.

"Dude," Trey drawls slowly. "Let's smoke a bowl."

Coby nods matter-of-factly and pulls out a big red glass pipe and loads it expertly. They alternate taking hits and before my eyes transform into high school freshman. In a language known and understood only by stoners.

they trade every usage of the word "dude" back and forth for the next five minutes, using it as subject, verb and noun - often in the same sentence.

"Fuck this shit," I finally say. "Let's go see the NHB guy." I'm on edge after getting out of jail and just don't have the patience for this anymore. I'm not the same and want a new direction in my life.

"Dude," Coby says sharply, as if that explains everything.

I laugh at their stupidity despite myself and wait while they each take one last hit and then get up. Smoke belches out of the office door as we leave and go outside to his dually. Despite being stoned, Coby drives the three of us towards Sea Lion Beach on the far side of the Naval Weapons Yard. I can see the water tower house in the glare from the setting sun over the ocean. We pass the tilt-up development where Fred's new office is and go by the huge McDonald Douglas aircraft factory, where I spent the formative years of my youth drinking beer in the parking lot. We finally pull into an out-of-place strip mall.

"This is the place," Coby says in a stoned voice.

He goes a third of the way down to a glass-fronted business suite with Japanese characters on the window above English words identifying it as a karate dojo. He backs into a spot in front and parks the dually facing towards the weapons yard with its wild grass covering the storage bunkers. I take stock of my present situation. I'm with two stoned idiots sitting in front of me talking like morons, trying to get into a no-rules fighting event by going to a wannabe fighter karate dojo. Life couldn't get any stranger. Before I went to jail, I wouldn't have put up with this bullshit but I need to get into this show to give me a way out.

We get out of his truck leaving Trey inside, walk a few feet, and pull open the swing door of the small karate studio. Inside are wannabe fighters who want to see if I know how to fight. *How about I just fuck you up to show you instead of you interviewing me?* Inside, there are awards all over the walls. It's just bullshit that people give themselves to cover their insecurities. We walk down a hallway to a room with blue pads on the walls. The carpet is short and looks like fuzz on a tennis ball. Martial arts equipment is everywhere and the blue sponge carpet looks familiar to me. I suddenly laugh aloud as I realize I've been here before.

I used to go around to karate dojos hoping to fight people but nobody ever wanted to get down with me. That's why I ended up in wrestling rooms and boxing gyms; at least they will train realistically. Nobody in any of the dojos I went to ever wanted to fight. They wanted to talk about fighting but not really fight. There was never any fun to be found in these types of places, just excuses. A girl comes out and Coby tell hers we have an appointment with the owner.

"This way, she says. "Sensei Monk is in his office."

She walks us to the back of the dojo where there's a guy behind a desk dressed in pajamas with a beard and long strawberry blond hair.

"I'm sorry to interrupt you, Sensei Monk," she says. "But they said they had an appointment."

"That's fine, Elaine," he replies. "You can go now."

"Yes, Sensei Monk," she bows, giving this guy crazy respect. "Thank you, Sensei Monk."

It's like she's talking to David Koresh in Waco, Texas. I wouldn't be surprised if she was sleeping with him. This is just like that: a bunch of fools worshipping a guy who couldn't punch his way out of a wet paper bag.

We sit down at his desk on two flimsy folding chairs. There's a pen-filled cup on it and a back issue of Black Belt Magazine with Bruce Lee on the cover addressed to "Chip M".

"You're the tough guy Coby has been talking about," the PJ clown says. "What's your expertise?"

"What do mean?" I ask. "I'm just a real fighter."

"Yeah, right," he answers. "I need to know your discipline."

I can see his face underneath his beard. It's pink like a cherry and I doubt this guy has been in a single fight his entire life.

"My discipline is whatever you want it to be," I say.

The PJ guy shrugs. "I need to know if you're ready for this no-rules kind of fighting."

"There's no doubt," I say confidently. "I saw it on TV and the guys didn't look all that tough."

"You should have a strong martial arts background," he says sternly. "The cage is no place for amateurs."

But the karate dojo is, I think, looking around. "I have a lot of hands-on fighting experience," I say. "I guess you could call me a wrestler."

"You mean like an NCAA All-American or something?" he asks, giving the application to Coby.

"What does that mean?" I say testily. The guy is starting to get on my nerves. "Does that make you a good fighter?"

"Well, yeah," the PJ guy says.

"Oh, really," I say. "I've crossed paths with a lot of those guys and I could tell you different."

"Sure you have," he says, like I'd just claimed to be from Mars. He turns away from me and looks at Coby. "Here's the application for your fighter," he says. "Fill this out and then call Big Bart Shady. He's the man. His card is with the application."

We walk back down the hall to the parking lot. The asphalt is brand new and has just been paved but the day has turned dark and cloudy. We jump in the dually and I get in the back seat and close the door. The two stoned idiots are looking over the legal-sized application the PJ guy gave us. As I sink back into the cloth seat a small Japanese car pulls next to the dually and Coby looks over.

"Jesus H. Christ!" Coby says.

"What are you freaked out about?" I ask, thinking he read something in the contract.

"Look next to me," Coby says.

Getting out of a brand-new Japanese SUV is a huge Samoan guy. He's well over six feet tall and has to be at least 400 lbs. He looks big but I can tell he's soft by the way he's built and moves. He casts a quick glance at us and then walks into the dojo.

"Walt," Coby says. "Do you think you could take that guy?"

"Coby," I answer, "I hope you're joking. "I'd rip that fuckers head off."

"Dude," Trey says with a stoned laugh. "That's fucking crazy."

"Yeah, I am," I answer. "Let's go fill out this application."

Coby fires up the dually and hits the gas. The tires screech as he backs out. He drives like he's seventeen all the way back to Decisions where we go into his office. The two geniuses share another bowl and Coby sits back in his chair. His big, bulging globe-like eyes are half-closed and I'm afraid he's going to drool all over the application. He lays out the contract on the desk and he and Trey go over it like they're working a crossword puzzle. The usual questions of height, weight, and age come up. Then it asks about martial arts background.

"Write 'none,' Coby," I say.

We finish the application and I leave before the room can fill up with smoke again and give me a contact buzz. I go down to my truck and head back to my parent's garage to pick up Adolf, my only friend. I head to the grocery store and do my usual march for vodka and cranberry juice. How many steps does it take? I know, but I'll never tell. I pay for my usual booty and then go outside and mix up a rooster in the parking lot in the safety of the night.

I go through the residential highway, into the harbor, and down past the waterfront homes. *Fuck!* Three-quarters of the fifth is gone but Adolf is happy and The Smiths are playing loud, so all in all it's a good night so far.

"Fuck it, Adolf," I say. "Let's go to Sea Lion Beach."

Should I go to that town? No way. But am I going? Hell, yes. The turn signal indicator clicks at me as I turn left into the city, breaking into The Smiths music. I search inside myself to decide if Jerome has paid his debt. I decide he hasn't and drive towards his last known address. Maybe karma will be there and truth will find him. I drive by his still-empty house and go by the

church just around the corner. In my head, his blood is
still fresh on the weathered stones near the crosswalk. I
pass the liquor store on Main Street but the town is dead
so I head north towards Wong Beach with my best friend
Adolf riding shotgun.

As I drive over into Naples, I see a couple walking
hand-in-hand towards Second Street. I stay on Ocean
Drive until I hit Pike, deep into an area I got very stupid
in a bunch of times. Adolf looks at me over the top of his
snout and his big black eyes shine at me. *I know how
stupid you can get*, he seems to say to me. I keep going
down past the Queen Mary. I never understood what the
big deal is. It's just a big ship to look at that hasn't sailed
in many years. It's just moored with nowhere to go and
nothing to do, just like me tonight.

I grab my red cup, drop some rocks into it, and pour
the last of the bottle, trying to steady my hand as I hit a
series of potholes. Parts of Wong Beach are so run down
it feels like being in TJ. I've done 120 days and now I've
changed. I don't need to hang with anyone all the time, -
I just need Adolf and a rooster now. I get back onto the
highway and go a little way then turn off when I see a
small liquor store ahead. I pull in to get supplies and get
stared at hard by the black and Mexican locals drinking
in the parking lot.

"What's up?" I ask the Korean clerk behind the
counter.

"Same old shit, Homie," he says in an inner-city
accent.

I pay for a sack of ice and a fifth of Stoli and then
make a freshy in the parking lot with the locals looking
on. I take a sip, pull out, and turn left back towards Wong
Beach. I drive without incident, anonymous in the

deepest section of the run-down part of the city. I go past a row of high-rises, turn left on Chestnut, and stop at the bottom of a short hill in front of a dark, seedy corner building. It's a tattoo parlor that's been inking generations of Navy men since the Japanese bombed Pearl Harbor. Oh, the stories these walls could tell.

I creep into the parking lot, rolling over the cracked and broken asphalt that lies in the armpit of Wong Beach. I open my glove box and grab a paper that I've had for a long time. My siren is blaring as I walk into the parlor that I remember all too well. When I was young, I picked a couple of nice ones for myself: a dagger with a skull on one calf and a love poem on the other. It was short lived and in two months I had the poem cut off and nothing but a scar remains now.

A rockabilly guy hears the bell ring when I walk in and comes out from the back.

"Can I help you?" he asks.

"Yeah," I say, putting my siren on the glass counter. The display case below has a collection of hardcore silver jewelry of skulls and demonic faces: hard cold stuff. "I need a cover up. "Can you do this?" I pull out the old crinkled paper and show him.

"Yeah, no problem," he says, after glancing at it for a few seconds. "It's an elephant, right?"

"Yeah," I confirm.

I picked it out a while ago. It's a charging rogue bull with ears back and head down coming straight ahead in full trample mode. I think back to what Juan, from Mort's warehouse, said about tattoos before he jumped probation: *Homie, don't get color. Only bitches have colored tattoos. They look like Easter eggs.*

"Just hit it with black ink," I say. "Only bitches get color."

"You got it," he nods.

He looks at my leg where I want the cover up. It's a girl's name on my calf that represents eight years of bullshit. Now that it's long over it's time to cover that shit up. While he gets ready, I go back to my truck and make another freshy and to make sure Adolf doesn't think he's been abandoned again. I slam the truck door and go back inside the parlor. The tattoo guy has made a copy of the elephant and is waiting for me. I take the top off the siren, put it on the counter and lay down on a table next to it. He shaves my calf with a straight razor and puts the copy of the elephant on my leg. It transfers perfectly.

"What do you think?" he asks.

"Fucking great," I say.

The tattoo machine fires up with a shrill whine and the needle starts to sing. Even though I knew it was coming it still hurts like hell, but nothing like the pain that was received from what it is covering up. I take another rip off my siren and put my head down. I have an elephant covering up the mistakes of the past, trampling them into dust.

"How's it coming out?" I ask.

"Outstanding," he says.

He finishes me off by putting on a bandage that covers my new elephant under a thick layer of anti-infection gel. I walk out and Adolf is lying patiently on the bench seat, loyal as usual and calm, knowing that he's in my truck. As I climb into the truck, he tries to climb over me and I have to push him away back to his side. I swerve all the way home out of Wong Beach and back to Happening Beach into the garage where my king-sized bed is and crash hard.

I wake up in the morning around 11 am and gradually come out of my coma. I'm up earlier than I thought I'd be and go into the bathroom to take a shower. I look down and see the patch on my leg. *Oh, yeah, I got an elephant last night.* I take off the bandage and admire how cool it looks. When I walked away from her, I said I would never look back and I haven't. The last of her has been trampled under the hoofs of the wild bull.

10. The Real Bart Shady

I get dressed and have my morning O.J. then decide to go over to Coby's to see if he wants to eat lunch. I'm on automatic pilot as I take the truck down the cul-de-sac and park in front. I walk through the reception area and up to the office in back.

"Did you hear anything?" I say as I walk in and shut the door.

Coby looks up with eyes wide and drool coming off one corner of his mouth. He is stoned as usual and it takes him a second to understand what I'm talking about.

"Oh, yeah," he says. "Hold on. I'm going to put Big Bart Shady on the speakerphone."

He pushes some buttons and I hear the phone ringing on the other end through the speaker.

"Hello?" a thin, reedy voice says crisply. "Bart Shady speaking."

"Hey, Big Bart," Coby says. "It's Coby. I'm here with that guy who wants to fight."

"Okay, Coby," Shady says. "What are his qualifications?"

Coby looks at me with a perplexed expression on his face and raises both arms with his palms up. "He's a wrestler...uh, and a boxer...but mainly he's a street fighter."

Shady pauses on the other end and then his wormy voice comes back over the speaker. "We need a black belt or something."

"Why don't you ask Bimbo who Walter Foxx is," Coby fires back, coming out of his chronic stupor. "Or anyone else in Orange County for that matter. You can see for yourself if he's qualified or not."

"I'll do just that, Coby," Shady answers. "I'll get back to you."

The speaker phone goes silent and Coby pushes a button to disconnect, plunging the office into silence.

"I told you," I say. "This is an inside deal. Those guys in PJs control who they want to fight. They're not going to let me in. They aren't real warriors."

We go to Sizzler for lunch and then Coby goes back to his office at the end of the cul-de-sac. I decide to stop by Fred's new store and drive to his tilt-up in the warehouse district. A sign on top reads, "Fred Gold's Garage Doors". I go in and he tells me that the bids are still on for the day after tomorrow and so I head back home and call Tim up.

"Hey, man," I say. "Let's go out. I need to have some fun. Come pick me up."

Tim shows up a few hours later and we go out and pick-up a clip of Coors and head to Poppa Chulo's downtown apartment that he shares with his brother and Rolando. We walk in the door and it doesn't take the boys more than ten seconds to start in on me.

"Hey, Walt," Poppa Chulo laughs. "How'd you like jail? Make any new butt buddies?"

"Fuck you, Poppa Chulo," I say.

"And what was up with those letters you sent me," he laughs even harder. "You sounded like the Count of Monte Cristo wanting to break out of Devil's Island. You were at Camp Snoopy."

Oh, fuck. I do remember those letters and get a little red-faced thinking about them. I hated the place and might have been a little dramatic in my letters but after a week it was more boredom than anything. "Yeah, well, you know how it is when you're a county cherry. You don't know what's going to happen and you're a little freaked out."

"What about Shelly?" Poppa Chulo snickers. "I bet she got it even worse than me."

"I actually did write her a few times," I laugh. "It wasn't funny then, though. You do stupid things when you're locked up. I hope to God she didn't show those letters to anyone."

"Yeah, I bet," Poppa Chulo laughs. "What's going on with her now?"

"I heard she got back with Jorge," I say. "At least I hope she did. He didn't like her all that much until I started seeing her. I guess I did her a favor."

"Right on," Poppa Chulo says. "He's more her type anyway."

I'm more than glad to put that topic to rest and we leave the apartment and go downtown. It's cold and rainy and nothing is happening so we go to the MacDonald Douglas airplane company parking lot, the place I've been drinking for most of my so-called adult life, at least when I could get booze. We go to the empty parking lot next to the employee softball area. No games are being played on the outside fields and it's a safe place to drink. I'm fresh out of county jail and sitting in an asphalt parking lot overlooking a nine-to-five field of dreams. It might seem boring but it sure beats the hell out of sitting in lock-up waiting for count. Nothing is going on besides hard drinking and hard thinking and that's okay with me.

I make an early night of it and head back to my garage and fall into bed. In the morning I feel like it's time to get back into action so I climb on my Interceptor and head to

the boxing gym where the speed bag is calling my name.
I wrap my hands tight and know that it's fucking time to
go to work. All around me are guys grunting and banging
on bags hanging from the ceiling.

I look around for Penny because he's still on my list
but no luck. All I see around me are hope and wishes
built on a ship of foolish dreams. Most of these guys are
nothing and are built with faulty hardware that will never
take them anywhere. They don't have the strength or
speed to go anywhere in this sport. I want to kill them all
with my bare hands for their delusions. I finish up on the
speed bag and walk to the parking lot, the gym noise
behind me fading away. I cruise to Decisions to see Coby
and the girl in front just waves me in without a word and
I go into his second-floor office. Coby is sitting there
with his usual stoner blank stare and jumps a little when I
close the door behind me.

"Dude," he says, after studying me for a moment,
"where'd you come from? Never mind. You're not going
to believe this. That Shady guy called back."

"What did that poser want," I ask.

"No, dude," Coby says. "You got it all wrong. This
guy is money. He is gold. He owns and runs the NHB."

"Well, he sounds like a bullshit artist to me," I say.

"Well, you're wrong," Coby says. "I set up a meeting
with him for tomorrow at 1:00 PM. I told you I'd hook it
up."

"Coby," I say, "you're stoned. "Nothing is going to
happen."

"Look, Walt," Coby says. "This is real fighting. Like
you always said you wanted."

"Yeah, Coby," I answer, "but you haven't seen the shit I have in boxing. The guys in PJs run it. They won't let anyone fight that they don't think they can beat."

"Don't blow it off without giving it a chance," Coby says.

"Okay," I say. "You're right. I'll go."

"There's one more thing," Coby says. "Shady said he has a 6'8" 300 lb. guy that might be there to fight you."

"No problem," I say. "It will be my pleasure to fuck him up. Let's go to lunch."

Coby drives us over to Sizzler and we walk up to the menu board and Coby gets the salad bar while I order a chicken breast with a plain baked potato. I get my food at the table and a few minutes later Coby comes back from the salad bar. His eyes are completely bloodshot and his face is two inches from his plate. He studies it carefully as if trying to comprehend what is before him and then looks up at me.

"Bart asked me if my fighter was a 5'4" overweight midget who had watched too much pro wrestling," Coby says. "He says he's been getting a ton of those types calling up wanting to fight."

"What did you say?" I ask.

"I told him the truth," says Coby. "That you're the real deal. Not a wrestler or boxer or a martial arts guy but a true warrior and real fighter. Someone that would kill you if it was legal."

"What did Shady say to that?" I ask. "Did it freak him out?"

"No. He seemed to like it," Coby answers. He puts his stoned face two inches away from his plate because he's having a hard time hitting his mouth with his fork. "Bart Shady is the man."

119

We finish lunch and Coby goes into fade mode, staring off into the distance.

"C'mon, stoner," I say. "Take me back to Decisions."

We hop into the white dually and Coby turns up his stereo and rubs his stomach. "Man, I'm still pretty hungry. I need some chips or something."

We manage to make it back without Coby stopping at a 7-11. I switch to my bike and as I start it up, I notice that the sky has turned to gray and it starts to drizzle. The cold moisture falls on my head so I go home and park the bike and get in the truck and head to Fred's. There is no work today but he says that he should have some tomorrow. I was hoping for some money but there's nothing I can do, so I head home and pick-up Adolf then drive to the beach with a new freshy in hand.

When we get there it's cold and desolate and the ocean is rough with waves crashing onto the shore. Adolf is happy inside the truck in anticipation of a walk and is jumping around on the bench seat. He's so fat now that my days of being pulled by him on the skateboard are over. I'm going to have to get him in shape. The days of my dad cooking him breakfast, lunch, and dinner are also over. I get half a siren down and then unhook him and let him out and he runs around the cliffs that lead to the beach.

The weather is getting uglier by the minute and the gray skies have turned black and waves are breaking offshore, whipped up by a stiff wind. When the seas are rough, I'm drawn to them. All the morons come out when it's sunny and nice. I sip my siren and ponder what I'm going to do with my life. At least I have a couple of bids coming in tomorrow if I'm lucky. I'll make a couple of hundred off that. As the sun starts to set I kill my siren and load Adolf up and head back to the garage.

I take a long hot shower then go off to the grocery store and do my march to get red cups, a fifth of Stoli, cranberry and ice. Out in the truck I mix up a siren and then hit the residential highway with Adolf beside me and Nirvana blasting out of the stereo. Before I went away for my speed bump in life, I would drive around looking for people. Now I'm hoping to not see anyone. I'm happy to cruise around by myself, talking to Adolf and listening to music. It may seem boring from the outside but inside my mind my thoughts are going a thousand miles an hour. *What am I going to do in life?* There are so many people I want to strangle with my bare hands but it's not going to happen. Jail is still fresh in my mind and I don't want to go back.

It's a dead night and my buzz is coming on. I pass a few cops but they don't look twice at me. It's starting to sprinkle and they don't want to get out in the wet any more than anyone else. I pound my fifth and go home because I want to be fresh tomorrow when I meet Bart Shady and whoever he might want me to fight. I go into the garage and pass out on the bed and the next thing I know the alarm is screaming "Beep, Beep, Beep" at me that it's 11 AM.

I hit the fucking thing to shut it off and then grab Adolf and squeeze him like a log and get a plaintive growl in return. As I come out of my sleep the sound of rain rocks me into consciousness. It's coming down so hard its beating on the garage roof like rocks on sheet metal. I lay there for a while but finally give in and roll out of bed. The oiled-stained bare cement floor is freezing cold and feels like dry ice on my feet.

I scamper across the floor and go into the kitchen door and down the hallway past the bedroom where I grew up. I turn the shower on as hot as I can stand and jump in. When I get out, I glance in the mirror and my face looks fresh and alert and I don't feel tired at all. I put on my work clothes, which are the nicest things I own, consisting of a rip-proof Spooner, white jeans, and Doc Martens boots. Then I go to the garage where my mom keeps the old grocery bags and grab one with a blue Albertson's logo on front. I walk next to my bed, where I stack my clothes on a brick and two-by-four shelf I made, and grab my basketball high tops, an old tee-shirt, and Bike elastic coaching shorts.

I roll them up tightly and stuff them into the grocery bag and fold the top down. They are sitting inside now, like a rattlesnake waiting to strike when someone steps on it. I'm ready to go now and look out the kitchen window and see that the rain is coming down like cats and dogs. *Where the fuck is that stupid stoner Coby?* It's closing in on noon and we're supposed to meet Bart Shady at 1:00 PM. I glance at Adolf and he looks at me as if to say, *who's really stupid for having a stoner pick him up?*

Touché, Adolf, I think. I don't want to show up late. Whenever I'm supposed to meet someone, I always try to have some respect for them by showing up on time. *Where are you at, you stupid stoner?* It's 10 minutes past noon and if Coby is any later we're not going to make it. *Fuck!* The rain has flooded the streets but there's a break in the storm. A beam of sunlight comes through an opening in the clouds and I hear thundering punk rock music as Coby pulls up in the white dually. *Finally.* The rain starts pouring hard again and I grab my grocery bag off the dining table and run out the front door, trying to dodge the raindrops. I'm all wet when I open the door of Coby's dually and climb in. The punk rock music is blaring so loud I can barely think and Coby is stoned as usual.

"What's up, Coby," I say.

"Oh, you know, man," he says with stoner wisdom in his voice, as if he just delivered the Gettysburg Address.

The wipers are going full blast but it's raining so hard that I can't see a thing out of the windshield. I look at my watch and it's nearly 20 after the hour. "Looks like we're going to be late," I say.

"For what?" he answers. "We gotta see Big Bart now."

"Never mind," I say.

We get on the freeway and I read out the address on Coby' scribbled piece of notebook paper as we head towards Borrance. Coby has directions but as usual they're all fucked up and I give up trying to navigate by them and we just go from memory. The rain is coming down in sheets and flooding the freeway and everyone but stoner Coby is driving slow and cautious. I stare ahead and try to ignore his swerving and sudden braking and accelerating.

"Hey, Walt," Coby says. "What's in the grocery bag? You got some chips in there?"

"No, man," I say. "I packed some clothes to change into."

"What for?"

"Well, if this Bart Shady guy thinks that I'm an overweight midget that got into ten fights in high school then he'll see what is real. Right now, I'm clean-shaven, 220 pounds and look like a clean-cut cop, not some surf punk wannabe with bleached blonde hair. He'll see how real I am."

"I don't think he cares," Coby says.

"Shit!" I say. "You're about to miss the street. Get off at the next exit."

"Oh, yeah," Coby says. "You're right."

We get off the freeway just in time while cutting off two other cars who slide by in the rain. "Go up a couple of lights and take a left. I worked in Borrance before selling garage doors. I know the area."

Borrance is an older town and the buildings all show their age a lot more than in Orange County. The area we're in, especially, looks like it was first built in the fifties. This isn't the business district where the high-rises are.

"Coby," I say. "You're a stoned idiot. Are you sure this is where a TV show operation is located?

"Yeah, dude," Coby says. "Big Bart Shady told me. Look, we're outside his place."

Coby pulls over and grabs a parking spot in front of a two-story office building that looks like a hole in the wall that was converted from apartments. In my mind I had pictured Bart Shady being in a glass and steel high-rise, not this dump. As I study it, I suddenly know that I've been in this place before.

"What kind of an office is this?" I ask. "This can't be the place. I've been here before."

"What?" Coby says.

"Nothing," I say. "Let's go inside."

We jump out of the truck and run but the raindrops are faster and we get a good shower before we make it to the overhang in front. My grocery bag is soaked and starting to tear. We walk along the overhang looking at names on the doors until we find one that says No-Holds-Barred Championships.

"This must be it," Coby says, turning to me with his stoner eyes that look like oranges. They're red with a heavy cloud cover of eyelids and are open just enough for him to see. Coby reaches out to the door and pushes instead of pulls and looks at me mystified when it doesn't open.

"Get out of the way," I say, pulling it open.

As we walk in, I see that the furniture is from the same designer who decorated the place where I just spent the last 99 days of my life. It is classic probation house decor with a couple of old desks with mismatched chairs bought from yard sales whenever the budget permitted.

A large guy in his forties with dark crew-cut hair is sitting behind a steel desk wearing a black sweat-suit. He has a body that looks like he took steroids in the past. I would never guess in a million years that he would be the one to run the NHB. I thought he would more an executive type. If this was a grocery store, he would be a giant cucumber in the middle of the fruit section, the shape of which describes him perfectly. As he stands up and slips off his sweat top, I can see he's trying to make himself look tough by his cut-off sleeves.

This is Big Bart Shady, the guy running a pay-per-view show about fighting? The old desk he's sitting behind has mounds of paper on it and would look more at home in a used car lot. I ease myself into an old, ripped leather office chair in front of the desk and stoner Coby pulls up a metal folding chair and sits next to me.

"Okay," Big Bart says in the thin voice I recognize from the phone. "You think you're a tough guy?"

"Correction," Coby fires back, "he *is* a tough guy."

I sit there stone-faced, trying to get a read on this. So far, I'm not liking what I'm seeing. Big Bart is a fast talker who doesn't hit me at first glance as being on the up-and-up.

"What makes you so tough?" Shady asks.

"I don't know," I say. "I just like to fight."

"Really?"

"Yeah, I do it a lot," I say.

"Do you box, study karate, practice kung-fu? What?"

"Well, that's not fighting," I say. "I fight in the street."

"Oh, yeah?" Shady says.

"I've been wrestling since I was a kid and I've boxed the past five years but I fight in the street," I say.

"I get it, Walt," Shady says. "But this is a show about martial arts fighters. We need someone with a black belt."

"I thought the show was about fighting, not about black belts," I say.

"A black belt gives you credibility," Big Bart says, like he's explaining addition and subtraction to a third grader.

"Bart, you know Bimbo, right?" I say. "He fought in your show. Ask him about me."

"Did you see his fight?" Shady asks.

"No, Bart. I didn't."

"How come?"

"I was in jail," I say. "I kicked the shit out of a beggar who came looking for it."

"Oh, really?" Bart says. For the first time I see a glimmer of interest in his eyes. "Well, let me do some checking around. Maybe you can fight in NHB 5 in Harlot, North Carolina."

I nod and get up to shake hands with him across the old desk.

"You know, Walt," Bart says, "I see a lot of guys that say they want to fight but I can tell you're different. I can tell by looking in your eyes that you're a real fighter."

"Well, nice to meet you," I say.

I reach down to the floor and pick up my grocery bag holding my clothes. As I turn and open the door to walk out, the raging storm screams in and blows rain onto my face.

"Hey, Walt," Shady says, "I have one more question."

I shut the door and turn around. "Yeah?"

"What's in the bag?"

"Coby told me that you had a guy that's 6'8" tall and 300 pounds that you wanted me to fight."

"Yeah?" Shady asks. "He couldn't make it."

"Well these are my fighting clothes," I say. "I was going to change so I didn't get his blood on my work clothes."

"You were going to fight him here for no money?" Shady asks.

"As long as I wouldn't go to jail for it," I say.

"Wow," Shady says, a look of surprise on his face. "You're crazy."

"Do some checking around," I say.

Shady's demeanor towards me changes and I can tell he's suddenly more accommodating. "Yeah, yeah, I'll do that."

"See ya, Bart," I say.

I open the door again and Coby and I dash outside, splashing through the puddles and the pouring rain, and pile into his dually.

"You're in, dude," Coby says happily.

"No, it's not happening," I say. "I told you these guys aren't going to let just anyone in if they think you're too tough."

"Dude," Coby says. "I think it went pretty well."

"I don't think so," I say. "That Shady guy is a big goof. I don't trust him."

11. Man with a Plan

I get out of Coby's truck at my parents' house and walk in the door only to be greeted by the sight of my dad and Adolf sitting on the couch snacking on Cheetos. As I watch, my Dad eats one himself and then gives one to Adolf, going back and forth a few times. No wonder the fucking dog is so fat.

"How'd the meeting go?" my Dad asks.

"Not too well," I say, slapping my hands and trying to lure Adolf away from the snack bag. He ignores me, mesmerized by the crunchy treats. "This Bart Shady is a wannabe joker. His office is straight out of the 1950s. It reminded me of the probation halfway house, right down to his desk with all the stapled papers on it. These guys don't want real fighters, just phony martial arts guys in PJs."

"That's too bad," my Dad says. "After watching that show I know you'd do great in it."

"Yep," I say. "That's the way things have been going for me lately. I've got to figure out what to do with my life. All I ever really wanted to do was fight. I think I might get serious about boxing. That sport is swimming with sharks, though. You've got to sign your life away just to get some wins. In the meantime, I've got a couple of bids to do for Fred tomorrow. I've got to start working more so I can get out of the garage."

"Don't worry about that, Walt," my Dad says. "Why don't you move back into your old room for a while?"

"I can't do that, Dad," I say. "Come on, Adolf."

I grab Adolf by the collar and pull him off the couch. He looks at the Cheetos over his shoulder like he's saying goodbye to a long-lost lover. The rain has stopped so I grab my keys and go to the store and do my usual loop. I mix up a siren in the truck and take my first swig as I turn onto PCH and head south towards Dana Point.

The Smiths are playing on the stereo and I cruise for a while, trying to clear my head. I make a right before Laguna and then head back north to friendly territory. I'm not worried about getting a DUI because it's raining and the cops hardly ever want to get out of their cars. Besides, everybody drives like hell in the rain so no one can tell if you're drinking or not.

I think about finding an asshole that is begging for it so I pull into the Dead Grunion parking lot and go inside. I don't have that happy-go-lucky vibe anymore. It disappeared for good when I was in jail and I'm hard now. The regulars turn their heads to look at me and then cast their eyes downward to avoid my gaze. They all have a look like, *Holy fuck! Walt is back!* It's slow because of the rain so I take a walk around but nobody has that look like they want to have some fun. I leave and head down to Happening Harbor Café but it's dead too so I go to the bar, have some drinks, then go home.

I get up in the morning, get ready for work, and make it to Fred's office at noon. I get the addresses and talk to Skip for a while and then do three bids in three hours and sell all three. It seems like my magical touch selling garage doors has only been enhanced by my time in jail, which worries me. *Is that my fate in life?* I get back to the office and Skip tells me that Coby called and wants me to stop by Decisions.

"Did he say why?" I ask.

"Nope," Skip answers. "Just to come over."

"Okay," I say. "Call me if you have any more bids."

I'm in a good mood as I drive over to Decisions because I've sold three doors and have money coming in. Maybe Coby will go out and party down with me. It's gray and cloudy as I drive down the cul-de-sac and walk up to his office. I pass Mort who gives me a slap on the back. When I go into Coby' office his eyes are in their usual bloodshot state and he is stoned out of his mind.

"Dude," he says. "I was just going to call you to come by."

"You called Skip, Coby," I say.

"Smart," he says, like he just invented a car that would run on water. He's silent for a few moments and doesn't speak.

"Why'd you call?" I finally ask.

"Oh, yeah," he answers. "Bart Shady called."

"Really?"

"Yep," Coby continues. "He called me first, I didn't call him. He did some checking around and found that everyone knows who you are. He was asking if you were qualified and I guess one of Bimbo's guys said that you were overqualified and might kill someone if they let you in."

"Well, I might," I say. "What's the deal?"

"He said that he'll call you in a couple of days and let you know for sure what's going on," Coby answers.

"Do you think I'll be able to fight in NHB 5? I ask.

"It sounds that way," Coby nods.

"Way cool," I say. My good day just got even better and I see a light at the end of the dark tunnel I've been in for over a year. "You wanna catch a few drinks to celebrate?"

"I'd like to," Coby says, "but I've got to go home to the wife. She's been bitching that I don't spend any time with her since we got married."

"Well, I'm going out tonight," I say. "I've got to start training soon and need to blow it out before I get serious."

"Have fun," Coby says.

"You know me," I say. "I always have fun."

The sun sets fast in the winter and it's dark and stormy when I leave but it has stopped raining at least. I want to raise some hell but I don't want to go to jail now that I've got the NHB on the horizon. Besides, if I get hit up again, I'll be going upstate for a three-to-five stretch. It won't be the Farm and then a halfway house but hard time. The DA has me lined up in his sights and I'm in the system now with a conviction on my record that I managed to avoid for years. I'm between a rock and a hard spot now. I've never turned away from a fight, whether it was one guy or ten, but now I have to look the other way. Before, when someone got in my face, it was automatically on, but not anymore.

I get in my truck and slam the door shut and the sound pulls me out of my thoughts. I drive across town to Gonzo's house but he's not there and is also out with his new wife. All my friends have new lives and are moving forward and I'm fresh out of jail, living in my parents' garage, and peddling garage doors.

I drive back home, pick up Adolf, get my normal supplies at the store, and then head over to Poppa Chulo's apartment. The door is open so I just walk in. Poppa Chulo and Rolando are on the couch drinking beer and watching the tube. They tell me that they've just gotten done with a high school wrestling match with the team they coach.

"How'd you guys do?" I ask.

"We lost," Rolando answers. "All the kids are pussies now. They don't train hard. These kids are spoiled."

"Yeah," I say. "They have it too easy."

"What are you up to, Walt?" Rolando asks.

"Just selling garage doors," I say. "I'm going to start training again now that I'm out." I don't say anything about the NHB because I don't want to jinx it and because I don't know for sure it's on.

"Chill with us," Poppa Chulo says. "Everybody is coming over to hang out."

I take a seat on the couch, drinking and watching TV, and in no time the apartment is full of wrestlers. There are at least 10 of us and we all gas up with the stereo playing. When we reach critical drunkenness Poppa Chulo moves the couches to the walls and the round robin takedown session starts. They are all way too small for me to bother with so I just sit back and laugh and watch while Poppa Chulo takes down everyone and is crowned king of party wrestling for the night.

When the session finishes, I go to the kitchen to mix up another drink. I reach across the counter to grab my bottle, bending over at the waist, when a punk kid named Frito, who has been acting tough all night, grabs my hips and starts pumping me from behind.

"What the fuck are you doing, motherfucker," I snarl, spinning around. "I'll fucking kill you."

The little fake bitch takes a step back and the color leaves his face. "I was just playing, Walt," he says.

"Not with me you don't," I say. "I'll rip your head off."

He backs up even further against the wall now, and looks like he is going to start crying. He slides over to the kitchen door and starts backing into the living room.

"Leave him alone," Poppa Chulo's brother yells, "He's just a kid."

"Who cares," I say. "He's a stupid ass who needs to learn some respect. There are consequences for acting up and if you can't deal with them then don't do it. The kid can't count to ten unless his girlfriend helps him and I'm not going to let him do something like that to me. He's lucky I didn't just blast him. He's supposed to be a tough guy but he's a fake. If an older guy would have talked to me the way I talked to him in high school I would have hit the guy. If you're gonna act tough you have to be ready to go. He's just a poser and a bitch."

Poppa Chulo's brother is quiet now because I've left the kitchen and am walking towards him. The other guys in the room all move back nervously as I approach him from across the living room. Frito is nowhere to be seen.

"C'mon, Walt," Poppa Chulo says, getting off the couch and standing in front of me. "Nobody meant anything. That kid is a good wrestler and my brother is just looking out for him."

"He's just beating everyone because he's been held back two grades and is two or three years older than everyone else," I say.

"You're right, Walt," Poppa Chulo says.

"He's a dumb fuck who is going to have a rude awakening when he gets into the real world," I finish.

"Okay, Walt. You're right," Poppa Chulo says, patting my shoulder.

I turn away and flop down on the couch, the two guys sitting there jumping off to give me room. "I'm cool,

Poppa Chulo. I'm just on edge from jail. I would really like to crack him, though."

"Yeah, I hear you," Poppa Chulo says, moving back across the room now that I've calmed down.

"Fuck it," I say, getting off the couch. "I'm outta here."

I jump in the truck, waking up Adolf as I shut the door, and drive home and crash in the garage and brood. It's been a few weeks since I've been out of jail but it doesn't seem that long. Time flies when you're not counting the days like when you're locked up. I'm trying to be good but I don't know how long I'll be able to look the other way when these beggars ask for it. I know the consequences of delivering justice to these phonies and bullies but I can't live like this anymore. It was bad enough having to eat shit from low-ranked boxers in the gym, but now I have to let some punk kid who has never been in a fight off the hook. As I drift off to sleep, I wonder how I'm going to be able to live my life the way I want without going to jail.

I finally go to sleep thanks to the vodka and get up in the morning and get ready and then swing by Fred's shop on the Interceptor.

"Hey, Walt," he asks, when I sit down in his new office," what did you do with Coby the other day?"

"We went to the NHB's head office," I say. "Coby got me a meeting with the owner."

"Sounds exciting," Fred says. "How'd it go?"

"I don't know," I say. "I couldn't really tell. I thought he liked me but then he said I wasn't a real martial artist because I didn't have a black belt."

"What did you say to that?"

"I told him that I was a real fighter and not a martial art pretend fighter," I say. "I can get down in the street but I don't dance in dojos."

"Yeah," Fred nods, "with your wrestling background you could kick ass in that show."

"I didn't want to tell him that I was a wrestler," I say, "because that isn't real fighting."

"I hope it works out for you," Fred says.

"I'm giving it a shot but I'm not counting on getting in," I say glumly. "I'll probably end up turning pro in boxing."

"You should," Fred says. "Swing by in a few days and see if they're any bids to do. You did great on those last three."

I leave the shop, climb on my bike and head north, taking a small detour to go past Decisions to see Coby. I walk straight in and go to his office but he's stoned as usual. I stand in front of his desk but he is on the phone and doesn't even notice I'm there. I wait for a couple of minutes then open the door to leave.

"Hold on," Coby says to me, putting his hand over the receiver. "Where you going? You just got here."

"I've been here nearly five minutes," I say.

"Fuck, you're quiet," he says.

"And you're stoned," I say. "Get off the phone if you want to talk to me."

"Okay," he says. "Hold on. I'm talking to someone from the boat shop."

"No problem," I say. "I'll see you later. I am not in the mood for this bullshit."

"I'll call you back," Coby says into the receiver, hanging up the phone. "Bart Shady wants to meet you next Tuesday. He says he has a plan for you and if you agree to it then you're in."

"Agree to what?" I ask.

"His plan," Coby repeats. "He didn't tell me what it was."

"Is he going to give me something in writing?" I ask.

"I don't think so," Coby says. "He didn't mention it."

"Fuck it," I say. "It's all bullshit then."

"No, no," Coby says. "Wait a second. Let me call him. He moved into a new office so I need some directions anyway. Then I'll ask him if he'll give you something in writing."

Coby punches the buttons on his phone with his middle finger and nods at me almost immediately. "Hello, Bart. It's Coby. I'm sitting here with Walt. He says he wants a contract or something so he can start training. No contract? Well he needs something." Coby goes quiet for a minute or two as Shady talks on the other end. "Okay," he says finally. "I'll let him know." He hangs up the phone.

"He said he has a plan for you but that he can't give you a contract," says Coby.

"Fuck it, then," I say, getting up to leave.

"No, wait," Coby says. "He did say that he would give you a letter saying that you're in and that you'll be fighting in NHB 6."

"What?" I say in surprise. "He told me NHB 5."

"It has something to do with his plan and with promoting you before you fight," Coby says.

"I knew something was up," I say, more disappointed than pissed. "I'm not going to fight. This is all a set-up. I guess I'll just be selling garage doors for the rest of my life."

"Calm down, Walt," Coby says. "You're fighting. It's just one show later. We have a meeting with Bart on Tuesday and he'll give you a letter then saying you're in."

I take a deep breath and try to think rationally. I've come too far with this to throw it away without giving it the benefit of the doubt. "Okay, I'll go to the meeting," I say, "but Shady's plan better be good."

12. Hammer Time

Friday rolls around and I haven't got anything to do. I don't want to work out and I'm restless. *Am I in this NHB fight show or not?* I don't know which end is up right now. I don't want to get my hopes up about the NHB because it will probably get taken away from me, like everything else in my life. Well, at least I'm a college graduate now. It's supposed to be the start of my adult life but my real passion is street fighting except it isn't legal and I can't get paid for it. The only future I have if I keep fighting is going back to jail.

Maybe I could put my life on hold and go to law school? I could make a lot of money but I'm not passionate about it. It would only cost me three more years of homework but then all the years of going to court afterwards and sitting in a suit in front of a judge and jury would bore me to tears. Besides, I'm a judge and jury already. I hurt posers, assholes and bullies that beg me to give it to them. I'm the executioner who stands up to the wannabe tough guys when no one else will. I need to pursue something that gives me a dog in the race. I can't go to law school just for money, I'm like a doctor who studies medicine to help people, not just to get a fat bank account. I have a passion that is real.

Even though the frauds and phonies try to hurt me, they usually fall short. Handing out street justice is a dangerous and thankless job but I'm the man to do it. That worked for me until this lying punk got on the stand and lied his ass off, crying fake crocodile tears about how he was a victim. The days of the warrior code are gone.

Now sore losers who start fights want to get you back
any way they can when they get what is coming to them.

What a justice system. There is no room for giving big
mouths and bullies the beatings they beg for. I lay in my
garage bed, fresh out of jail, staring into the empty rafters
and thinking about how my current life can't continue.
No matter what the circumstances are, I know I can't be a
street warrior and keep my freedom. I hear the phone
ringing in the house and think it might be for me since
my parents are at work.

I rush in and answer and hear Big Cal's voice. "Yo,
Walter! What's up? Long time no see or hear. I'm in town
with Little Danny and we're going to see David Bass on
Meat Street in Happening Beach at JerQ's."

"Wow, Cal you're batting one thousand," I
sarcastically say. "It doesn't get any better than that."

"I know, right?" Cal says enthusiastically. "Get
Gonzo and let's meet up at eight."

My derision is completely lost on Cal. Meat Street is
ground zero for the dumb scumbags in Happening Beach.
Not in a scary way but in a pathetic way. I know because
I've hung out there for years. Most of the inhabitants are
at the top of their field in framing houses, swinging
hammers, and pouring concrete. I've partied with a lot of
them and most of the time they can't remember their own
names. I'm from the northwest side of town where the
houses are filled with college-educated people who can
count to 20 without taking off their shoes.

I hang up the phone, jump in the shower, then call
Gonzo and arrange for him to pick me up. Twenty
minutes later he pulls up in his light-green Blazer 4x4
with the top off, exposing the roll bar. We have a few
hours until 8:00 PM so we head to the grocery store and I

do my usual stroll, pick up my usual supplies and grab a
twelver for Gonzo. In the parking lot, he pops the cap off
a soldier, while I mix up a traveler and we hit the
residential highway listening to the Smiths. I'm quiet and
stare out the window.

"What's up, Walter?" Gonzo says with a serious tone.
"You don't seem like yourself."

"I don't know, man," I sigh. "I'm at this fork in my
life. I can't go on beating up these beggars anymore. I've
graduated from college and have to figure out what I'm
going to do. I didn't even go to the Wong Beach State
graduation ceremony. It really meant nothing to me. I
know I can't only be delivering justice to these clowns
anymore. For every idiot I set straight another ten pop up
who won't take a beating like a man but will call the cops
on me. I'm on a beatdown treadmill."

"Yeah, Walter," Gonzo nods. "I get you. This new
generation has no honor."

"There you go, Gonzo. Bingo! Let's not try to figure it
out and just get wasted."

I clink my traveler against Gonzo's soldier and we
pound a succession of drinks and the buzz gets stronger.
As the beverages go down the odometer spins higher and
the sun sinks into the ocean. As it gets closer to eight
o'clock, Gonzo turns towards downtown. All the bright
guys are there because it's beyond their capability to
leave that part of town. They are stuck for life but I go
there by choice. I find their existence entertaining
because it reminds me to not get stuck like them. The
trolls that are trapped there don't have the tools or the
desire to build a better life. We turn onto Meat Street and
pull into a diagonal parking spot on the JerQs side of the
street. The groan of the Blazer's V-8 comes to a stop and

we sit in silence. I take a mercy gulp to kill my traveler and take a deep breath.

"Let's go!" I say as I exhale. I open the door and jump down from the four-by-four to Meat Street. "Come on Gonzo, let's check out David Bass."

We walk through a couple of the diagonal parking spots to the front of JerQs and walk around the people coming off the beach as the evening breeze kicks up. There's a crowd building up around the front entrance. I go to the front door and look over the shoulder of the dumpy, short, Samoan doorman. He's an unathletic wannabe tough guy with his face strained into a scowl. The front door is open and I can't see anything but the crowd jammed inside and hear the sound of a jazz steel guitar echoing into the street. I ask the short poser if I can go in and see if my friends are there and to my surprise, he waves me in with a curt nod.

Big Cal is easy to spot, towering over the people around him. "What's up, Cal?" I ask, coming up beside him.

"Walt!" Cal says loudly, over the noise. "Great you made it cause I'm just in town for a bit."

I tell Cal I have to get Gonzo and push my way back outside to the front entrance. Gonzo is milling around with the gathering crowd who are all trying to push their way in.

I wave to him and catch his eye. "Let's go! Cal's inside!"

Gonzo pushes his way over to me and we start moving towards the entrance. I hear a loud voice from behind yelling at me with bad intensions. "You're going down, Foxx!"

This isn't my first BBQ by a long shot and if this unknown poser is looking for trouble, he's probably brought a few friends. I spin around and automatically drop into a fighting stance, ready for anything, clearing a 10-foot square space around me. The loud crowd suddenly turns silent and then ripples out of the way like the Red Sea parting for Moses.

A dark figure moves into the open area and I do my visual rundown and see he has thinning light brown hair with a widow's peak with thin strands sticking up around it. He looks to me like one of the many posers I know from the bars who take steroids to get show muscles with no power because they lack the discipline to work out. His face is covered by a carefully groomed stubble that he must have spent hours on trying to make it look casual. He's like a little boy who has been playing with Daddy's razor. His neck is a stack of dimes that hasn't seen a wrestling mat except on TV. It's perched on top of a frail body like a bird cage on a pole. *Who is this clown?*

He starts jumping up and down on his toes in front of the bewildered crowd. "Let's go, Foxx!" He barks out.

I suddenly make the connection and a half-smile crosses my face but I make no immediate motion. It's a loser named Estwing Punkle, who has been on my list for years. Punkle is the biggest sucker-punch coward in the beach cities and is known for going to house parties, cold cocking unsuspecting victims and then taking off running and bragging about it later. He's not a warrior. He's has no honor and no code. He's just another coward that has never been up against a true warrior who lives by the warrior code. For years people have been talking about me and him getting into it. He seems drunk enough to try now and is about to get a hard lesson.

I look around in front of me, as he puts his fists up. The crowd around us is growing by the minute as word spreads inside the bar that we're going to throw down. He starts to juke like a bad boxer, his tight blue jeans rising with every feint. He's wearing these ridiculous ninja slippers I've seen on Kung-Fu Theater late at night when I was surfing cable TV. They are low-fitting and made from black felt with pointy toes. They look like camel toes, which is fitting for such a pussy.

"No place for you to run to this time, Punkle," I say.

He stops jumping around as if suddenly realizing the crowd has blocked his retreat. This moron fancies himself a kickboxer but I been around boxing gyms for years and have never seen him once. I'm guessing he kicks a bag in his garage. I'm sure he has no discipline to train with others. A smile comes across my face as this roadrunner jumps up and down, clicking his ninja booties together like a cartoon character. I know he is going to run so I lunge into him, exploding like an NFL linebacker. His frail body crumples over my shoulder and I slam him to the pavement and drive the air out his lungs.

He is toast and knows it. He didn't land a punch, much less a kick. I take a deep breath as I hold his waist with ease. I take inventory of myself to make sure I'm not bleeding. then I climb the rope up his body, clear his arms, and settle on top of his shoulders with my shins. I reach down and ball up his thinning baby hair, preparing to smash his head onto the ground like a bowling ball. I put my thumbs on his eye sockets and squeeze.

Punkle begins to scream from the pressure. "I'm sorry, dude! Sorry, sorry, sorry! You're the man. Don't hurt me."

I know better than to let him up. I look around at the crowd, many of whom were Punkle's cheap shot victims and are now yelling for blood. Not one person is on Punkle's side. But in the back of my mind I hear myself saying, *I can't do this anymore.* My own words echoing in my brain louder and louder. I stop just as I'm just about to bounce his head off his steroid-abused body. *I'm going to ruin my life if I keep going. Fuck it.*

I go against my instincts and release him, standing over him while he rolls to his stomach and then gets up quickly. He looks at me like he just won the lottery and then runs across Meat Street and starts rummaging through his cheap, light blue, little GMC work truck. I turn away from him for a moment to look for Gonzo and hear Punkle's voice behind me.

"Foxx! You're dead!"

Not again! Why did I cut him loose? I don't even bother to look for him. The sucker-punch coward got it handed to him so now it's over for me. He is just a coward according to the real warrior code of the street where sucker punchers are looked down on. But the cheap shot artist keeps screaming at me.

"Foxx! Come on, Foxx! Don't turn your back on me!

I know I should leave him be but his whiney voice gets the better of me. I showed him mercy once but now this loudmouth is going to pay. I spin around and sprint towards him. He keeps leaning against the side of his truck with one hand braced inside the bed. He's a sitting duck. I get within grappling distance in seconds and lower my head and lunge…into inky blackness.

The next thing I know I'm on my back in the middle of the street and Gonzo is bent over me, lightly slapping me on the cheek.

"Get up, Walt," he says, his words coming like slow-motion to my addled brain.

What the fuck? I try to push myself off the ground but fall back heavily. "I think I just had a stroke," I say groggily.

"A stroke?" Gonzo says. "No, man. Punkle pulled out a hammer when you shot in for a double leg and bashed your head. You got knocked the fuck out! I gotta get you to the ER. You're bleeding like a stuck pig!"

I see that Gonzo has pulled his Blazer next to me and that there's a circle of people looking down at me. A few hands come out of the crowd and help me to my feet as Gonzo grabs a gym towel from his back seat and throws it to me. Blood is all over my nice Spooner and I press the towel against my face to staunch the bleeding. I struggle into the passenger's side door and shut it.

"I tried to tackle him after he hit you but he jumped into his truck and drove off," Gonzo says, whipping down the road towards the E.R. "You never even saw the hammer. Why'd you let him up in the first place?"

"Fuck, Gonzo," I say. "I don't know. I thought he was going to run."

"Yeah, he ran right to his truck and grabbed a hammer and then suckered you in." He pulls up to the E.R. entrance and slams on the brakes. "What a coward. You got to get stitched up."

He helps me inside and the nurses see the blood and take me directly into an exam room, sit me down on the paper-covered padded table and then pull the curtain shut. After only a few seconds a young doctor rushes in and starts to clean and treat the wound.

"What happened?" he asks. "That's a nasty cut."

"I got in a bar fight and got hit with a hammer," I say.

"Looks like he got you good," the doctor says, finishing his cleaning and then pulling opening the supplies drawer under the table. "We're going to have to stitch up your nose and chin."

"Yep," I say. "Not my first barbecue.

"You're going to have to see a dentist for your teeth. The top teeth are missing."

I start to chuckle. "Don't worry about that." I feel a little silly in the head as the painkiller shot starts to take effect. "My teeth got knocked out when I was a freshman in high school. I took my parent's car for a joy ride and was stopped by a tree. I have a bridge that's been knocked out dozens of times."

"Okay, that's a relief," he says, finishing up with the stitches. "It's bad but not as bad as I thought." He checks his work and then tells me he's going to write a prescription for painkillers and leaves through the curtain.

A few minutes later, as I start to come back to my full senses, the curtain opens again and Sargent Hatchet from the Happening Beach PD walks in.

"Hello, Walter," he says with a slight smile and nod. "The doctor called in about a felony assault with you as the victim."

Sargent Hatchet is cool for a cop and understands street fights so I don't feel threatened talking to him. I tell him about the fight with Punkle.

"Oh, yes," he nods knowingly. "The sucker punch coward. We have had a few reports on him but I think we have him now because of all the witnesses outside the club. If you want to press charges, we'll bring him up on an attempted murder charge."

Sargent Hatchet is old school and understands the laws of the street so I give it to him straight. "I'm a warrior and I live by my street warrior code," I say. "I'll take care Punkle on my own," I say grimly.

"Look, Walter," he says, shaking his head in disapproval. "You just graduated from college and you're going to start your adult life. You won't be able to pay him back without messing up your future. At some point you have to let these things go."

I'm surprised he knows I just graduated. "How do you know all this about me, Sarge?"

"Walter, you're famous around here," he chuckles. "Everybody knows you and what you're doing with your life. You're the Happening Beach Bad Boy."

I think for a moment about what Sargent Hatchet just told me before speaking again. "I didn't finish him off for a reason. I let him up when he begged for his life just to be a new Walter...a good boy. You can see where that got me. I'll think about what I'm going to do about this but I don't want to press charges. Although, I'm sure if the tables were turned and I beat him in front of witnesses there's no doubt he would press charges against me."

"Well, we know that has already happened to you," Hatchet nods.

"Well, if the success I think I'm destined to achieve, happens, I have to stay true to the warrior code. What's that saying? The best revenge is to live a better life?"

"Okay, Walt," Hatchet says, "Your call. Let me know if you change your mind." He looks at me thoughtfully, like he is seeing me for the first time and then walks out through the curtain.

Feeling a little woozy again, I lay back down on the exam table and look up at the ceiling. It might be hard to do, but in the future I will have to learn to have the discipline to sit back and watch phonies and wannabes pass by me without taking them all down. I'll listen to the fantasy lies that cowards such as Estwing Punkle spew out and not say a word. I'll smile at them with pity from the mountaintop of my future great life. I don't know when I'll climb that mountain or how I will do it but I know that I will. I won't press charges or say a word to the cops. I'll just bide my time and get payback on all the posers by having a rich and full life. That's something that no sucker-punch coward can ever hope to match.

13. Krazy is Born

"Aren't you even going to ask me what it is?" Coby says.

"A party," I reply. "That's good enough for me.

"It's not just a party," he says. "It's the Christmas boat parade."

"Okay, whatever," I say. "A party is a party. I'll go change. Pick me up at my parents' house."

I head home and get ready and wonder about my fast change of heart. It isn't that I can't be different and stop partying it's that I don't want to. I'll just have to keep an eye on myself. I hang out and watch TV until evening comes around. As I sit on the couch with Adolf the windows start to vibrate from a low bass noise like a jet plane taking off or a locomotive rolling by and I realize that it has to be Coby's monster stereo. I look out the window and sure enough his dually is parked on the street facing the wrong way. I grab my jacket and head out. Luckily, Adolf is fast asleep so I don't have to deal with his looks of abandonment.

I walk down the driveway, pass in front of the hood of the truck, and open the passenger door. Punk rock music pours out the door accompanied by a cloud of smoke. A twelver of Coors is on the floor.

"Thank God you have something to drink," I say, coughing the dense smoke out of my lungs.

"What?" Coby asks.

I shake my head and climb in the passenger seat and reach between my legs and grab a soldier out of the cardboard carton. He pumps his head back and forth to the beat of the hard pounding music and takes off as I crack the soldier and take my first swig. As the sweet nectar falls into my stomach the houses pass by. Coby turns the residential landscape into a blur with his high school-level driving skills. He finally turns down the stereo.

"We're going to Fred's house," he says.

We wind a few miles down the residential highway to Fred's place, just one main street across from my parents', and pull into his driveway. I grab another soldier and jump out with a stupid smile on my face from the contact buzz I got from Coby's dually. Before we even get to the front door, Fred opens it up and ushers us in. He makes Coby a Bacardi and coke and then comes over to me.

"What do you want, Walt?" he asks.

"Pour me a rooster," I say. "I'll add the cranberry myself."

"I know, Walt," he smiles.

Fred puts on old school ZZ Top as I look around his place. The inside of the house is nice and clean with two-story vaulted ceilings, white walls with green carpet, and soft leather couches arranged around a high-end glass coffee table. We burn through a few songs and three drinks later are talking about which parties we're going to hit that night. Coby and Fred are properly lubricated and Fred stretches his legs, pushes back into the white leather of the couch, and digs his hand into his pocket and pulls out a white piece of paper folded into a rectangle.

"Yeah," Coby says.

Fred unfolds it on the glass table and they both fidget in anticipation. Fred puts his hand into an empty vase that is sitting on the coffee table, pulls out a razor blade, and scrapes the white powder off the paper and into lines on the glass. The drinks have managed to make ZZ Top actually sound good but I'm not going to ruin it by bumping it up. As they sit there and begin to snort, I think how similar they are: rip-off, big mouth, wannabe tough guys. The lines disappear from the glass table and their eyes get big. Fred turns into a camel, his jaw swiveling back and forth to the beat of ZZ Top like he's chewing his cud. They are both on the edge of the couches like they're getting ready for the start of a hundred-meter dash.

Fred is wearing a cheap flowered print shirt with blue jeans and Coby has on a red velour sweat suit like he's a hardcore rapper. They have been doing coke for as long as I've known them, which is 15 years for Fred and three for Coby. One good thing is that it quieted Coby down from his earlier buzz.

"Hey, guys," I finally say. "Where are we going?"

"To Nugget's party," Coby says. "We better get over there."

We head towards the Harbor and the road is crowded. The closer we get the water the thicker the traffic is. Nugget's mom is at her friend's house so he has the waterfront place all to himself. Coby pushes the doorbell until Nugget finally opens the door with a laughing *Ho, Ho, Ho*. His laughter stops, though, when he sees Coby and me. We clearly weren't on the invite list.

"Oh, hey guys," he says flatly.

I can see the wheels start to turn in his head as he looks at us. Fred has been supplying all the twenty-somethings with coke for years. Nugget clearly likes the possibility of a white Christmas.

"Come on in," he finally says.

I walk in and see many of the same people I knew from high school. Most of them are still trying to live off mommy and daddy's money as they finish college or waste time in dead-end jobs. The problem is that mommy and daddy don't have money for twenty-something kids anymore. Their second mortgages are spent and life will soon hit them in the face like a left hook. All the adult kids have on Christmas Spooners and exchange Merry Christmases with me as I walk through them to the back patio in search of the beer. The smell of cloves floats through the salty air as I grab a bottle from a cooler.

Across from me are two sisters that I had some classes with. They are tall blondes with nothing between their ears but air. I hear their whiny voices complain about how Nugget is still living with his mom. *Oh, my God*, I think. They're doing the same thing. I can't believe they can even remember to breathe. Their daddy is a dentist and they're dumb enough to think that makes them better than everyone else. They think they look like runway models and have money but they haven't figured out that daddy's money isn't their money and that they don't have two nickels of their own to rub together. They haven't changed a bit since high school.

"Hey, Walt," the taller of the two says. "What have you been up to?"

"Nothing much," I reply. "Just working for Fred selling garage doors."

They look at each other and giggle as if that's the funniest thing in the world but I just ignore it. She takes a drag off her clove cigarette and starts talking to another guy who walks outside. I drink my beer as other people come out to the patio to get ready for the boat parade. Everyone knows me by name but I just know faces.

154

"Hey, Walt," a short guy in designer clothes passes by. "Got anything coming up?"

"Nope, nothing," I say.

"Right on. Happy holidays."

I'd like to shove my happy-holidays foot up his ass. These people aren't my friends. They're all wannabes and posers. The boats start to float past the patio, all decorated with Christmas lights. A big cabin cruiser passes by with a team of reindeer taking off to the sky pulling a big fat Santa with a long beard and big belly. Fred and Coby are running back and forth to the bathroom keeping their holiday cheer going while I check out these familiar faces that I went to high school with many years back, when they thought they had the world by the tail. Now it seems that we're all in some kind of prison of our own making.

I've been pounding beers and I can tell that I'm drunk. Coby and Fred are going full throttle with the amperage pumping. They're acting like the coked-up idiots that they are, talking non-stop gibberish about nothing. Fred finally has the good sense to suggest to Coby that we leave and we head out the front door. The night is cold and the fog is rolling in from the ocean. The streets are clear since it's late and we quickly drive away from the expensive houses and head to a duplex in a big tract of apartments. Fred has a destination in mind and says he knows where there's another party. There's one complex after another filled with nothing but renters. It's a short drive from the harbor to the duplex and as we drive up, I can see that it's quiet. It's not a party but rather a place that Fred wants to party.

We walk up the quiet stairs to the landing that only has a dim porch light on. He knocks quietly and I can hear footsteps inside and then the door cracks open.

"Oh, it's Fred," a man's voice says. "Come in."

Now it's clear to me that Fred is making a delivery and dropping off a bindle. Their palms touch and the small folded paper container changes hands as the deal goes down.

"Let's hang out for a while," Fred says to me. "Do you want a bump?"

"No, I'm good," I say. I've got plenty of booze inside me but not enough to take a bump.

I sit at the small kitchen table with Coby while Fred searches the entertainment center for a tape to put on. He finds something and plugs in the cassette and I hear *La Grange* come on. *Holy fuck, more ZZ Top.* Fred comes back to the table and unfolds another bindle while Coby pulls a picture off the wall. Fred dumps the white contents on the glass of the picture frame and starts lining it out. Coby snorts a line with a dollar bill then passes it to Fred who does the same. Fred leans back and tilts his head up.

"I'm doing good now," Fred says.

A few moments later the conversation goes into full gibberish mode as the two chatter back and forth a mile a minute. After several minutes of talk that I don't even try to follow Fred turns to me.

"How are the bids going, Walt?" he asks.

"Real good," I say. "I've got the pitch down to a science. I was three-for-three the other day."

"Yeah," Fred says. "I saw that. I get you some more to do. I think I've got a couple more coming in on Tuesday."

"Cool," I say. "I could use the money."

"Coby said you have another meeting with the NHB," Fred says. "Do you think it's for real?"

"I hope so," I say. "But even if it is, I don't think they'll let me on the show. I don't think they want someone who can really fight."

Coby leans forward and does another bump and then looks at me. "Don't worry, Walt," he says. "I'll make it happen."

"We'll see what happens on Tuesday," I say.

The conversation turns to gibberish again and the sun starts to raise its ugly head over the horizon, peeking through the windows. I've been drinking all night and I can barely keep my eyes open.

"Hey, Coby," I say. "I'm not doing drugs and I'm about to fall asleep. Can you drop me off at home?"

"Yeah," Coby say. "I gotta go, too."

I fall asleep on the way back and stagger out of the dually and into my bed. Adolf dutifully followed me into the garage from the living room, where he was waiting on the couch. I don't even remember getting undressed but when I open my eyes in bed it's already 2:00 PM and stuffy inside from the afternoon sun. Adolf is next to me and I decide to take him for a long walk to try to burn off some of the fat my Dad has packed onto him. I hang out at the house on Sunday and then hit a workout on Monday and take Adolf for another walk. He seems to look thinner but it could just be wishful thinking on my part.

When Monday rolls around I decide to not risk trying to get Coby to come by and get me there on time. I look up the address of the new NHB office and drive over myself. Big Bart has upgraded from the converted 1950's hotel and moved to a modern part of Borrence that looks only 20 years old instead of 40. I go inside the two-story building and go upstairs, where I look out the hallway windows and can see my white truck parked below in the parking lot. I have no idea what to expect this time, and come more normally dressed in my Doc Martens boots, light blue jeans and a Spooner.

I walk into the NHB suite and the mirrored glass door slowly closes behind me. A little Mexican girl is sitting behind the front desk and Big Bart walks up behind her when he sees me.

"Hey, Walt," Shady says. "You found us. Let's go back to my office."

We walk into the small back office through an open door. Cardboard boxes are lying all around with the tops of most of them off. He clears two boxes off the chair in front of his desk and motions me into it and sits down across from me. The light from the single window bounces off his jet-back dyed hair cut into a flat-top. He sits back into a leather chair and his 6'2" frame makes it disappear beneath him.

"You remind me of this Russian guy who's applying to get in," Shady says. "He also sought me out. But the problem is that he's a black belt and you're not."

I look at Shady hard, waiting for his next words. *Here it comes,* I think. *I should not even have come here. He's just going to blow me off.* "So that's it then," I say, pushing back in my chair.

"Hold on, Walt," Shady says. "I know you're a fighter. I've done some research on you and all the bouncers in Orange County know who you are and were very careful to not say anything that might get back to you and make you angry."

"Good for them," I say. "They know better."

"I talked to my partners," Shady continues, "and I want to call you "Krazy" Foxx with a K".

"Why with a K?" I ask.

Have you seen that movie with Flint Westwood and the tame bear?"

"No, I don't go to movies," I answer. "I live them."

"Well, in it," Shady continues, "there's a street-fighting legend named Krazy Gridlock that Flint goes all over the U.S. trying to find so he can fight him. You'll be the real-life version of him – street-fighting legend Krazy Foxx."

"Bart," I say. "I don't care if you call me Lucy, just let me fight. I really am a street fighting legend. That is no bullshit at all."

Shady gets an even bigger smile. "Fantastic! This is going to be great." "You're sure you know how to fight, right? This show is insane. It isn't like anything the world has ever seen before"

"Don't worry, Bart," I say calmly. "I'll be fine."

"Okay, great," he says. "You're the real life Krazy."

We both start to laugh but for different reasons. I'm laughing at the absurdity of it all but I can tell that he's laughing at me not with me. This big cucumber of a man thinks he's playing me, but in reality, he's the one who's getting played. Shady thinks he just created a cartoon character that is going to get the stuffing knocked out of him by real martial artists and I'm thinking what a fool this guy is. I'm going to hurt some people.

"One thing," I say. "Can I get it on paper that I'm fighting in NHB 5?"

"Oh, I forgot to tell you," Shady says. "You can't fight in NHB 5. We're getting a lot of heat right now.

No-rules fighting is taking a beating in the media so you're going to fight in July when everything cools down."

"Okay," I say. "I just want something on paper so I can train."

"No problem," Shady says. "I'll write something up right now."

"Make it out to Walter Foxx," I say. "But when I fight it will be as Krazy Foxx."

Shady calls in the secretary, gives her instructions, and she goes out to her typewriter and comes back in a couple of minutes with a one-page letter with one line on it: "Walter Foxx will fight in NHB 6." Then on the bottom it's dated December 20, 1994. He signs it "Bart Shady, NHB Matchmaker." He puts it on the only clear part of the desk in front of me and I take it, stand up, and shake his hand.

"Walt," Shady says, "I want you to know that this is a very serious and dangerous business. It's not a boxing match. It's no-rules fighting. Frankly Walt, it's just crazy and I hope you're ready for it."

"Crazy sounds just like me," I say. "I'll keep in touch. I've got some training to do."

"You look like you're in good shape already," Shady says.

"I've been running a lot but I need to get into fighting shape," I say. "They're two different things."

"Whatever you say, Krazy," Shady says.

I turn and walk out of his office through the mirrored door. I look back as I walk along the hallway and there is no flash off the glass due to the cloudy and gray day. I walk through the parking lot to my truck, put it into reverse, and back up until the front of the truck is pointed directly at Shady's office. A ray of sunlight has burned through the cloud cover and bounces off the upstairs window into my eyes. The letter is still clutched in my hand. I don't want to let it go for fear it may disappear like something from a dream. In a few months I'm going to be fighting in the NHB.

14. The Letter

"I'm Krazy," I say aloud.

Then I start laughing. What kind of bullshit is this? I cruise through the old Borrence neighborhoods towards the freeway, eager to get back to Orange County where everything is new. I change the radio from KLOS to KROQ and hear the Ramones come on singing, "I want to be sedated." That's pretty much how I feel right now. I drive to Decisions at the end of the cul-de-sac and go inside to Coby's office. His eyes are less red than normal and he actually seems semi-alert.

"What happened?" he asks eagerly.

"I'm in," I say.

"Yeah!" Coby yells. "I told you!"

"For the first time I believe it," I say. "He even gave me a letter. But they want me to fight as Krazy Foxx, with a K."

"You mean like in the movie with the bear?" Coby says.

"Yep. Krazy Foxx," I repeat. "The world's toughest underground street fighter. It's stupid, I know."

"No, Walt," Coby says. "I like it. It's perfect."

"They think they're getting over on me and setting me up but the joke will be on them when I destroy these PJ guys," I say. "Also, it isn't until July so I have plenty of time to get ready."

"This is fucking great," Coby says. "The NHB was made for you."

I'm anxious to spread the word after thinking it wasn't going to happen. I leave Decisions and drive the short distance to Fred's office, but Skip is the only one there when I walk in.

"What's up, Walt?" he asks.

"I just got done meeting with the head honcho of the NHB, Bart Shady," I say.

"What's the NHB?" Skip asks.

It's that no-holds-barred fighting show on pay-per-view," I say.

"Oh yeah. I heard about that. That's perfect for you," Skip laughs.

The office door opens and Fred walks in.

"Walt just got invited to be in that NHB fighting show on pay-per-view TV," Skip says to him. "He's going to be a star."

Fred takes a second to digest the news and gets a jealous look on his face, like someone else just got the last slice of pizza. "That's cool," he says with a slight nod and faint smile. "I mean, if you like that kind of thing."

"Check out this letter they gave me," I say.

I pull Bart Shady's letter out of the folder I carry to do bids. Skip grabs it, makes a copy, and staples it to the wall. Fred looks it over and the smile leaves his face.

"Okay, Skip," Fred says. "Back to work now."

I can see what Skip means about Fred. He really is a controlling prick in the office.

"Well, I'm going for a run now," I say, to break the awkward silence. "I have to formulate a plan. I need to be big and strong and ready to take on the world."

I drive home, still in a little bit of a daze, and get my running sweats on. I lace up my running shoes, put a rubber band around the Walkman headphones to keep them from falling off, and jog out of the housing tract and onto the main drag. With Ice T's "Colors" blaring in my head I pick up the pace and start to push myself. I have something to run for now, and a direction to go. My sweat is cool in the air and I run hard, pushing myself to that moment of pain you need to get to when you train where you're just about to throw up and your heart feels like it's going to explode in your chest.

I back-off and sigh and a smile crosses my face. *It hurts so good.* I need to get back on the mat and wrestle. All real fights end up on the ground after a few seconds. Ice T turns into NWA and I start to pick up the pace. The earlier pain has gone away so I push harder until it comes back then back off again. I ran so much at the halfway house that my cardio is good. As the cinder block fence passes by in the corner of my eye a million thoughts run through my head. I need to get big and strong. I need to go to Poppa Chulo's high school wrestling match tonight and show him the letter.

I get to the far end of my parents' street and push myself hard, sprinting down the asphalt. I glance left and see a neighbor scrubbing pots through her kitchen window. She stops and stares out the window as I haul ass by her; a rampaging elephant shaking the ground beneath her feet. My heart is pounding and my lungs burning as I make it to my front yard. As I bend over at the waist and take in huge gulps of fresh air my dad pulls up in the driveway and rolls the window down.

"Jump in," he says. "Let's go get some food, on me."

"Sure, Dad," I say.

I cool down for a few more minutes, then hop-in and my dad drives to Steve's, a burger place run by a cool Greek family that is a step up from all the fast food chains. We order our food and sit down to eat and then I pull out the letter.

"Dad," I say, putting it on the table. "I got a signed letter from that big goof who runs the NHB."

My dad stops in mid-bite. "Seriously? What does it say?"

"It says I'm fighting in their July show, not in May," I say. "There's too much bad press going around about no-rules fighting right now and he wants to give it a chance to cool off."

"You're going to be on TV?" my Dad says. "Like what we watched that one night?"

I nod at him.

"That's great!" he says. "Just wait till I tell everyone."

"Yeah," I say. "It's going to be a lot of fun. I'm going to do a lot of wrestling and hit the weight room and put on size and muscle."

"Good, Walter," my Dad says. "You need to give this your best shot. It's what you've been talking about for years."

We leave and go home and I take a shower. *I've been here before*, I think, as the water falls down on me. Except now instead of looking forward to getting out of jail I'm going to be fighting on TV. It almost doesn't seem real to me still. I get dressed and go to the high school's main gym. The mat is stretched out in the middle of the basketball floor with the two high school teams on each side, ready to go to war. The wood bleachers are sparsely filled with some parents. I don't even see any cheerleaders. I spot Rolando and Poppa Chulo on the other side, getting their kids warmed up and walk over.

"Hey guys," I say, producing the letter from Shady. "Check this out. It's from the head honcho of the NHB fighting show."

Poppa Chulo reads the one sentence letter and his eyes pop open. "This is great, Walt."

I pass the letter over to Rolando, expecting to see the same response. He reads it though and shoves it back in my hands.

"Fuck!" Rolando says. "This is bullshit!" He stomps away to the mat.

"What is his problem?" I ask Poppa Chulo.

"Ignore him," Poppa Chulo says. "It isn't about you. He's been trying to get in this show since you went to jail. He knows some clown who said he was going to get him in but it was all bullshit."

"But Rolando is not a fighter," I say. "He's a wrestler."

"Yeah, I know," Poppa Chulo says. "I told him that. He has no rep on the street at all. But some guy from downtown has been pumping him up, telling him that he's a killer."

"Come on," I say dubiously. "Rolando?"

"Yeah," Poppa Chulo says. "I have no idea where he got that from."

I shrug and walk away and grab a seat in the bleachers by myself. There are guys everywhere who are closet gladiators. They think they're tough but they have never gone to war, just played around on the mat or in the ring. That's not real fighting at all. It's hard when they find out the truth about themselves.

I watch the high school kids get down and don't really even start to really pay attention until the bigger kids come up. The lightweights bore me. When I was in high school, I would wrestle with the older guys that were smaller. They were so weak that I would beat them even then. It is a curse to be small, I muse. You spend your entire life trying to prove yourself but you never really do.

After the 190 pounders wrestle I walk out of the gym and get on my Interceptor. The high school parking lot is empty with no kids anywhere. I've got seven months to get ready for the rest of my life. I need to let people know who I am. I need to get big and sharpen my wrestling and I decide to get started in earnest in the morning.

After tossing and turning in bed for a while from the excitement of the letter I finally fall into a deep sleep. I am awakened only by the beeping of my alarm clock in the early morning. Rather than turn it off, however, I spring up, hit the shower, put on my running gear, and then go outside and hit the throttle on my cruise to Pain City. If you're not hurting, then you're not doing anything. After a long jog followed by a heart-pounding sprint down the long stretch of road back to my house I lean against the garage door to catch my breath. Behind the wooden swing-up door is my bedroom and my life. But that will change if I can just keep training hard and getting ready.

I get cleaned up and presentable to the rest of the normal world and jump on the Interceptor. My thoughts race even faster than my bike as I twist the throttle hard and make the scenery pass by me in a blur. My Mom's words echo in the wind rushing past my ears: "Life is passing you by, Walter. Make something of yourself." I end up at Fred's office and walk in the dark tinted glass door. Skip is on the phone so Fred comes out of the back to see who chimed the entrance ringer.

"It's me, Fred," I say. "You don't need to sell anything."

"Oh, hey Walt," Fred says in a neutral voice. "Looks like you've started training."

"Yeah," I say. "I just got done with a hard run."

"Are you even going to want to work?" Fred asks.

"Yeah," I say. "Why do you think I'm here? I need a few bids to do each week, until just before I fight."

"I think I can do that," Fred says. "What are you going to do after the fight?"

"I don't know," I shrug. "I haven't thought about it. Go back to full time I guess, if you have enough bids."

"We'll see how it goes," Fred says noncommittally.

I'm surprised by Fred's reaction but say nothing. I thought he would happy but he's acting more like he's jealous. I get on my bike and head home. It's weird how Fred reacted to my good news. He's a wannabe tough guy but except for a sucker punch now and then he never had the balls to throw down in a real fight. It's his problem not mine, I decide.

I get back home and go into the kitchen to start the other part of my training plan which is to get big and gain weight. I grill up three big cheeseburgers on the barbeque and wolf them down. Then I mix an entire blender of chocolate ice cream and non-fat milk. Adolf stares waiting for a snack but I ignore him. I have to get bigger and he has to get smaller. I eat till it hurts and then eat some more. I stare mindlessly at daytime TV until the food digests then I grab my weight belt and workout bag and head to the gym on my Interceptor.

The weight room is half the size of a basketball court with high ceilings and tall windows looking outside. One third of the room is taken up by blue Nautilus weight machines and their chains rattle as I pass them. They are mainly being used by women, who move the shells that the chains wrap around to get in shape. I cross the brown shag carpet in the middle of the room and go to the back where my old friend, the old-school weight bench is. It's an old but sturdy bench I used when I drove up 600 lbs. the first time on the bench press. The long steel bar sits on top of two posts instead of sitting on welded pegs that cantilever out.

I cinch up my weight belt tightly and get to work punching out four sets of four, loading up the bar with enough plates to make it sag on the ends. Then I switch to dumbbell bench, upright rows, dumbbell curls, and Nautilus neck and trap machines. If I keep this up, I know I'll get big in no time. I finish up with a light cool-down on the treadmill then head over to Rolando's and Poppa Chulo's high school wrestling practice. Practice is just finishing and Rolando kicks the kids out of the room when he sees me.

"Okay," I say. "Let's train."

We all look at each other unsurely. We've never trained for a no-rules fight and are not sure what to do.

"What do you want to practice?" Poppa Chulo asks.

"I guess let's do takedowns," I say, "then mess around with the fighting stuff." I can see that I'm going to have to call the shots in training.

We do a good session of takedowns but always end it when we get to the ground. I know that is where the fight will actually start in the NHB and decide to do some of the chokes we saw on TV. We rest up a little bit and then start rolling wildly on the ground, applying chokes to each other anytime we can and then trying to break them.

After just a little bit we're all red-faced and gasping for air.

"This is crazy shit," Rolando says. "We're just copying what we've seen on TV. I hope we're doing it right."

"Well we got no choice," I say. "We're all that we have. Let's go some more."

Rolando and Poppa Chulo take turns sparring with me, none of us stopping when we get to a position or hold that would be considered illegal in wrestling. This is the first time any of us has done real no-rules grappling and we try different chokes to see which ones actually work and which are bullshit. Our arms quickly get flooded with lactic acid and become exhausted, and after an hour we can barely move them. Our eyes have been forever opened by the first squeeze around the neck and we realize just how little we know about no-rules wrestling.

15. Baton Beatdown

We make plans to train every day after wrestling practice with the three of us trying chokes and different moves. As the training days go by, we stay consistent and I also keep visiting the weight room. In just a matter of few months I've added many more 45 lb. plates to the bar and have gone up from 220 lbs. to just a tad over 260 lbs. My strength is back and I'm going 505 lbs. for four sets on the bench and hitting upright rows at 335 lbs.

My takedowns are sharp and I've been fighting against Rolando, who has copied the guard that the PJ guy has been doing on TV, to get used to that style. I've been getting my chokes down and my arms are not getting flooded anymore and I've learned how to relax on the mat doing no-rules wrestling. Rolando and Poppa Chulo and myself have been doing moves that are nothing like traditional wrestling. Before I know it NHB 5 is coming up and Poppa Chulo is sitting on the mat with me after one of our usual training battles.

"I ran into an old wrestling buddy we both know the other day," Poppa Chulo says.

"Yeah?" I answer.

"I used to work with him at Baton Sportswear," Poppa Chulo continues, "and I told him you're fighting in the NHB. You remember Mark, right?"

"Yeah," I say. "He wrestled in the lighter weights."

"Well, he watches the NHB and thinks it's cool," Poppa Chulo tells me, "and he said to call him up and he'll line you up with a whole new wardrobe."

"Really?" I say. "How much will it cost me? Do I get a discount?"

"That's what I asked," Poppa Chulo says. "But he won't charge you a dime if you wear it on TV."

"Well, set it up," I say. "You call him. I can't beg people for stuff. It's against who I am as a person. I hate to ask people for things. It makes me feel weak."

"Okay, Walt," Poppa Chulo says. "I'll talk to him and let you know."

Another thought suddenly pops into my head. "See if he'll buy me an airline ticket and a hotel room to NHB 5 in North Carolina. I need to see this stuff in person to get ready for it. Then I'll call him later after you talk to him, when I get done with my bids for Fred."

"You got it, boss," Poppa Chulo says.

I go home and shower and change and go out on the road but both appointments are a waste of time; just window shoppers who aren't ready to buy. With no money to be made I go back to the office and sit glumly at my desk and look at the letter on the wall that Skip stapled there; the one with the one sentence from Bart Shady that has the power to change my life. No one is around so I pick up the phone and dial Poppa Chulo.

"Did you talk to Mark?" I ask when he picks up.

"Yeah," Poppa Chulo says. "He was really friendly. He says he can get you clothes and also get you a room and an airline ticket to North Carolina."

"That would be fucking cool," I say.

"He's serious but he's expecting a call from you now," Poppa Chulo says. "Call him, okay?"

Poppa Chulo gives me the number and I hang up and dial the new digits. When it gets picked up, I instantly recognize the voice.

"Hey, Mark," I say. "It's Walter Foxx."

"Walt," Mark answers. "Great to hear from you. Poppa Chulo told me that you're fighting in that no-rules fighting show. It's been years since I've seen you last, since junior college. I'm at Baton Sportswear now so come down and get some clothes."

This is all going a little too easily and I'm suspicious. "You know I'm not fighting in the next one," I say. "I'll be going live in July."

"Yeah, that's no problem," Mark says. "Poppa Chulo already told me."

"I just want you to know I'm not taking anything without making sure I do something in return for it," I say. "I'm not a rip-off."

"Don't worry, Walt," Mark says. "As long as you wear it then everybody will be happy. Just come down now and we'll work it out."

Mark gives me directions and I get into my white truck and drive down to Orvine, about 30 minutes away. I get off the freeway and drive into a business park near the airport that is filled with the ever-present tilt-up concrete buildings that seem to drive the southern California economy. I find the building and open the mirrored front door and walk into the lobby and ask the receptionist for Mark.

"He'll be right out," she says, after picking up the phone and announcing me.

I sit down on the green fabric sofa in the lobby and look around at the windowless walls, which are filled with picture of volleyball players, all a little too pretty even as they dive in the sand or spike the ball over the net. They have slim bodies, not tight or rough, and have soft faces. *They wouldn't last a second with me*, I think.

175

It seems funny that a volleyball company would want to sponsor a fighter but I'm not going to look a gift horse in the mouth. The door to the corporate back offices open and Mark walks out.

"Hey, Walt," he says. "It's been a long time."

Mark is wearing a button-down shirt and blue jeans and has grown from the 130 lbs. weight class he wrestled in on the junior college team to around 180 lbs. He looks like Opie from the Andy Griffith show with an honest and open face. I follow him into his office in the middle of the big clothing corporation. He sits behind the desk and I sit across from him.

"Fuck, Mark," I say. "I'm going to get down. I'm going to show these posers how to fight. They don't know what's up, but they will."

"That's great," Mark laughs, "You haven't changed a bit from college. I actually thought about you when I saw that show on TV. It was perfect when Poppa Chulo called and told me you were doing it. That show is made for you. Poppa Chulo said you also needed a plane ticket and hotel room for the next event. Is that right?"

"Yeah," I say, "if possible. But I don't want to put you out on a limb."

"Don't worry about it," Mark says. "I already talked to Ted, the owner, and he agreed to it. You're all set. We have a person that books that for the volleyball players we sponsor. We're used to doing it. Now let's go grab some clothes."

I follow him back into the building and the office workers there look at me like, *Who the hell is this guy?* I look around a little bit self-consciously, but Mark introduces me to a few of them as an NHB fighter – but they have no idea what he's talking about.

176

"Don't worry about it," Mark says as we walk out of the office and into the warehouse. "They'll know who you are soon enough."

We take a big bin with wheels and Mark takes me down aisle after aisle of shirts, pants, shorts, socks of every color size and style imaginable. I take a little here and there but am very respectful about the amount I take. The only thing I take a lot of are socks, which I've been going through from my running and mat work. We take the halfway full bin out to my truck and load the clothes into the back.

"Mark," I say. "I feel bad taking these clothes from you before I've done anything to earn them. It doesn't feel right."

Mark looks at me quizzically for a moment and then laughs. "Walt, we have not yet begun to shop. I thought you were just checking out what you liked. These volleyball players leave here with truckloads of this stuff. This is nothing, Walt. Take it and run. Trust me. Now I'll show you how we really do things around here."

We walk back into the warehouse with me pushing the cart and with Mark in the lead pulling product off the shelves by the handful. He grabs everything in my size that even looks halfway good to me. As I walk around the warehouse among the ten-foot tall shelves of clothing Mark takes over and goes crazy, grabbing three of everything and throwing them into the bin. He puts in shorts, shirts, jackets, and pants.

"You like this?" Mark asks, holding up a short-sleeved shirt with vertical stripes.

"It's cool," I say.

Mark nods he throws in five of them in different colors. When we fill up one bag, we leave it by the door and go back with another.

"I feel guilty, Mark," I say after the third load.

"No, Walt," he says. "This is nothing."

"I'm just not used to people giving me things just because of who I am," I say.'

"Well, get used to it," Mark replies.

He just keeps loading up boxes and we eventually have four of them stacked by the rear door.

"Hold on," Mark says. "I'll get you a sports bag. We just got them in."

He goes to the loading docks and opens a big container and pulls out a four-foot long bag and goes back and stuff it with clothes until we can barely zip it shut. Finally, we finish and the rear door is stacked with four big boxes and the giant bag. I wonder if I can even get them in my truck. Mark calls over a couple of workers to carry the boxes to my truck.

"You don't look like a volleyball player," one of the Mexican workers says to me as we walk out with the load and put it in the back of my truck. "You're too damn big."

"This is Walter Foxx," Mark says. "He's going to be fighting in a no-rules fighting show."

The Mexican's eyes get really big. "You mean the NHB?"

"I'm going to be fighting in July," I say.

The guy grabs my hand and starts shaking it like he just met the President of the United States. "I love that show. I never miss it. I'm gonna watch you on TV. Kick ass!"

16. Fly Like an Eagle

I pull into the parking lot of Fred's office and rummage
through the boxes and the big sports bag from Baton just
looking at all the free stuff they gave me. I manage to
close the boxes but the bag is so full that I can barely zip
it up. I have to compress the sides with my knees to get
the teeth close enough together to mesh. I wrap both
hands around it in a bear hug when I get out of the truck,
then lumber to the door and push it open with my back.

"Hey, Skip," I say as I drop the four-foot-long bag in
the middle of the blue carpeted floor. "Check it out.
There's even more stuff in my truck."

I go back outside and bring in the boxes one at a time,
pushing the door open with my back each trip, barely
able to see where I'm going. By the time I've brought in
the final box Skip already has the clothes from the bag
laid out on the office floor. With no room left I stack the
boxes on the desk where I do my bids.

"Holy shit, Walt," Skip says. "This is crazy."

The door chimes and Fred walks in and looks over the
front office which is strewn with new clothes from front
to back.

"What is all this stuff?" Fred asks, with a little bit of
an attitude.

"Baton Sportswear is sponsoring Walt," Skip says.
"They gave him all this stuff for free. Cool, huh?"

Fred nods with an annoyed look on his face and walks
down the hallway to his office in the rear. Skip shrugs his
shoulders and we go through everything, sorting the
pants and shirts and organizing and repacking them. I

have a whole new wardrobe, I realize, and a new look. I sit in the chair at my desk and look at the bulletin board on the wall where Skip stapled the letter.

"That one little sentence carries a lot of weight," I laugh.

"Yeah, I guess so," Skip answers.

"I don't get it," I say. "I haven't done anything yet but get a piece of paper and people are giving me stuff. It's too soon. Maybe someday it'll make sense to me."

"That's the power of TV," Skip says.

"Yeah, I guess," I answer. "I'll check you out later."

I drive home and put the stuff in my garage next to my bed. I reach into one of the boxes and pull out the thick socks I liked and slide them on and lace my running shoes tightly. I'm determined more than ever to chase the pain and push it till it hurts. I go outside and settle into a brisk jog that gets my heart pumping in my chest. It bothers me a little that people want to give me so much. I thought I'd have to prove myself. Do I owe them something if I don't do well? I just want to be upfront with everyone so there are no misunderstandings.

I start to open the door of pain and when it almost gets unbearable, I back off and ease into something less intense, like sunburn pain. I know it's there but I can control it deal with it for days if need be. I go into cruise control and do four miles quickly but not without a struggle. Now that I'm getting heavier, running long distance is getting harder. But that is all part of my edge and when I climb into the cage, I don't want my fitness to be an issue.

I finish my run and grab my grappling gear and meet Rolando and Poppa Chulo at the wrestling room. We bang around in the room until we're pouring sweat mixed with a little bit of blood from crashing our heads together doing takedowns.

"Mark dialed me in," I say to Poppa Chulo as we take a break. "He gave me a ton of clothes and a whole new look. You really think Ted will get me a plane ticket and a hotel for NHB 5?"

"Don't worry," Poppa Chulo says. "You're in. They like you."

We finish the workout and I go home and eat a big meal to keep my weight up and then go to bed early. Now that I'm training my mind is focused on what I have to do. I wake up in the morning in my garage and realize that I'm sore from my long run yesterday. I'm just too big for long distance jogging, I realize, and am afraid I might blow out a knee or ankle. I change up and run a two-mile loop around the housing tract instead and add that to my workout routine every day. It's still hard but I can do it without fear of injury. I'm sitting in the living room one morning, after two weeks of this, when the phone rings.

"Hi," a crisp, official-sounding voice says. "I'm looking for Walter Foxx."

Oh, shit, I think. Did someone from my not-too-distant past that I beat up call the cops?

"This is Ted from Baton Sportswear," he continues, not waiting for me to answer. "I'm the owner."

"Oh, Ted," I say in relief. "Yeah! How are you? Hey, thanks for those clothes. They're really cool. I really appreciate it."

"No problem," Ted says. "I was wondering when you wanted to fly out to the show in North Carolina? Mark said you needed a ticket and a hotel room."

"Yeah," I say. "That would be great if you could hook me up for that. I don't know the particulars yet, but I'll call Bart Shady and figure it out."

"Call my secretary when you get the info and we'll book everything from our office," Ted says.

"Cool, Ted," I say. "You're the man."

"Not to worry," Ted replies. "We do a lot of that for promotional purposes."

I start to feel a little guilty and decide to clear the air. "You know, I'm not sure I'll be on TV at this show," I say. "I'm not fighting but I'll try get it on."

"Don't worry about that now," Ted says. "Just get on in the summer and it'll be all good."

"I will," I say. "The world doesn't know what's coming."

I hang up the phone, get into my truck, and go over to Decisions and walk up the stairs to Coby's office. He's sitting behind his desk looking at the back of his hand with an expression of wonderment on his face.

"Coby," I say. "Snap out of it."

"Oh, hey," he says, not looking up. "Dude, the human hand is amazing. You ever thought about how when you think it to move, it actually does what it's told. What if it went on strike? We'd all be so fucked."

"Look, stoner," I say, "that's like the tenth time you've told me about your hand. I just wanted to let you know that Baton Sportswear is sending me to NHB 5 in North Carolina."

Coby pulls his gaze upwards from the joys of his own anatomy with a look of puzzlement. "Why do you want to go there?"

"I want to watch the show in person and get the lay of the land," I say. "I don't want to get there when I fight in the summer and have it all be new. I want to know everything."

"Exactly," Coby says, with unfocused stoner gaze. "I'm glad you're finally seeing things my way. I'll call Big Bart and get all the information you need."

"Look," I say. "Write this stuff down so you don't forget it. Find out where to go and where to stay. Find out how I get to the arena from the airport. Get me passes to the backstage area so I can see the fighters myself."

"I don't have to write it down," Coby says. "I'll call Bart right now."

He dials a number and I coach him through talking to Shady, several times having him put his hand over the receiver so I can remind him of something. After 10 minutes he hangs up.

"Bart says you're dialed in," Coby announces. "No problem at all. Front row tickets on the floor, backstage passes, and tickets to the press conference, weigh-in, and after party."

"Okay," I say. It sounds a little too good to be true. I hope it all works out. "Make sure you call Ted's secretary at Baton and give her all the info. She'll book everything. Just don't screw it up. I don't want to get on a plane and end up in Alaska."

"Dude," Coby says. "It's all good. What could possibly go wrong?"

I leave that question hanging in the air and head out to do a couple of bids but don't sell either one. I go back to Fred's office a little deflated because I really need the money and give Coby a call.

"How'd it go?" I ask when he picks up.

"You're lined up, man," Coby says. "You're going to NHB 5!"

"Cool," I say. "I really have to hook Baton up with exposure when I get the chance."

"You're not just going but you'll be in the same hotel as all the NHB staff," Coby explains. "Ted took care of everything."

"Yeah," I say. "He's a very cool guy."

"You leave next week out of John Wayne Airport," Coby finishes. "I'll take you there myself. Come by later and I'll give you all the info."

I hang up the phone and lean back in the office chair and stare sightlessly at the wall, tapping my pen on the desktop. *This is really going to happen.* Just a few months ago I was in jail with nothing to look forward to in life and now I'm going to the NHB and having a sponsor pay for it. You just never know when good things will turn on a dime and go to hell, or when bad things will make a U-turn and start heading up. You just can't get too down when you're in the dumps or too up when you're on top of the world.

I tell Skip what's going down and he's dutifully impressed. Then I head to my garage, get my workout bag, and go to the gym where I pump some heavy iron. My excitement gives me a lot of energy and I get in a good lift. I change clothes and then get on the Interceptor and go over to see Coby in his office.

His eyes are a little puffier than earlier this morning with little slits to see out of. It's obvious 4:20 came early today. If possible, he's even more stoned than he was earlier. He hands me the itinerary that Ted's secretary faxed over to him and I check it out. Everything looks good so I guess this is all on the up and up.

"Let's go to Sizzler and eat," I say, folding the paper and putting it in my back pocket. "I've got to get big."

Coby drives over in his truck and we stand in line and get to the register.

"What will it be?" the Mexican guy behind the counter asks.

"I'll have a chicken breast and a plain baked potato," I say.

"Will that be it?" he asks.

"No," I say after a moment, "actually it won't. Give me a steak and the all-you-can-eat shrimp too."

The guy raises his eyebrows but says nothing and rings me up. Coby is the one who's stoned and should have the munchies but instead I'm the one who is trying to pack it in. I sit down and I eat till it hurts. Coby keep pace with me at the salad bar for a while but finally falls by the wayside and watches me chow down. I'm so full I can barely talk but I know that I have to get big if I'm going to fight the 300-pounders in the NHB.

Coby drops me off at my Interceptor and I drive home, my thoughts turning over even faster than the pistons underneath me. Even though I have all the paperwork, there's a nagging feeling in the back of my head that it just isn't going to happen. I've been down this road before, where things look like they're turning around only to run straight into a brick wall. Nevertheless, I force myself to remain positive and hit hard workouts the rest of the week doing my running, wrestling and boxing.

When Saturday rolls around I'm ready for a break and pick up some supplies from the grocery store and head to Poppa Chulo's apartment to get my mind off my training. I feel like blowing off some steam but know that I have to be careful to not have too much fun because the DA is still out there with his legal sniper aimed straight between my shoulder blades. He'd like nothing better than to pull the trigger and send me away. So instead of going out to the bars we chill in the apartment and watch the tube and get drunk on Stoli and cranberry. I go home late at night and lay in bed looking up at the garage rafters with Adolf next to me.

With the trip to NHB 5 in sight, it's unbelievable how many beggars I've let off the hook who normally would have paid the price for their evil actions. Looking from the outside in you would think that I'd changed; but from the inside looking out I'm about to explode. I can't live like this but I also can't fuck it up when I'm so close to my lifelong dream of doing real fighting without going to jail. I've gotten big and strong and sharp and have been training hard to legally kick the shit of some phony beggars on television. *Fuck it. I've got to be a good boy.* I can't be in prison for life now that I've got something to shoot for.

The week goes by slowly because all I can do is think about the upcoming trip. I do a few more bids early in the week and make some much-needed money and then for my passion I lift weights, wrestle, box and run every day, making for a busy schedule. The day before I'm supposed to leave for the NHB I run into Albert, one of the coaches in the junior college weight room.

"Hey, Walt," he says. "How are you?"

"Just getting ready to head out on a trip, actually," I say. "I'm going out to a fight show in North Carolina."

"Boxing?" he asks.

"No," I say. "It's a new no-holds-barred fighting show in a steel cage. It'll be on TV so you'll be able to watch. I'll be fighting in the next one this summer."

"For real?" he asks with a laugh. "Walt, that's perfect for you. How many times has the athletic trainer here taken stitches out of your face from street-fighting?"

"Fuck, Albert," I say. "I can't count that high."

"Well, have fun," he says. "Just stay out of trouble and don't mess it up. I wanna see you kick ass on TV. This could be good for you so don't be stupid and throw it away to beat some fool's ass in a parking lot."

"Yeah, I know," I say. I've known Albert for a while and he knows me better than most of my casual acquaintances. "I won't blow it. I've been playing it cool since I got out of jail."

"Alright," he says, walking off. "Let me know if you need anything."

I go back to driving heavy iron and finish after an hour and walk out to my bike, slapping my weight belt on the asphalt as I go. It's a familiar sound that rings true in my ears. I've perfected it from many years of practice. You can hear it from a mile away – it's a signal to my enemies to clear a path to the weight room and run the other unless they want trouble. I get back home and clean up and then go out to the garage to pack. I'm leaving tomorrow so I load up the big Baton sports bag with new clothes. I set it by the front door, watch some TV, then go into the garage and fall into a restless sleep.

I wake up in the morning and get ready and it's obvious that Adolf senses something is up. He looks at the bag by the door and then at me and lets out a whine.

"Don't worry, boy," I say. "I'll be back in a few days."

I walk outside with my bag and wait for Coby to show up. I should have asked someone a little more reliable to drive me but he offered so now I just hope he shows up.

He's five minutes late and I'm just about to go inside and call him when his white dually appears at the end of the street with tires squealing and his punk rock music leaking out through the closed windows.

"Come on, Coby," I say. "We're late. We have to hurry."

A wicked smiled comes over his face and I'm sorry I said the words as soon as they leave my mouth. We race to the airport, weaving in and out of lanes at 90 miles-per-hour, and the stoner gets me to the airport half-scared out of my mind but on time to make my flight to my first NHB.

17. Federal Bureau of Intoxication

The typical flight holds no surprises, just the lame boredom of modern economy air travel. I eagerly stare out the oval window of the plane as the jet hits the tarmac in Harlot, North Carolina. My thoughts are going crazy with the improbability of it all: *What the fuck am I doing and how did I get here?*

I walk out of the plane and through the airport and spot a guy near the outside curb holding a sign with my name on it as promised. It seems that maybe Bart Shady is the man if he can get me a curbside shuttle. It's light outside even after a long layover in Atlanta to change planes but I'm here. The guy with the sign leads me to a van where a short blonde chick and a red-headed guy are already sitting on the front bench seat.

"Did you hear about the Jeet Kune Do guy that's fighting?" the blonde says as the door slides shut.

"He's a badass," the redhead comments. "Fred E. Mercury, the NCAA wrestler, is on the card too."

"He's tough," the woman says.

A smile slowly creeps across my face as I stare out the window at the passing scenery and listen to them talk about all the fighters on the card in the seat in front of me. Finally, the blonde woman turns around and looks at me.

"Who are you?" the blonde asks.

"I'm nobody," I say. "Just Walt."

"You're not a fighter?" she says.

"I'm just here to check it out," I say. "I'm nothing like these tough guys you're talking about." *I'm actually a fighter and not a wannabe.*

"Nice to meet you, Walt," she says. "I've been to all the shows and know everyone. Do you know Mick Puffer, the announcer?"

"No, I don't know anyone," I say sarcastically.

As the van winds down the tree-lined landscape of North Carolina I marvel at how green it is. I've never been in a place like this and wonder if the entire South looks the same. It's starting to get dark when the van turns into a long driveway and pulls up to the front of the hotel. A couple of bellhops come out to the van pushing a luggage cart with brass bars arching on top. They pop the back door of the van and I get out quickly and grab my Baton bag before they can put it on the cart.

"No, bro," I say. "I got it."

He's probably looking for a tip which is okay except for the fact that I'm currently living in a garage. I sling it over my shoulder and walk in the lobby. Just inside the door I see an older black guy, maybe in his mid-50s, wearing a tuxedo and standing in front of a table stacked with NHB tee-shirts. He has a surreal look to him with gray around the outlines of his curly black hair like a bad dye job. He is old with an unnaturally smooth complexion and tight smile that makes me think a face lift has been performed. I cast my eyes downward and attempt to walk by but he sticks out his arm to offer a handshake.

"Hi," he says a little too cheerfully for my liking, "I'm Ron Disbleef. What's your name?"

"I'm Walt," I say.

"You're a big one," he says, suddenly a little guarded. "Are you an NHB fighter?"

"Just a spectator," I say, "here to watch the show."

"Well, then, welcome, Walt," He says.

I shake his hand and then quickly walk off before anyone can try to sell me a tee-shirt. If I'm going to wear anything it's going to be Baton Sportswear. I walk up to the black granite front desk across from one of the dark-suited clerks.

"I think I have a room waiting for me," I say hopefully.

"Your name?" he asks.

"Walter Foxx," I reply.

He checks a list in front of him then and looks up and smiles at me. "Here you are. You have a suite."

"Are you sure?" I ask. "I think it was just supposed to be a regular room."

"All our rooms are suites, sir," he replies. "Many people live here and use the room for extended business stays. Here's your key."

I take the paper sleeve he offers me and see that he has written 255 on it, which means I'm on the second floor. He points across the lobby and I walk across it, keeping my distance from Ron Disbleef and his unnaturally smooth skin, and walk to the elevator. I get out after a quick ride up and walk down the hallway to my room, which is at the corner of the hotel.

I walk in and see that it's larger than a normal room and has a living room and bedroom area. It's nicely furnished and everything is clean and new but I doubt the clerk's story about people living here. I throw down my Baton bag and sit down on the couch in the living room area and flip on the TV. There's nothing on but I didn't come all this way to watch the tube anyway. I splash some cold water on my face and head out to find some fun. It's time to party.

I leave the room and walk down the hallway, assaulted by green floral print wallpaper and white carpet. I walk to the elevator and press the button to go down and it stops on my floor and slowly opens. I walk in and see three goofs standing at the back of the mirror-lined elevator with a brass handrail halfway up. All of them have on sweat suits and one has a towel wrapped around his neck and is wearing wrestling shoes. As the doors close, I recognize him as the wrestler that got choked out by the skinny guy in pajamas.

"You're the guy who got choked out by the PJ guy," I say.

"You mean the guy in the gi?" he asks.

"Yeah," I say. "I'm a wrestler so don't ever get choked out again like that."

"Okay, man," he says, a little taken aback by my forwardness, "I won't."

"Good," I say. "Don't ever let down the sport of wrestling again if you know what's good for you."

The three guys look at me like I'm crazy but the door opens and I walk away from them into the lobby. I scan the area and see Ron Disbleef on the other side. Across from him is a table with NHB tee-shirts and other gear on it. Those must be the shirts that Coby saw being made when he got my application.

Sure enough, behind the table is Chip Monk, the cherry-blonde sensei whose ass everyone is kissing at the dojo in West Minister. I walk up to the table and he does a double take like he's seen me before but can't figure out where. He doesn't recognize me from his dojo, where

the big Samoan walked in, because I'm 50 lbs. heavier
now, my arms are five inches bigger, and I've grown a
goatee. He just knows my eyes.

"How you doing," I ask.

He stands behind the table with tee-shirts, beanies,
programs and all the other stuff posers love to wear who
aren't real fighters. I'm wearing the clothes that Ted from
Baton gave me: a black-and-white striped collarless shirt,
green corduroy shorts, thick white socks with Baton
embroidered on them, and Doc Martens low-top boots.
All of a sudden, his eyes pop open as he realizes who I
am but yet still can't believe it.

"What are you doing here?" he asks.

"Just checking out the scene," I say nonchalantly, as if
running into him 2,000 miles away from home is the
most normal thing in the world.

He starts to sputter a reply but I turn and walk away
and go out the front doors to a guy sitting in a uniform at
the taxi stand.

"Can I help you, sir?" he asks.

"Yeah," I say. "Where's a good place to get a drink
around here?"

"Do you have a car?"

"No," I reply. "I just flew in for the fight. I need
someplace I can walk to so I can stretch my legs."

"Okay, sir," he nods politely. "Go across the front
lawn and climb the hill to a long, skinny brick building.
There's a bar and restaurant on the first floor and only
offices on the second."

I follow his directions and go through a set of big
wooden doors in the brick building and walk into the bar,
which has 15 people or so scattered around. Most of them
have on white long-sleeve dress shirts and dress slacks,

telling me that it's the after-work crowd. I find a place at the long, straight bar and order a double-Stoli with a cran back. I drop a few straws of cranberry juice into the Stoli and take a sip and inhale the Southern spirit. The vibe is good. People are being really friendly to each other but not in a phony way like they're trying to get over on you, like in L.A.

The bartender returns when my drink is done and asks if I want another. I get another double-Stoli without cran, because I still have a lot. I look around and see people eating big burgers all around me so before he leaves, I also order a plain cheeseburger with cross-cut fries. He comes back almost immediately and plants a freshy on me and the burger appears five minutes later and is delicious. The juice from the patty runs out of the corners of my mouth as I finish it off.

The fans hanging from the ceiling swirl cigarette smoke around the room. It looks like in the South that everyone smokes, especially in North Carolina where I suppose a lot of tobacco plantations are. Now that I've finished putting down a blanket in my stomach, I'm ready for another drink, as ice is the only thing left in my glass now. I order another rooster and then another and am feeling no pain and am ready to talk to strangers.

A man in his 60s sat down next to me while I was eating and has the look of what I imagine a true Southern gentleman to be. He has on gold wireframe glasses and his salt-and-pepper hair is parted neatly on the side. His wife, sitting next to him, is an older blonde and a true southern belle with an age-appropriate white suit that is very flattering on her. He matches her in style with a white-collared short-sleeved shirt and dress slacks and polished leather shoes. I judge him to be around 5'8" tall and 160 lbs. from his height on the bar stool.

"How ya doing?" I ask, the Stoli buzzing in my head.

"Just great," he replies. "Judging from your clothes I'm guessing that you're not from around here."

"That's right," I say. "I'm staying at the hotel down the hill. I'm here to watch the fighting show this weekend."

"Oh, nice," he says. "Hey, bartender. I need another drink and get my friend here whatever he's having as well." He turns his attention back to me. What do you do for a living?"

"Not much," I say. "Right now, I'm selling garage doors in Southern California."

"That's a long way from here," he says.

"What do you do?" I ask.

"Oh, I'm retired," he says. "I used to be with the FBI."

"What a coincidence," I say. "Same here."

"Really?" he asks.

"Yep," I say raising my glass and taking a long sip. "The Federal Bureau of Intoxication."

He laughs aloud and clinks his glass against mine and then introduces me to his wife and tells her I'm here to watch the fight show. She tells everyone that I'm an NHB fighter and spreads it around to the other regulars in the bar and after a few drinks more the whole bar is circled around me and the couple, all toasting to the NHB. This always seems to happen to me in bars; like iron to a magnet people just like to drink with me.

"Are you really here to fight?" says a cute brunette in her 20s from the middle of the group.

"I'm here to watch," I say. "I'll be fighting in the next show.

"You know, Walt," the FBI man says. "Part of my job was reading people and doing profiles on them. You're a real nice guy at heart but I can also tell you're a fighter."

"I don't do it for money or for fame," I reply. "I'm doing it because I'm passionate about fighting."

The whole bar is around me now, captivated by my telling them about my training and how I'm getting ready to get into a cage and fight. Rooster after rooster rolls out and soon its 10 PM and getting late. The FBI agent and his wife leave and two guys in the crowd in their 20s take their place at the bar. They're wearing jeans and tee-shirts and are clean-cut southern boys fresh out of college.

"Hey, Walt," says one of the guys, "this place is going to close soon. Would you like to go off to more of a nightclub type place and get some more drinks?"

"Sure," I say. "Let's go have some fun."

We pay the tab and leave the neighborhood bar with a barrage of friendly handshakes. Nobody I've met so far has an attitude like in Orange County. They have all been very cool. Nobody wants to go to war or to disrespect you but only to have fun and get to know you. As I sit in the back seat with my new friends I get lost in the streets of Harlot. As we drive, all I see are endless rows of tree-lined streets. We end up at a nightclub with big windows that take up the entire two-story walls. The lights are bright and so is my buzz. As I get out of the car the windows flex to the booming bass of the music.

We get a table inside and order drinks and the place gets more and more crowded. It's obvious to me that this is the happening place in Harlot. I look around and a after while see a bunch of people from the NHB show walk in wearing tee-shirts with logos of gyms and dojos. The feel of the local bar is gone and I'm getting the more aggressive vibe of the bars in Orange County.

"All these guys are from the show," I say to my new friends.

With an edge in the air and an element of potential conflict from the fighters I realize that I'm actually feeling more at home than in the friendly local bar. This is my real scene no matter where I'm at. The big guys wearing the NHB clothes are walking around drunk with attitudes and acting like they're superstars when they're really a bunch of posers. I watch carefully to make sure there is no trouble, as I have a habit of always being on my guard. I see Big Bart across the room, towering over a group of people and point him out to my new friends.

"There's the NHB super-boss," I say. "Let's go say hello."

We leave the table and walk up to him and I wait for a break in the conversation he's having with two fighters. When they move away, I walk up, playing it cool.

"Hey, Bart," I say, catching his eye. "How's it going?"

He looks at me with a complete blank on his face. "Who are you?"

"Walter Foxx," I say. "The guy you want to call Krazy."

A look of amazement comes over Shady's face. "No way. You don't look the same at all. You've doubled in size. That's unbelievable. I can't believe you've gotten this big."

"I told you I was going to get ready," I say.

He doesn't have the same swagger that he had in his office in Borrence. He's with two guys in suits who are standing a few steps behind him. He steps close to me and stoops down so he can speak into my ear privately.

"These guys are the big cheeses in the company," he says, nodding his head slightly towards them.

One of the guys is young, about my age, of medium build and height, has a clean-cut baby-face, short curly hair, and is dressed like an attorney. The other guy is older with a short Abe Lincoln-looking beard and is 6'1" and in his 50s. They are both wearing dark suits that look out of place with the tee-shirts and sweats all around them. Neither one of them even acknowledges my existence, like I'm less than the furniture in the room. *They'll know about me soon*, I vow to myself. Without a word the two big cheeses disappear into the milling crowd.

"Bart," I say, "these are some new friends I met here. They're showing me around town. Do you have my pass for the show?"

"Sure, Walt," Bart says. "Come find me tomorrow at the NHB office at the hotel. I've got to get back to the bosses table."

I look at him for a few seconds as he walks off. I knew he was full of shit the first time I laid eyes on him. He's just a big oaf of a guy in every sense of the word, from his body aura to the way he talks. He's nothing more than a big, dumb guy trying to act important. On the West Coast he's the boss, but when he's on the East Coast he's kissing ass to the powers that be. I almost say something as he walks off but decide to keep my mouth shut. *Fuck it. I'm here to have fun.* Almost on cue, one of my new friends brings me a double Stoli and I slam it down in one gulp.

"Let's get crazy!" I yell.

The whole bar turns their heads and starts to notice me as I pound more drinks. I'm dancing to the music and burning down the house.

"You wanna sign up for karaoke?" one of the college boys asks.

"Fuck yeah," I say. I'm on a roll and would sign up for cake decorating if somebody asked.

"What do you want to sing?" he asks.

"The Doors are cool," I say.

The Southern bar crowd is cool and we're tearing it up, getting drunker and louder. The only idiots in the place are the NHB posers, walking around in their tee-shirts and sweats acting like rock stars that they'll never be. Nobody knows who they are but they're strutting around like they can beat up the world. I can tell by looking at them that they've never been in a real fight in their lives between them all. They will only fight when they have the safety valve of a referee to save them or when it's a friendly sparring match that is predictable and not dangerous. That's the bullshit they call a fight. Just wait till they see me in the cage. None of them are coming anywhere near me. Something must tell them to stay clear. I'm huge and I'm loaded and I'm loud and my realness must scare the phonies. Every time I turn around, I see Big Bart Shady staring at me. It's like he is studying my every move and action. I ignore him, though, and act like I don't notice.

"Hey, Walt," one of the college boys says. "It's your turn to sing."

The DJ calls out over the PA system that NHB fighter Walter Foxx, the Bad Boy from Happening Beach, California, is going to sing, and asks for the crowd to give me a warm Southern welcome. When I walk up to the podium the DJ asks if I'm fighting on the weekend and I tell him it won't be until summer. He gives me the microphone and the Doors music starts to come alive on the speakers. The lyrics start scrolling across the karaoke screen in front of me and I start to belt them out.

"Come on, come on, touch me babe," I belt out, in more of a scream than a song, but I don't give a fuck because I'm having a good time.

This my first-time doing karaoke anywhere, much less North Carolina at an NHB pre-fight party, and the whole bar is watching me. None of the other fighters wanted to get up and ruin their self-perceived toughness but I don't give a fuck about that. I'm real and I'm having fun. The lyrics pour out of my mouth and transfer over the speakers and the Southerners go wild, cheering my every chorus. When I finish, I give up the mic and walk off the stage into the crowd around me and we go to the bar to get more drinks.

"That was good," somebody says to me. "Too bad you're not fighting tomorrow."

"This summer," I say. "Watch for me then. I'm gonna shake things up."

"This martial arts stuff is bad-ass," somebody else says.

"I'm not a martial arts guy," I say. "I don't train in that stuff. I'm just a street fighter who likes to fuck people up."

"Those guys are all full of themselves," another person says. "I really want to see you mess those guys up."

"Yeah, me too," I say.

Pretty soon closing time comes around and I've been drinking for hours and am a wreck, barely able to stand. I've been rolling hard the entire day and it's catching up with me. My two new friends take me back to my hotel and we go up to my suite and sit in the living room area. All these people are buying me drinks and hanging out with me because they can sense that I'm a real fighter and a real person who acts like who he is, not like who he thinks people want him to be. They can feel that I'm a man who has the balls to go when nobody else will and to take action when others will just stand around and talk. We get into the mini-bar and have some more drinks and start to laugh and yell again and I hear somebody pounding on the wall from the room next door.

"Fuck 'em," I say, pounding on the wall back at them. "They should come party with us."

The college boys laugh and we start up again even louder and after a while the phone rings.

"Mr. Foxx," a voice says when I pick up. "This is the front desk. We've gotten several calls from the room next to you complaining about the noise. Please tone it down or we're going to have to send someone up."

Just what I don't need is to have them call the cops on me at my first NHB. "Okay," I say. "No problem."

I hang up the phone. "They're getting calls about us from the fucks next door so I'm going to call it a night," I say. "I'll be at the bar across the street tomorrow so I'll see you there."

They stumble out of the room and I fall back onto my king-sized bed and am instantly out.

18. Outside the Cage

I wake to the sun creeping around the edges of the blackout curtains. It's 2:00 PM and my head is pounding more than usual. I can't believe I got up this late. Then I remember that because it's the East Coast I'm awake three hours earlier than normal. I pull myself together and get to the lobby. I've got my weightlifting clothes on with a tee-shirt, coaching shorts, and untied basketball high-tops. I go up to the front desk and ask a young girl working there where the NHB office is. She directs me down the hallway to the right, across the courtyard, and through a door that opens from the grass quad.

I start the trek and pass the table of NHB tee-shirts with the Senseless Sensei behind it. A bunch of karate guys with evil eyes, with nothing to back up their aggressive gazes, are surrounding it. I just laugh to myself. These idiots are certainly ignorant and just don't know what a real fight or real warrior is. As I walk down the hallway, I pass a small banquet room where some guys in hotel uniforms are setting up for a party. I go outside across the courtyard, breathing in the fresh air, and open the door at the far end.

Inside is Bart Shady, the loser who claimed to be the head honcho. He's talking to a girl in a light brown, knee-length skirt, wearing a white blouse, with brown shoulder-length hair and short bangs. I have a flashback to last night, remember the two guys in suits that Shady was calling his bosses, and laugh to myself that he isn't the head guy after all. Shady has on a suit and looks like one of the after-work crowd I met at the neighborhood bar last night.

"What's up, Bart," I say. "Do you know where Gold's Gym is at? Somebody last night told me there was one close to work out at."

"Hey, Walt," Shady says. "It's up the road a bit behind the hotel within easy walking distance." He puts his arm around the brunette next to him. "I'd like you to meet the future Mrs. Shady," he says. "She'll be giving you your ticket in a couple of hours."

"Nice meeting you," I say. "I'll hit a workout and stop by on my way back to my room."

I start up the hilly road. Trees are everywhere and well-kept green grass is on both sides of the street. As the trees clear after a few hundred yards I see another brick building with one wall made completely of glass. I can see weight machines inside so I walk up to the front door and go in. The front desk is empty and no one is around so I go inside, see a guy with white hair who looks like he's a trainer, and tell him I'm from the NHB and staying at the hotel. He tells me to help myself so I walk up to the first sturdy-looking bench I see and he follows me over. He looks to be in his late 40s and is fit and I can tell that he lifts, even though he isn't that big.

"Do you need something from me?" I ask. "Should I sign in? The guys from the NHB said I could grab a workout here."

"No," he says. "You're cool. Have a good lift."

He wanders off and I look around the club. It's basically deserted with only a couple of girls working out. As he walks away, I think that he looks a lot like that pro-wrestling guy, Rick or Dick or something like that. My head is pounding from the night before, but I have to get in a good lift to clear my brain. I do some light reps with 225 lbs. to warm up and then put five wheels on each side of the bar. The warm-up felt light but I don't like the bench so I decide this is as heavy as I'm going.

I look at the girls but there's no way I'm going to have them spot me. I go to the office and find the guy with white hair sitting at a desk.

"Can you give me a spot, man?" I ask.

"Well, I really don't do that," he says.

"But nobody's here," I say. "I really don't need a spot, just a lift-off."

"Okay," he says. "Let's do it."

We go back through the machines to the bench and he sees how much weight I have stacked on both sides of the bar.

"Whoa!" he says.

All of a sudden it hits me. The white-haired guy is Dick Blair, the pro-wrestling legend.

"Just give me a lift-off," I say. "Once I get it up, I'm good."

"Are you sure?" he asks doubtfully.

"Yeah," I say. "I got this easily."

I lay down on the bench with him behind me and count to three. I push upwards and he lifts the bar into the air right in the groove. I drive if for a quick and easy four reps and set it down on the racks.

"Good job," the guy says. "Let me know if you need another one."

As he walks off, he passes the two girls and one of them speaks to him.

"Hey, Dick," she says.

He waves at them and continues out of the lifting area. I continue my workout and when I'm done my hangover is gone and I feel much better. I feel energized as I leave the gym and walk down the hill to the hotel. If it was bad before it's even worse now, with a bunch of posers walking around with bullshit fighting tee-shirts on – it's like it's a Star Trek convention for phony tough guys. These guys are just chasing the latest fighting fad in hopes it will make people think they're tough. Oh, how I would love to kick all their asses.

I walk out of the lobby and across the courtyard, snapping my weight belt on the ground with loud cracks. I walk into the NHB office and the future Mrs. Shady hands me an envelope with my name on it. I take it and walk back through the lobby of losers and go to the elevator and go to my room. I open the white envelope to find that Bart Shady has given me a regular ticket, not the all-access pass that he had promised.

That fucker! He's like the big oaf on the playground that thinks he's smarter than everyone else. But I know his game. I've seen it a million times before. Big Bart Shady is nothing more than a small-time joker. His office at the converted Motel 6 said it all. He's just another loser clown trying to get over on me. I'm trying my hardest to get Baton on TV to give back to Ted what he did for me, and all I get is a regular ticket up in the stands with the herd of humanity.

I laugh aloud in my empty room. This is the kind of guy I've been beating up my whole life: he's a nine-ball swindler with a big mouth claiming to be something he's not. *Fuck it!* I'm not going to let this get me down. I learned that a long time ago. I would like nothing better than to put my fist into his face, while all he can do to me is to tell stories and lies. I know that I need to get a drink to calm down. I shower and change and walk up the hill to the neighborhood bar I was at the night before. I go into the big wooden doors and belly up to the bar.

The two guys from last night see me and come over as does a different bartender. He's a Steve Garvey lookalike including the oversized forearms from mixing up drinks, I guess. I order a double Stoli rocks with a cran back.

"You're the fighter everyone was talking about yesterday," the bartender says when he brings my drink.

"Yeah," I say. "I guess. I'm not fighting until the summer, though."

"Well, you made an impression," he says.

"You need to make an impression on me with a plain cheeseburger and another double," I smile.

"Coming right up," he laughs.

I make short work of my first friend and notice how lonely the ice looks at the bottom of my glass when I've downed it. I can tell it's going to be the first of many tonight. The show starts at 10 PM so I'm drinking fast and hit the throttle hard. The bar is full and the cigarette smoke is billowing down from the ceiling. Many drinks go down before it's time to go to the Harlot Coliseum for the NHB. The two college boys are giving me a ride and as we walk out of the front door it seems like everyone else wants to also. Everyone wants to watch no-holds-barred fighting and it's what I'm going to be doing when summer rolls around.

We drive through the city of Harlot on our way to the outskirts of town where the arena is. As we get closer the night gets brighter due to all the lights from the long line of cars going there. We drive into the parking lot and it's jam packed. I drink one of the beers that my two Southern friends brought and it seems that every parking stall is full so it takes us a while to find an open one.

"This show is going to be good," one of the college boys says.

"I hope so," I say. "These grappling guys can be really boring once they get the fight on the ground."

"Well, I'm psyched anyway," my other friend says. "Do you know how to grapple, Walt?"

"Well, I've wrestled for a long time," I answer, "but I'd rather punch people. I just like to fight and to get down. I hope I get a good seat so I can see what is going on."

"It's gotta be good," the first college guy says. "You heard it from Bart Shady himself."

"Let's cross our fingers," I say.

We kill our soldiers and head into the arena. As I walk through the smallish front entrance it reminds me a little of the old days, when I would go the Fantastic Forum arena to watch boxing. Every time the owner of the arena would go through the porthole, I would yell out at him.

"Walter Foxx," I'd scream. "Don't forget it."

He was an old geezer that was fucking all the dumb wannabe L.A. starlets – young girls who ended up getting old dick and nothing else out of it. They got their integrity taken for nothing at all. But I guess they never had any to begin with if they were trying to fuck their way to the top. We called them the Forum Groupies and used to laugh at them. Where are they now? Most likely dumb, broke ex-hookers who realized too late in life what the real score is.

Fuck! Where's my seat! I get tired of walking around aimlessly and walk up to an usher dressed in his red uniform and show him my ticket. The arena is dark already and the cage looks like a gold ring below me sitting in a sea of people hoping to see warriors battle. I get pointed in the right direction and make my way towards the floor, down past G, F, E, D, C and finally to B, on the second row above the floor.

Fuck! I'm in the stands! This is bullshit! I was supposed to have an all-access pass. I sit down in my seat and try to look over the three-inch diameter steel railing but it blocks my view. Wouldn't you know it? It's the perfect height to keep me from watching the fights. Why am I here in the bleachers with the normal people? Down below I can see all the karate fucks sitting on the floor and walking in and out of the backstage area. Oh well, I feel more comfortable with the fans than I do with the phonies anyway. I sit back to take in the show as best I can.

The music starts and the production crew starts to run around like ants then settle down as the lights go down. The music gets louder and the lights come up and the first fighter walks out. He's a martial arts fighter from Miami. He squares up with his opponent and they start to fight as the noise from the crowd builds. They don't fight at all but rather roll around awkwardly like freshman in a high school wrestling match. It's over fast and out of the corner of my eye I see Shady walking out from the backstage area wearing a tuxedo.

"Hey, Bart!" I bellow.

Even though the arena is full Big Bart hears me and walks across the arena floor and up to the wall the separates us. I can barely see Shady as his head is just under the bar that is blocking my view.

"Yeah, Walt," Shady says. "What do you want?"

"What the fuck is with this seat?" I say. "You told Coby I had an all-access pass. I wanted to see what this is all about from the inside, not like some fan."

"It's just a show, Walt," Shady says.

"No, Bart," I reply. "It's more than that to me."

He looks at me speculatively before answering then shrugs his shoulders. "Well, I thought you had a pass."

"The view from this seat is blocked," I say. "I can't see shit. The guys selling tee-shirts have a better view."

He shrugs again and his tuxedo pulls tight. He turns around and walks off as his rented cummerbund threatens to fall off. He walks back into the lighted cage area as I seethe with frustration. *Fuck this!* I get up from my seat with the blocked view and walk up the stairs to the upper deck where my two new friends are with a couple of other people from the bar.

"This is boring," says one of the girls from the bar. "I thought they were going to fight not wrestle. All they do is roll around on the ground."

"I hear you," I say glumly. "Wait till you see me fight in the summer. I promise it will be different."

"I hope so," she says.

The matches continue on much the same way for the rest of the evening, with the crowd getting more and more subdued. As the show comes to an end the lights come up and the crowd flows out of the arena with a generally letdown feeling and mood. I feel much the same way as I leave with my new Southern friends.

19. Party Crasher

We make it back to the bar and people are so disappointed with the NHB that I feel like apologizing, even though I didn't have anything to do with it.

"That was really slow," one of the girls sitting with us says.

"I know," I reply. "These guys don't know how to fight and the matchmakers don't know how to put a show together. I'm going to show them what real fighting is. I swear I'm different. I don't go out there to stall; I go out to kick your ass. It will be completely different from what you just saw. I don't fuck around."

I power another few roosters and decide to go across the street to the after-fight NHB cocktail party at the hotel. My buzz is strong but the bar crowd is unsure we should go.

"You said you weren't invited, Walt," says one of the college boys.

"I'm not," I say, "but we're going anyways."

Me and six local guys pour our drinks down our throats and march out of the bar towards the hotel. We cross the grass field and go past the desk at the taxi stand where I got my original directions to the neighborhood watering hole. The lobby of the hotel that holds the contingent of the NHB posers is empty and the man with the tuxedo is gone and the table of NHB shirts with Chip Monk is nowhere to be seen. All I can spot are two guys behind the front desk talking quietly to each other.

"Where's the NHB cocktail party?" I ask, stopping in front of them. "I want to get down!" Just for good measure and because I'm in the South I let out a rebel yell.

A second later another man in a suit appears from a room behind the desk. "Sir, you need to keep it down."

"Yeah, yeah," I say. "Where's the NHB cocktail party?"

"Down the hall and through the doors to the right," he says, pointing to his left.

"Okay, thanks," I say.

I walk down the hallway with my crew of locals in tow and go through the wooden doors, hoping to see the big cucumber, Bart Shady, to ask him what was up with my ticket. He's nowhere to be found, though. Across the room I spot the referee, Little Winchell Duncan, walking around like he's a superstar, thinking he's famous for doing nothing besides standing around in the cage watching other people fight. Other delusional nobodies in suits are standing around chit-chatting about who they think the next badass will be, as if their opinion meant anything. I hope to spot that skinny PJ guy, Garcia, but he is a no-show like Shady.

Disappointed, I go to the portable bar they've set up and order a double Stoli but they don't have it. I change my order to whatever vodka they have and then mix in a little cranberry juice at a table we park ourselves at next to the bar. My new party crew is doing fine with drinks they've ordered and we settle into our lair at the end of the small banquet room. I've got to know the lay of the land at all times to spot any potential threats so I survey my surroundings. All the tables have white tablecloths that reach all the way to the floor. A long table in the middle has crystal bowls of crackers, cheese, fruit and other appetizers. A big crystal chandelier hangs from the wood ceiling with mirrored panels set into it and I see my reflection. I have to admit to myself I am one scary-looking motherfucker.

I decide to mix it up a bit with the other people there and get up and walk around the room. My crew of six one step behind me, following me with star-struck expressions as they see some of the fighters, they know from the show that night. I bounce past a couple of idiots who fought earlier and then walk past the alternate referee, a black guy, and he sticks out his hand to me.

"Hi. I'm Sly Flack," he says.

"What's up," I reply.

He's 6'1" tall and is very fit. He's the first guy I've met so far that doesn't seem to have an attitude. As I turn away from him, I see Olympic wrestling champion Jerry Blockneck, one of the commentators. I saw him win the gold medal in person.

"Hey," I say. "I'm Walter Foxx. "I watched you win the gold medal in Anaheim. Good job, man. You really represented."

"Oh, thanks," he says, seeming to be happy that someone remembers his wrestling career. "You going to be fighting in an upcoming show?"

"This isn't a show to me," I say. "Fighting is my life."

"What do you mean?" Blockneck asks.

"I love to fight," I say. "It's all I ever think about."

"You gotta be a little crazy to do this," Blockneck laughs. "I guess you fit the bill perfectly. Good luck."

"I don't need luck, Blockneck," I say sourly, my patience wearing thin. "I just need a chance."

I leave Blockneck with a stupid-looking expression on his face and walk off with my crew to the snack table in the middle of the room. I grab a roll, cut it in half, and grab some roast beef and slam in on the bread like I'm slamming an opponent into the mat. I smash the roll together and then push it into my mouth in one piece. I drunkenly devour it in a matter of seconds and circle the table, seeing if there is anything else I want.

I spot a large, muscular black man, wearing a raspberry beret, sitting near the middle of the room. I know who this guy is: it's Tim Black, another of the announcers and an NFL football legend. He's a man that would run right at you and then trample you wearing nothing more than an old-school suspension helmet with barely any padding.

I was more of a Chicago Bears fan, though, and suddenly find myself wishing that I was another Nick Buttress. Try to cross the chalk goal line and I will knock the fuck out of you. Bring your Cleveland Browns bucket at me and I'll end your run for negative yards with a Buttress body tackle. Out of all the announcers, he's the one who keeps saying how much he loves Garcia, that skinny Mexican PJ boy. For some reason, in my drunken state, I conclude that Tim Black just might be my enemy.

"Hey, Tim," I say, walking up drunkenly. "Where's the PJ boy you've been pumping."

He looks at me appraisingly. "What are you talking about?

"That Garcia brother," I say. "I'm surprised you aren't hanging out with him. That's why you're one of the announcers. You keep pumping him up like he's big stuff."

His eyes get bigger and his lips compress into a thin line. He's not used to having someone tell it like it is. "Hey, big guy," he says. "Take it easy."

I step back one stride. "Take it easy*?*" I say menacingly.

"Uh, Walt," one of the college boys says behind me. "He didn't actually say anything bad to you. He's actually being kind of nice."

"You call someone getting in my face, nice?" I say drunkenly and without reason.

"Listen to your friends," Black says evenly.

"And you listen to me," I continue, well beyond any attempt at rational thought. "You're the best running back the NFL has ever seen but you have no idea who I am. I'm benching over six hundred pounds with no drugs. All natural. All me. All real."

I can hear myself talk, and I know it's jumbled, but the words keep coming out.

"Uh, Walt," the other college boy says. "Maybe we ought to go check out the buffet instead."

The sensible words roll off me like water off a duck's back. I look at this football legend who is one of my Dad's sports heroes. This football star standing in front of me is a monster but I'm not scared. I'm just getting ready. My heart is pumping and I can feel my blood pressure spike inside my body.

"I'm thinking you should maybe have a cup of coffee," Black says.

I glare at him silently. He has no idea what I'm thinking or else he wouldn't be sitting there so calmly while I'm seconds away from beating him to a pulp. He is taking this way too lightly. I reach up and grab his raspberry beret that no NFL legend should be wearing anyway. Maybe that is what is infuriating me about him. Would Nick Buttress ever be caught dead in such a thing? Never!

"That ain't cool," he says. "You want a souvenir or autograph just ask. I'll sign a picture for you. Don't be taking my hat off my head."

My eyes get small and I'm ready for war. Despite all my words he just doesn't get it. I will show him what it's like to be a legend: not for carrying the ball but for beating the fuck out of somebody because they dare to wear a raspberry beret in a public place. Beret in hand I walk back to the snack table. The college boys don't follow me this time but rather mill around uncertainly.

I take a glance back and see that Tim Black is trailing me. I move around the table and see his reflection behind me in the crystal chandelier in the middle of the room. He wants his beret back but he doesn't get it. I would never wear a raspberry hat any more than I would get a colored tattoo. Fuck that. The only proper color for either is black or green. As I stop in the middle of the banquet room, I start to laugh aloud at the football player. His mood changes as he approaches me. I'm pretty sure I can see it in his eyes. It's like fear, or maybe extreme annoyance, or maybe just regular annoyance; but he is definitely annoyed. I have his identity in my hand. I have what makes Tim Black, Tim Black: the raspberry beret. *Fuck! Where's Buttress? We could stick Black on the goal line right here and now.* Black's eyes leave my face and travel down to my hand that is holding his beret. His beret is sitting at my waistline, clutched in the hand at the end of my arm. Good luck if he tries to take it from me. I'm not a PJ boy.

"Look, man," he says reasonably. "What are you doing with my beret? My head gets cold. Can I just have it back? What the hell are you going to do with it anyway?"

I walk away again to the other side of the snack table opposite him. He stands there passively, not following me. But he's right. What am I going to do with a raspberry beret? I'm damn sure not going to wear it. I don't even want it in my luggage. I pull the beret across my body, take aim, and let it fly across the room like the Frisbee I used to throw for Adolf to chase at the beach. It flies straight into his chest and he grabs it without looking and pulls it onto his head. He goes around the table, walks towards me, and gets right in my face. *He's got balls, I'll give him that.*

"Are you riding me?" he asks.

"If I was riding you, I would knock you out," I say.

He looks at me closer and his features get hard and then after a few seconds they relax. It's as if he's seeing a bit of himself from 40 years ago in me. An ease comes to the muscles in his face. He now knows who I am. It's been many years back but he once had my eyes. The spell between us is broken. The walk across the room has cleared my head and I become aware of my surroundings. Someone has called hotel security and two muscle morons have come over, unnoticed by me, and are standing on either side of me.

"Is there a problem, Mr. Black?" one of them asks.

He shakes his head. "No problem. He's a good kid."

Tim Black walks away and the security guys shrug at each other and melt into the crowd. All around me I can see that the party is thinning out. There's now just a bunch of wannabe idiots wearing martial arts tee-shirts, looking for someone to recognize them. These martial arts phonies are just like the long-haired rock-and-roll pussies that got replaced when punk rock came along. Pretty soon they'll be exposed as well. It's not about the scene you're from it's about being you and kicking ass. It's the beginning of the end for them and they're desperately trying to hang onto their own self-delusions. I definitely don't want to be here with them.

I go in search of my party crew and find they have dwindled down to three, including the two original college boys and one of their friends.

"The rest of them took off," says college boy number one. "They were afraid you were gonna slug Tim Black and get us arrested."

"Nah," I say. "We've got an understanding. Let's go."

We walk out the door of the banquet room and go back through the lobby to the elevators. We're laughing and joking about me stealing Tim Black's hat and one of the hotel security guards comes around the corner and asks us to keep it down. We nod, get into the elevator, then scream as loud as we can when the steel door shuts and we start to move upwards. We stumble down the hallway to my room, sit on the couches in the living room facing each other, and raid the mini-bar and keep pounding drinks.

"That show was really boring," says college boy number two. "How are you going to make it more interesting when you fight?"

"Like this," I say.

I pull him out of his chair and take him to the carpet. This Southern boy is game but is all of 180 lbs. His back is on the dark blue carpet and I jump on his chest. As he pushes me away and extends his arms, I spin like a top, pinch my thighs around his out-stretched arm, and fall back for the Garcia Brother's arm-bar. As I go backwards, though, I hit my head on the edge of the couch, nearly knocking myself out. The Southern boys all wail with laughter as I release his arm and rub the back of my head.

"I'm just playing around," I say. "I don't know how to do that Mexican jiu-jitsu stuff."

"Well, if you don't know how to do it," my arm-bar victim says, getting back up on the couch, "how can you win?"

"I have things that people can't learn," I say. "That's what makes me different. It all goes back to who you are and not what you know. If you're educated but not tough, strong, and mean then you're vulnerable. Education is something you can't count on. Even if you know how to use a hammer, if you're not strong enough to pick it up then you can't swing it. Big and tough will beat small and educated every time. But if big and tough fight against each other, then the most educated will win. But it all starts with having size and strength. These guys winning now are just the head of the nail waiting to get wacked by the hammer. I promise you guys I will show the world how a real warrior fights in the next show."

The phone rings and startles me because nobody knows I'm here. I pick up the phone and it's the front desk.

"Hello, sir?" the voice says. "The gentleman in the room next to you is complaining that you're being too loud again."

"I don't care," I say. "Fuck him!" To emphasize my point, I pound on the common wall between us.

"Sir," the voice says. "You're being too loud for the hotel. We prefer to not have to send people up to address the situation personally."

"Okay," I say. "I'll shut it down." It's late and I have to get some sleep anyway to get ready for my flight.

I tell the Southern boys the party's over and they exit the room and stumble down towards the elevator. I watch them go and then shut the door. *Fuck the people in the next room.* The living room is littered with half-full drinks the Southern boys left. I'm ready to leave anyway, because the management had been complaining about me since I arrived. The king-sized bed looks like a landing pad and I take aim and fall face first onto the mattress.

20. Wake-Up Call

The ringing of the phone jars me into wakefulness out of my alcohol-fueled sleep. I pick up the phone and a recorded voice informs me that I've just received my wake-up call. I roll out of bed and take a long, hot shower, letting the stream of hot water pelt my body and wash away the bar smoke smell from my hair. It's so relaxing that I curl into the corner and let the water beat on the top of my head. As I stare down at the water swirling down the drain, I think about the night I just lived. As the swirling water climbs higher my thoughts also swirl around in my head.

What is up with Bart Shady and why did he put me in the cheap seats? I thought he had big plans for me. I'm still trying to figure out why Tim Black would be wearing the raspberry beret whose sole purpose seemed to be to infuriate me. Most of all I wonder who the idiot next door is and why he kept calling hotel security on me for making so much noise. None of them have seen a warrior like me and maybe that threw them for a loop.

I turn down the shower handle and the pool of swirling water disappears down the drain. I slide my feet underneath me and push myself up the tile shower wall and turn off the water completely. I step carefully out of the slippery shower and onto the bathroom tile. I don't want to miss my flight so I dry and dress quickly and then throw my stuff together. My bag is mostly packed so I throw in what I'm not wearing, do a final visual sweep of the room, zip up the Baton bag and exit the room, shutting the door behind me.

I pause and look at the door of the complainer's room next to me. I seriously consider knocking on their door and confronting them: *Who the fuck do you think you are, fucking with me?* I would like nothing better than to get in their face but I take a deep breath to slow my breathing. I look down at the carpet and squeeze the handle on my Baton bag like I imagine squeezing the complainer's neck. My sweaty palms slide on the leather handle but with a force of will I turn away and walk down the hallway and take the elevator to the first floor.

As I step out, I spot the bearded guy in the suit from the pre-fight party at the downtown bar that Shady pointed out to me as being the NHB's big cheese. He's putting a small bag onto a luggage cart as he gets ready to leave. He looks over at me with a barely contained sneer on his face, like I'm the world's ultimate scumbag. Instead of slinking away I decide to go over and speak to him like a man.

"Hey, man," I say. "What's up?"

He seems surprised by that and throws out a fake smile. "How are you?"

"I'm fine," I say. "Better than you will ever know."

I wait to see if he has any smartass response to that but he just nods and then follows out a woman who I assume to be his wife, to the front of the hotel with the luggage cart. I let him get a 10-yard head start and then catch up with them in the driveway where a line of taxi cabs are. He has on expensive goofy clothes that look like total New York country club bullshit to me. His white tennis shorts make his pink shirt with the alligator on the chest stand out even more. *What an old school East Coast geek*, I think. He has no idea what fighting is all about. *Just wait till you see me fight next summer.* I side up to him as he waits for his bags to be loaded into the limo that has appeared for him.

"What did you think about the fights?" I say.

"I don't know," he says, obviously sharing the same opinion as everyone else about the event. "These guys were supposed to be the toughest guys in the world."

"Well I can tell you," I say. "That isn't the case."

"Yeah," he says. "I'm starting to wonder." His wife has come over and is standing next to him expectantly. She's a small woman with short brown hair and a nice warm smile. "This is Ellen."

"Nice to meet you," I say.

"My pleasure," she says. She yawns deeply and I can see she has dark circles under her eyes. "Excuse me," she says. "I didn't sleep very well."

"Tell me about it," I say. "I spent half the night on the phone with hotel security."

They exchange a long glance with each other and without a word climb into the back of the limo and are driven off. *Typical country club types,* I think. I look around the driveway and it seems like everyone is leaving town. The driveway is full of wannabe NHB tough guys acting like badasses. These midgets are walking around like they're hardcore just because they have on an NHB tee-shirt, but in my world they're just bad jokes. If they only knew what was in store for them when I fight. Everyone will think they can beat me until I blast them in the face.

The thought brings a smile to my face as the hotel's white Lincoln Town Car airport shuttle shows up. I hustle over and throw my bag into the trunk and see two other guys inside as I climb in to escape the circus of clowns.

"We saw you singing at the bar," one of them says. "How'd you like the show?"

"It was okay," I say.

"Just okay?" the other guy says.

"Yeah," I answer. "Nobody knew how to fight. They were all goofs."

They both turn quiet and I can tell that they're part of somebody's team and have never punched someone in the face in their entire lives. I decide not to waste my time trying to educate them and look out the window as we travel through the grassy hills and tree-lined highways. We get to the airport and I grab my bag from the back of the white Lincoln and go inside. As I check myself in and go through security, I think about what a crazy experience this was.

I get on the plane, go past the big seats in first class and find myself a seat in the economy section. *I'll be in first class someday*, I promise myself. I buckle up and the plane roars down the runway and into the air. I pull the seatback switch on the arm rest and recline back a whole two inches. I twist the air vent and a cool blast hits me in the face. I consider everything I saw the past few days and decide I've never seen such a collection of phonies. Can I really be a part of all this?

These guys have never been in a real fight in their lives and everyone in the audience can tell. A chimp could own this company and do a better job of matchmaking. Oh well, I'll show them what a real fighter is when the summer rolls around. At the very least it will beat selling garage doors for a living. I close my eyes and drift off, only to be awakened seemingly seconds later when the wheels screech on the John Wayne Airport runway in Orange County as we land. I exit the plane and walk out to the arrival area, where my mom is waiting at the curb to pick me up.

"Well, Walter," my mom says, after I stow my bag in back and settle down in the passenger seat, "how did it go? We watched it on TV but didn't see you. It looked like something you'd like, though,"

"They screwed me out of my all-access pass," I grumble. "I really wanted to get on TV for Ted and his Baton clothing company."

"What did you think about the Russian fighting the wrestler?" she asks.

"I have no idea why they would stop a fight just because someone was bleeding," I say. "The wrestler was going to kill him. But maybe it was good they stopped it before it really even started. That way the world will see when I fight in the summer what a real warrior is."

"Adolf is acting upset that you left again," my mom says.

"I'll see him tonight when I get in," I say.

"You're not staying in tonight?" my mom asks.

"Nope," I say. "It's Saturday. I need to see some people. But I'll play with him before I go out."

My mom pulls into the driveway and I carry my Baton bag into the house. I pass Adolf in the hallway and try to pet him but he turns his head and walks the other way, his head down and somber. I put my bag down onto my bed in the garage and call Adolf.

"Where's my boy?" I say loudly. "Where's my Adolf?"

He doesn't come in so I walk into the living room where Adolf is lying next to my dad on the couch. I clap my hands to call him but he turns his back to me.

"C'mon, boy!" I say again. 'Come over here."

225

Finally, his tail starts to beat up and down on the sofa. I get onto my hands and knees, crawl over to him, and pull him off the sofa and start to wrestle with him. He groans and growls in excitement and fights back, trying to get on top of me. I let him get the upper hand and then push him off me. He runs around in a small circle and barks at me happily.

"Don't worry, Adolf," I say, grabbing him around the neck. "I'm not going away again." I get up and walk to the front door and open it. He stays near the couch and looks at me and then I clap my hands together. "Let's go, Adolf!"

He dashes out the front door and runs to the truck like a bullet, hopping in when I open the door. I drive to the grocery store, make my usual round trip to the liquor section, and then go outside and mix a traveler. I start to cruise the residential highway as I drink another and then another. Before long I have on a good glow and make the short drive to Coby's house and see a light on in the garage. I park on the street and walk up and look in through the partially raised door. The smell of pot comes out and I see Coby inside smoking a bong with a teenage punk.

"Hey, what's up?" I say, ducking my head and walking in.

Coby looks up with his usual red-rimmed eyes without surprise. He is so stoned that it would take a nuclear blast to surprise him.

"I saw the show," Coby says. "How was it in person?"

"It's just a bunch of posers running around like they can beat up the world," I say. "I can tell you that none of them have ever gone to war when there is nobody to save them and no rules except the possibility of death."

"Did you get in any scrapes?" Coby asks.

"No," I say. "I played it cool. I didn't want to fuck anything up before I fight in the summer."

"Good going," Coby says. "Did you get good seats?"

"That Bart Shady is a worm," I say. "He didn't even give me an all-access pass. I told you the first time I saw him that he was piece of shit. He isn't for real. He's a peon. He isn't the head man of anything. The guys from New York in suits own the show. They're the real movers."

"No way!" Coby says. "I can't believe he fucked you over. He had big plans for you. If you weren't backstage then where were you?"

"I met a bunch of good ol' Southern boys at the bar across the street from the hotel so I hung out with them," I say.

Coby looks like he's going to say something but then stares off over my shoulder and falls back into his stoner world. I can see he's not going to be any good to me tonight or any fun to be with.

"I'm out of here, doper," I say.

"What, dude?" he asks, not really even hearing me.

I bend down to clear the half-opened garage door and go to my truck and jump in with Adolf. I mix another freshy on the way home and make it back to my parent's garage and fall into bed with Adolf snorting happily beside me. I get up late the next morning and kick back with my dad all-day Sunday watching football and taking it easy. Monday comes and I get back into my workout routine and start training with a sense of urgency. With the summer fight coming up I want to be ready to destroy these posers I saw.

For the next three weeks I train hard, only drinking on the weekends. I keep my nose clean, walking away from beggars in bars that I could have killed with one hand. I can't go back to jail now that I have a direction and purpose in life and my big break is just around the corner. I'm going to the show the world how a real warrior fights. After so much hard training I call Coby for to meet for lunch to see how things are going. I hit a hard run in the morning to get my appetite up and then get on the Interceptor and ride down to Decisions and into Coby's upstairs office.

"Hey, Walt," he says, as I walk in. "How's the training going?"

"Fucking great," I say. "I just got a great run in and have been lifting like a madman at the gym. What's up with the NHB? It's been a while since we heard from them. Call that worm, Shady."

"Okay," Coby says. He picks up the receiver, pushes the buttons and then nods at me when the phone is answered on the other end. "Hey, Bart, it's Coby. I'm sitting here with Krazy."

He listens to Shady talk for several seconds and then answers.

"You're busy," Coby says. "No problem. I'll talk to you later." Coby hangs up the receiver and looks at me with his pie-eyed stare, stone cold stoned as usual. "He couldn't talk. Let's go get lunch."

We eat but don't say much so I head home and go train. A few more days pass and I don't hear anything so I call up Coby again. It's getting closer to when I'm supposed to fight so I want to make sure I have the dates right.

"Hey, Coby," I say. "Did you ever talk to Shady?"

"It's weird, Walt," he says. "He won't talk to me for some reason. I left him a bunch of messages and talked to his secretary but I can't get him to call me back. Don't worry about it. He's probably just busy."

I hang up the phone with a sense of unease around me. I knew Shady was a worm when I first met him and now he isn't returning Coby's calls. Despite what Coby says, I have a bad feeling about this.

21. Playing by the Rules

Knowing that my NHB fight show match is coming up, I start looking for some way to protect my hands when I punch someone but yet will still let me grab and wrestle. Basically, I want to be able to smash someone's face without hurting my hands. I've been waking up with sore and bloody knuckles my whole adult life from getting into real fights. Only posers say they want to fight without gloves. If someone says they prefer bare knuckles I know they've never been in a real fight before.

I tell Rolando my idea and we drive to the martial arts store on Beach Blvd. that I used to pass on the way to my job when I was living at the halfway house. I remember it because it's where I bought my Mushashi heavy bag. We pull up into the parking lot and walk through the swinging glass door. In the far corner to the right is a heavy bag with a yellow price tag hanging down and a sign printed in black magic marker on white paper that declares *DO NOT HIT!* There's a shelf of black and white gi tops and pants on the back wall and a rack of martial arts books and magazines by the counter. We walk by the fake Asian Mexican guy sitting on a stool by the cash register and thumb through some of the magazines.

"Hey, Walt," Rolando says. "One day you'll be on the cover. They'll call you Master Krazy."

"Oh, god," I reply. "Please don't say that dumb name."

"Okay, Master Krazy," Rolando laughs, "whatever you say."

I start to reply but the guy gets off his stool and comes over to us. "You need some help?" he asks in his fake accent.

"I'm looking for some gloves that I can wrestle in," I say.

The clerk gives me an odd look. Like I'd just asked for running shoes that you can scuba dive in. "They only make gloves for striking," he says.

"But what if you're a wrestler and you want to throw down?" I ask.

"Wrestlers don't punch, ese," he says, giving up the Asian accent. He turns away and goes back to his stool.

"Hey, look at this," Rolando says, pointing to a stack of flyers at the end of the magazine rack. I pick one up and see it's an ad for a Mexican jiu-jitsu school in Anaheim run by a seven-time world champion.

"This guy must be good," Rolando says.

"Are you serious?" I ask. "You've been lying on your back for a couple of months while we train, getting me used to fighting Mexican jiu-jitsu guys. I would knock the shit out of this guy."

Rolando stuffs a couple of flyers into his pocket and we leave the store and get into my white truck. Rolando jams the flyers into the side compartment of the passenger door and we head back across town and go to the college and bang out a good workout in the wrestling room. Rolando spends most of his time on his back doing what he says is called the guard. He's getting pretty good at it and I'm feeling confident that I won't get taken by surprise if someone uses it on me. We go into the weight room and catch a hard lift then I drop Rolando off and head home, where I decide to call Coby. It's been a week since we tried to talk to Bart Shady and I wonder what is going on.

"Hey, stoner," I say when Coby answers. "Have you talked to Shady?"

"I've tried, dude," Coby says. "He won't take my calls. Did you do something at the show to piss him off?"

"Nothing out of the ordinary," I say. "I was just being myself."

"Well, your ordinary is everyone else's extraordinary," Coby says. "But don't worry. I'll keep trying. I'll get him eventually."

"Okay," I say. "I'm just getting a little freaked out."

"You have that letter, right?" Coby says. "It says you're fighting and we haven't heard differently so nothing is up."

I say goodbye and hang up the phone but I still have an unsettled feeling and toss and turn in bed all night. The next day I get up and do a couple of bids in the morning and then go to the weight room in the late afternoon with Rolando and Poppa Chulo. I warm up with 135 lbs., hit some easy reps at 225 lbs., then rack up 495 lbs. and press it twice slowly before letting it slam down on the hooks and then popping up to my feet.

"Fuck it," I say. "I'm sore as hell. Let's do something else to train."

"Like what?" Poppa Chulo asks.

"I got an idea," I say. "Grab your gear. Let's go out to my truck."

We leave the weight room and walk across the parking lot. I lead the way, cracking my weight belt on the asphalt as I go. I climb behind the wheel and Rolando and Poppa Chulo both squeeze in beside me on the single cloth bench seat with Poppa Chulo in the middle.

"Fuck, Walt," Poppa Chulo says. "I don't like riding bitch. Where we going?"

"Grab that flyer you got from the martial arts store, Rolando," I say. "Let's go to Anaheim and check out this seven-time world jiu-jitsu champion." Rolando reads off the address and I get onto the freeway for the long ride across Orange County.

"Are you sure about this?" Rolando asks.

"This won't be the first time I've gone into a martial arts dojo looking for a fight," I say. "You've never done that before?"

"Never," Rolando says.

"Me either," Poppa Chulo adds.

"What a couple of pussies," I laugh. "None of these martial arts geeks know how to brawl. I want to see what a real guard feels like. If they fuck with us, I'll rip their heads off."

We transfer from the 405 freeway to the 22 and end up near Garden Grove which is away from the beach and hot as hell in the summer. I make another transition to the 55 East and get off after a few minutes on Harbor Blvd going north. We head towards the foothills looking at the addresses and finally see what we're looking for at a strip mall on the left. I pull into the parking lot and see the school, Champion MJJ, in the corner.

"Look, Walt," Rolando says. "I don't know if we should be doing this."

"Rolando, it's cool," I say. "Nothing is going to happen. These dojo boys never have the balls to fight."

"You know these Mexican guys all have secret video cameras to film their fights," Poppa Chulo says.

"I don't give a flying fuck," I say. "Let them film it. Then all their friends can see them getting their asses kicked by me."

We drive by the Circuit Town store that anchors the strip mall. As we come up on the dojo, I can see guys rolling around on mats through the big front window all dressed in PJs. I back into a parking space in front of the dojo and we sit cramped on the truck's bench seat, craning our necks and looking in. The PJ guys are all rolling around on blue fold-up mats you see in gymnastic rooms.

"Can you believe this?" I say. "Look at all these geeks trying to be tough. These guys couldn't beat their way out of a wet paper bag. Let's go."

I get out of the truck and walk up to the front door with Rolando and Poppa Chulo behind me. I walk inside to the small office that consists basically of a single desk. Behind it, a long skinny room stretches about 50 feet. As we walk in, a guy who looks like he's the head PJ stops talking to a small group in the middle of the room and walks out to us.

"Hey, guys," he says in a Mexican accent. "What's up?"

"We just wanted to check out this jiu-jitsu stuff," I say. "I'm Walt and this is Rolando and Poppa Chulo."

The jiu-jitsu guy nods and looks into my eyes, ignoring the other two. "Walter Foxx?"

My head jerks up in surprise. "How do you know me?"

"From the West Minister boxing gym," he says.

"I've never seen you there," I say.

"I've just heard about you from guys who train there," he says. "What brings you here? You're not looking for anyone are you? I don't want any trouble."

"Nothing like that," I say. "I just want to check out this jiu-jitsu stuff they do in the cage."

"You've fought in the NHB?" he asks.

"No," I say. "Just wrestled and boxed a little. I just wanted to see how this jiu-jitsu stuff measures up against wrestling. My friends are wrestlers too." The guys face brightens up. Unlike the karate and kung-fu geeks he doesn't seem to be afraid at all of getting on the mat with strangers.

He turns around and looks back at the class. "Demonstration!" he yells. "Everybody make room!" He looks back at us. "I just help out here. I'll get the head instructor to roll with you."

Everyone quiets down and you can hear the ticking of the clock on the wall as the 20 guys in class stare at us and size us up, wondering who the hell we are. The Mexican guy who talked to us disappears into the crowd around the center of the front mat and another guy comes forward and goes to the center of the 20-foot square space.

"Let's go live," he says. "Pick who you want to go first."

The guy is around 180 pounds and just under six feet tall. He isn't really muscular but looks confident. I smile to myself because he has no idea what he's in for. Poppa Chulo is a junior college state champ and Rolando was an All-American wrestler at Husker A&M.

"You go first," I say to Poppa Chulo.

As the wannabe geeks look on as if they are tough themselves my excitement climbs. The PJ guy is 40 pounds heavier than Poppa Chulo but I've seen him beat guys a lot bigger than that. The guy gets on his knees and waits while Poppa Chulo takes off his sweats.

"You know what he's going to do," I say quietly to Poppa Chulo. "Just control the position and watch your neck."

This skinny guy in white PJs jumps around on his knees in the middle of the blue mat. The floor vibrates as he hits the mat repeatedly. Poppa Chulo goes to the center and faces off with him on his knees as well. The PJ guy is so focused on Poppa Chulo that he is completely open for a kick to the face by me. I can see he's never been in a street fight where he has to worry about his opponent's friends. I think about kicking him in the head to teach him a free lesson but discard the idea for now. With a sudden move forward the two clinch up.

"Go Poppa Chulo!" I scream. "Kill him!"

Poppa Chulo tries to grab the guy around the neck but the PJ guy falls onto his back with his legs up. Poppa Chulo stands up between his legs then lunges forward, reaching out for his neck with both hands. It's just a matter of time before Poppa Chulo squeezes this fuck into bye-bye land. As he lunges forward, though, the PJ guy passes one leg over Poppa Chulo's head, puts his elbow between his legs, and straightens his right arm from the bottom, making Poppa Chulo tap on the mat like a machine gun. *Fuck!*

Poppa Chulo goes again and gets between the guys legs one more time. This time, instead of reaching out with both hands, he just puts one hand out and goes for the guy's neck. Instead of bending the arm between his legs, this time the PJ guy wraps his legs around Poppa

Chulo's neck in a figure-four and squeezes hard, making him tap again from a leg choke!

I remember what Poppa Chulo said about a camera and look around and see the manager we talked to first walking around in the back near a small door that leads into a changing room. Above the door in a small box with a hole in that looks just about right for a video camera. The guy is undoubtedly turning it on now. Poppa Chulo comes off the mat and I turn to Rolando.

"Poppa Chulo is too small for this guy," I whisper to him as he takes off his sweat shirt. "You weigh the same. Get in there and kill this fuck."

"I know, Walt," Rolando says. "Don't worry."

As Rolando's sweat shirt comes off it reveals a blue Husker A&M Cornstalks wrestling shirt underneath. The PJ guys on the fringe of the mat murmur among themselves as Rolando's NCAA Division I experience is exposed. This is going to be good. Rolando and I have been practicing this guard stuff for a while and I know he is going to do just fine. They square off with both of them on their knees, the cast of PJ wannabes behind them forming a white wall. From their expressions I can tell that they are all wishing they can someday be warriors if they learn enough. They don't get that being a warrior comes from inside you and is something that can't be learned.

PJ Boy and Rolando start in and PJ pulls Rolando back into his guard, between his legs. Rolando floats on top because PJ has put both legs inside of Rolando's thighs, lifting him off the mat.

"Watch it!" I yell.

Now PJ lets his legs go wide and Rolando falls inside where PJ wraps his legs around him. Rolando is held in tightly and can't move. He looks over at me with a befuddled expression that says, *What the fuck?* PJ moves his legs up Rolando's back and wraps them around his neck and squeezes hard. Rolando's face turns red as his air is cut off and he taps PJ's thigh, making him release the hold so he can gasp for much-needed air.

They face off again and I can see Poppa Chulo beside me looking on intently. The wannabes are all focused on the center of the mat and the manager is in back taping away for some future greatest tap out tape to sell to their students. Rolando is much more aggressive this time around and more at ease. They tangle together with intertwined arms and legs fighting for position: the seven-time world champion and the Husker A&M All-American wrestler. They go for two minutes and it looks like Rolando is going to get him. Rolando straightens his legs on top and puts pressure downward on PJ Boy's neck. His hips are high and his hands are around his neck. Rolando is going to make him tap. Then out of the blue, PJ Boy swivels his hips and kicks his leg across the front of Rolando's face. The back of his leg presses against Rolando's face and both of his legs stick into the air. Rolando's arm is stuck in the middle as PJ Boy's back starts to arch. Rolando taps out quickly as his elbow joint starts to invert. *Rolando got caught with an arm lock. You've got to be kidding me.*

All around me the wannabes smile. They think that knowledge alone will make you a warrior. Rolando walks off the mat with a mixture of rage, frustration and disappointment etched on his face. The PJ Boy is now pumped up. He is nodding at the other PJs who are slapping him on the back in congratulations. He looks over at me and catches my stare. He has taken care of the

239

small guys and now he is ready for the big guy; except this big guy is pushing around six bills in the weight room. He motions me forward onto the mat with his arms: *Come to my world*, his body language says.

I step onto the mat with my wrestling shoes and the manager runs up and tells me that no shoes are allowed. I slip them off quickly and approach him in my bare feet. The PJ wannabes are smiling like this going to be a piece of cake. As the foam compresses under my feet, my muscles compress under my skin getting ready for war. I don't know jiu-jitsu but I do know that knowledge is not the Rosetta Stone to being a warrior. It won't make you tough if you don't have heart. He is waiting for me on his knees and I put myself into his world by rushing in as he falls to his back.

As he falls, he grabs my shirt. It's a polyester fabric shirt I wear because it doesn't rip. He's on his back right in front of me and my arms are free. If this was a real fight, I would blast this idiot's head into the mat. I seriously consider unloading on this fucker then putting my knee on his chest and rattling his cage by slamming his head into the cheap mat. Maybe even just dope slapping him a little bit would get his attention. But we're playing by his rules so just like in boxing I don't turn it into a real fight.

We've been holding this position for a couple of minutes and he has gradually grabbed both sides of my tee-shirt collar and crossed his arms, getting leverage to choke me. The fabric is tight around my neck and his face is straining under the exertion required to apply the hold. He's almost got me and I'm starting to get lightheaded from the lack of oxygen. Rules or not, I'm not going out without a fight and I ball my hands into fists and put them inches away from his face. His eyes get big as he thinks I'm going to hit him, but instead I put my knuckles on his neck and grind them downward, putting my full weight of nearly 270 pounds all on his neck.

He continues to pull me inward to apply the choke but the more he pulls the more my knuckles dig into his neck. I'm ready to go out but just before I do, he gives into the pain and releases his hold from my neck, looking at me somewhat fearfully. If he would have just fought the pain for another few seconds I would have been out, but now I'm free. He is not a warrior but just another wannabe. He has a relieved look on his face, glad that he didn't get hit when I gouged his neck with my knuckles. He stays on his knees looking at me carefully, waiting for me to make the first move.

The PJ students on the edge of the mat are suddenly pensive; the pleased looks of their faces now ones of concern since I broke the choke. They've realized that I went face to face with their hero and he backed down first, releasing his hold rather than face the pain. The big guy with the comic book arms just kicked sand in their hero's face. They know if this was a real fight that he would have been in for a real beating.

We start again and his energy is faster. He can really move and I can feel his multiple positional changes but I keep up with him as his hips roll back and forth searching for an advantage. He's a seven-time world champion but I'm a seasoned street fighter with the strength to rip your ears off your head with my bare hands. I keep him off my back and pinned to the mat. His legs with their white gi pants are locked in place around my waist and we stay there for two minutes as I keep his hands from getting a firm grip on my collar. I push down on his knees with my hands and feel his feet unlock.

Not missing a beat, he swings his hips around to the side. I'm bent over at the waist with my arm extended out from breaking his waist lock. I push down on his shoulder to keep him from sliding to my back and he snaps his leg over my head and puts it against my face. I feel him trying to straighten my arm so I get to my feet with him still holding on. Like a baby possum holding onto its mother's side as it runs down a backyard fence, PJ Boy is bouncing up and down trying to extend my arm at the elbow for the tap, but this is not going to happen.

I've doing dumbbell curls with 140 lbs. and I've got the strength to resist his hold because he has no leverage hanging in the air. As I look down, his white PJ karate suit looks like a cast hanging off my left arm. I put my right arm up, make a fist, and smile. His head is hanging upside down from my arm, both feet in the air. I dig my fist into his leg and twist it, ripping into the quadriceps painfully. He lets go and falls to the mat, his back crashing onto the floor. Mr. PJ Boy has no taste for pain.

I follow him to the mat and crash on top of him, covering him like a blanket. His eyes are full of surprise that I was able to resist the arm bar but his hips again begin to move. This fucker is like slippery as hell. I put my weight on his chest and pin him down with my arms, being careful not to extend them like Poppa Chulo did. I pin him down and get one arm free and am in position to blast him to the other side of the globe. All credibility he had with me disappears, just like the air from the blue mats I'm smashing him into. The surprised look in his eyes has turned to one of concern. I hold steady as he tries to slide his hips out. His eyes move back and forth, looking for me to react to his movement so he can escape. I smile at him and my smile gets bigger as his panic grows. Size matters and I'm proving it right here and right now.

I'm not just an experienced wrestler, I'm a warrior who won't be intimidated and who won't back down from pain. I've turned world class wrestlers into sacks of bones and into soup-filled bowls of skin. He may know jiu-jitsu but that isn't fighting, that's rolling around with rules with guys in your own weight class with no pain involved. They get just to the point where it starts to get fun and then tap to end the possibility of pain. That isn't being a warrior; that is just gaining knowledge and being safe. Warriors live in the pain zone. You can be tough in a sport and have no idea how to fight when you not inside a controlled environment. The street is not a sport. There are no rules, no guarantees, and no safe endings. There's just survival.

Me and PJ Boy have made it to the edge of the blue mats in our dance of death. He has moved his hips continuously to try to escape and I have changed positions to follow. The Velcro holding the mat pieces together has started to rip apart at the edges. I need to get him away from the wall so I quickly pick him up by one shoulder and hip and toss him to the center of the mat in one smooth motion. I follow him to the mat and cover him again chest-to-chest with his legs around my waist. I look at Rolando and roll my eyes to let him know that this guy has nothing that can hurt me. I'm too big and too strong.

I put my forearm on his neck and press down in a pure power move. He can feel the pressure and his face goes from surprise, to concern, and then to panic as the force increases. If this was a street fight this fuck in his white karate suit would be crimson red in his own blood. This long skinny Q-Tip shaped dojo is the right shape for him and his Charles Atlas wannabe tough guy students that he is stealing money from. He can't do anything to me. If this was a fight without rules, I would be using his karate uniform for a Q-Tip and this 180 lb. dope would be beaten into unconsciousness in 28 seconds and dead in 30. He is trying to be safe and submit me but now when the pain starts is when it gets fun.

I can't bash this guy's head in with punches because of the rules of sport. I'm not going to fuck this moron up with the real answer to a fight: a stiff punch to the face. Two more minutes of stalemate go by with me on top pressuring his neck and him trying to slide his hips to the side and around my waist to get to my back. This bullshit is getting old so I reach down and push down with one hand on his left leg wrapped around my waist. He responds by squeezing with his legs but it doesn't hurt me. He just isn't strong enough.

I push his left leg down further with my right hand. He fights to keep his leg on top but he has no power so I push it down and hurdle the leg of this wannabe warrior and vault to the side of his body with both legs flat on the mat, free from between his legs. I keep my weight on him so he can't move. I could punch this dumb fuck's lights out but I'm playing nice. He tries to slide his legs around me again but I don't want to go back to where I was so I grab his white karate gi pants. They bunch up in my hand as his fights to slide his legs around me but he can't. I'm on the side with my weight on him and in control.

I put my shoulder on his chest and reach around his neck in a wrestling head lock and squeeze hard like a boa crushing a rat. My arms are getting flooded with blood and my hands are getting tired from squeezing his head. His PJs are hanging out from the black belt around his waist and he is lifting his hips up and moving them back and forth trying to swivel. Playing by the rules sucks and I wish I could blast this fucker. Finally, I lose my grip and his hips swivel around and his head pops out.

I roll to my stomach and he gets on my back like he has done something great and puts his heels inside my inner thighs. The truth is he hasn't done anything except be lucky that we weren't fighting for real. He fights to put his arm around my neck and I tuck my chin down to block it. After a minute of this I get really bored of the entire game. I could stay here until next Tuesday but what is the point? I tap the mat to end the match and he rolls off me and stands up with his arms in the air, then he bends over at the waist gasping for breath.

I get to my feet and the PJ guys in the dojo look at me curiously, not sure what to make of me. They know that he just got his ass kicked at his own game by a guy who had never played by their rules before. If this was a real fight, he'd be dead. I just laugh as I walk off the mat. I'm tired of rules holding me back in wrestling, in boxing and now in this submission shit, whatever it is. I need to fight no rules matches where anything goes.

I'm not worried about fighting the jiu-jitsu guys after this. It took him 20 seconds to tap little Poppa Chulo, three minutes to get Rolando twice, and ten minutes to get me once. But I wasn't punching; I was just bellied down on the mat and on him for most of the match. This was a seven-time world champ and I got his neck good with a high school head lock. As I look at him, I can see that the side of his face is still red from the pressure I put on him. I try to catch him in eye to eye contact but he looks away and doesn't meet my gaze. I stopped his submissions twice with the promise of pain, then cleared his guard, then nearly tore his head off with a forearm choke, then finally tapped just because I was bored.

His students go back to rolling around on the mats and the PJ world champion goes to the back wall and takes a seat on the mat with his head down, still trying to recover his breath. We put our sweats back on and the manager comes out of the back room just as we open the front door to leave.

"I'll see you at the West Minister Boxing Club sometime," I say. "Maybe we can spar a little."

The guy slaps my pumped biceps and laughs. "And maybe not, my friend. I don't have a death wish you know."

I laugh despite myself and we go outside to the parking lot and get into my truck and drive away.

22. The Worm Turns

We all crowd together on the cloth bench seat with Poppa Chulo unhappily in the middle as I pull out of the Circuit Town parking lot and onto the main street heading towards the freeway. The truck is quiet until I get into the flow of traffic then it starts.

"Fuck!" Rolando says angrily. "We've got to learn this shit! That guy toyed with me."

"Yeah," I say, "that was pretty crazy but you did good, Rolando. What happened to you, Poppa Chulo? He got you twice in a minute."

"I don't know, Walt," Poppa Chulo says. "When he wanted to start on his knees it threw me off my game. I didn't know what was going on."

"Well, he got you in no time," I say.

"Yeah, I know," Poppa Chulo says disgustedly.

"He would have had me, too," I say, "if I wasn't too strong for him. It's not what you know, it's who knows it."

"You're right, Walt," Rolando says.

"Well, I can tell you that you'll never see the tape the manager took through the box on top of the dressing room," I say.

"That's for sure," Poppa Chulo says. "He couldn't do anything with you. It made him look bad. If you were punching, he would be dead."

"He's a seven-time world champ and then some guy who has never done jiu-jitsu steam rolls him," I say. "The chokes he did were the same ones we did as freshmen in the high school wrestling room. He couldn't even tap me out with an arm lock. I'm too strong for that shit to work. He got to be better than the Garcia brothers. I just gave into the choke because I got bored. I wish I would have punched that fucker!"

"I hear ya, Walt," Poppa Chulo says.

But one thing's for sure," I continue, "is that we've got to learn this shit. Even though I don't know jack I still passed the seven-time world champion's guard. But I can't rely on strength. I need to know what I'm doing and what they're doing. All those guys in that dojo didn't know what being tough is. They're all technique and no heart."

Rolando is sitting silently in disbelief at the far end of the bench seat, brooding unhappily about how he got worked by the jiu-jitsu guy.

"Yo, Rolando," I say. "Don't worry about it. We'll figure it out. Did you guys pick up anything? I know I did. I got a whole new perspective on fighting these guys. Now we just have to learn their game."

The ride back home is quiet as we all think about what happened. It used to be that wrestlers ruled but now there is something new to learn or get left behind. I drop off Rolando and Poppa Chulo at the college parking lot to get their cars and then go back to my garage and fall asleep quickly with Adolf curled up beside me.

For the rest of the week the three of us hit the gym hard, spending more time on chokes and arm bars and trying to recreate the positions we got stuck in at the jiu-jitsu dojo. I increase my weight training intensity as well in order to get my strength up for the NHB. By the end of the week I'm happy with my training but unhappy that I still haven't heard anything from Bart Shady. After I do my morning run on Friday I get on my Interceptor and ride over to Decisions to see Coby in person. I park my bike in the front parking lot and walk in the front glass office door and go through the lobby door to Coby' upstairs office.

"What's up, stoner?" I say to Coby as I shut the door behind me.

"Nothing much," he says, more lucid than normal.

"I had a really good week for workouts," I say. "I've been running hard, lifting like crazy, sparring at the boxing club, and practicing that jiu-jitsu shit with Rolando and Poppa Chulo. I'm ready, man. You talk to Shady yet?"

"Fuck, bro," Coby says. "I've called him every day but he won't take my calls. Are you sure you didn't do anything in North Carolina to make him mad?"

"Nothing I can think of," I say. "I was just myself."

"Being yourself isn't always the best thing for you, Walt," Coby says.

"You don't think he kicked me out, do you?" I ask.

"He can't, Walt," Coby says. "You have a letter of intent."

"Yeah, but that doesn't mean anything," I say.

"Yes, it does," Coby says. "You can sue his ass."

"I wouldn't sue anyone over money because I wouldn't want anyone to sue me," I say. "If someone did, they would be signing their own death warrant. I would kill them with my bare hands and then smile as they take their last breath."

"I don't think it will come to that," Coby says. "I'll just keep trying to reach him. Hopefully, I'll get him next week."

"Okay," I say. "This is just kind of weird."

"Don't worry," Coby says. "You're in."

"You wanna go get something to eat?" I ask.

"No," Coby says. "I'm not that hungry and I've got some work to do."

It figures that Coby isn't hungry when he isn't stoned so it doesn't surprise me. "No problem," I say. "I'll go hit a workout at the wrestling room and do some drills."

"You doing any bids for Fred now?" Coby asks.

"Just a few," I say. "I'm basically done until after my fight then I'll start back up."

"You really want to work for him?" Coby asks.

"Yeah, right," I say. "And I love root canals, too. But I've got to do something."

"I guess so," Coby says. "You going to party tonight?"

"Fuck, yeah," I say. "I need to get my mind off this Shady business."

"Cruise by my house after you train," Coby says.

"No problem," I say. "I'm going to hit the heavy bag for a while then roll with Rolando and Poppa Chulo in the wrestling room. They're bringing in a big guy for me to train with that used to be a state champ in junior college. Rolando thinks he'll be good for me since he's more my size. See ya later."

I take off and cruise to the college and walk up the stairs to the wrestling room. The dirty green mats shine from the sun coming through the high windows, highlighting the caked-on dirt. The coach in charge of the program lost his passion for the sport long ago and is just collecting a paycheck and going through the motions. He could never get where he wanted in life so he ended up as a wrestling coach at a junior college. I guess it's a good life for a midget but I don't want to end up settling for less than I know I can be. I need to make my mark.

Rolando and Poppa Chulo are waiting when I get there so I strap on my high-top wrestling shoes and do takedowns with them. We bang with each other for about 40 minutes and then start training how to beat jiu-jitsu. Rolando gets on is back and I get on top and he moves his hips around like that seven-time world champ as I try to fight him off and get out from between his legs. After 30 minutes the door opens and a big guy in his mid-forties walks in.

"Hey, Walt," the guy says.

It's Craig, a guy I knew years ago, who used to come into the wrestling room and train with guys 10 or 15 years younger than him when I was on the wrestling team. "Fuck, dude," I say. "Good to see you. I didn't know you were coming out to train with me."

"Glad to help out," he says, coming up and sitting down by us and taking his wrestling shoes out of his gym bag. "What's this thing you're training for?"

"I'm doing that NHB show in a few months," I say.

"I've seen that," he says. "Pretty wild stuff."

"I'm going to do it in the summer," I say.

"Really?" he asks. "You know martial arts?"

"Nope," I say. "I just know how to street fight."

"Will that work against a black belt?" he says dubiously. "Are you going to use wrestling?"

"Fuck, no," I say. "That isn't fighting. I will stomp those black belts' asses if there are no rules. Wrestling isn't fighting any more than boxing is fighting. They all have rules that limit you but in the NHB anything goes. The NHB is for me."

"I think it's a good fit," he laughs. "You always were a little crazy. Let's do some takedowns."

251

We square off and go at each other. He's older and I'm able to get him pretty quickly but he's strong and has a lot of size so it helps me just to feel his weight after going with Poppa Chulo and Rolando all the time. After 30 minutes he's tired so we call it a day and get ready to leave.

"Let me know if you need any more help getting ready," Craig says, giving me his number on a scrap of paper. "Be happy to train with you whenever."

"Cool, man," I say. "Thanks."

I head out and make a quick stop at the grocery store for essential rooster supplies then head home and shower up and change into my party clothes. I cruise over to Coby's house and go in through the partially opened garage door, which has smoke seeping out from inside. This is the Coby I know. My heavy bag is hanging in the middle of the two-car garage and he's hitting a two-foot tall bong with three neighborhood high school wannabe tough guys. They all give me a hard look and I feel like beating the fuck out of them on general principals but they're Coby's friends and they keep their mouths' shut so I let it go.

Coby is sitting at an old, cheap wooden desk in a matching chair that has the back broken off. The garage is full of pot smoke. Their eyes are closed into slits narrower than the half-opened door. These three dumb high school kids are sitting around listening to Coby's bullshit, as he spins himself into a bad ass fighting guru.

Do they really believe this bullshit? Maybe it's the pot or more likely they're just plain stupid. On the wall behind the desk are sports medals and trophies from his first two years in high school before he turned into a pothead. His new wife won't let him smoke or keep that crap in the house so he has his own pathetic hall of fame in the garage.

"Hey, guys," Coby says slowly. "This is my good friend, uh..."

"Walt," I say, finishing Coby's pot-fueled non-sentence. "What's up?"

"You wanna hit the bong?" one of the kids asks.

"No, man," I say. "I got a bar in my car."

"Dude, you rhymed," the kid says, looking at me like I'm William Shakespeare. "That's fucking awesome."

"I need a drink," I say. The alcohol will dull my sensitivity to their stoner stupidity.

I go out to the truck, make a freshy, and then come back in under the garage door. As I do, I hear Coby telling them that I'm going to be fighting in the NHB in the summer.

"No way, dude," one of them says as I lean against the desk and take a long pull on my rooster. "You're big and all but those guys are black belts. They're trained killers. Are you a black belt?"

"No," I say. "I'm a street fighter. Being a black belt doesn't mean shit."

"Oh, dude," he says. "Don't you watch those karate movies where Chuck Norris kills like 50 people in a single fight? You're going to get destroyed."

"That stuff is all Hollywood martial arts," I say.

"They're going to call him Krazy with a K," Coby says, "the real-life street fighting legend. Like in that movie."

The smoke-filled garage erupts in laughter and one of the skinny punks chimes in. "No, dude. You can't beat a black belt. That shit is crazy. You're going to get seriously fucked up."

I smile and feel strangely calm. Most likely from a
contact buzz from the garage smoke. "Just watch me
when I fight. You'll see."

Coby packs another bud into the bong bowl and takes
a long rip. Smoke escapes from his lips and he starts to
hack and cough. The high school stoners all sit around
and stare at Coby on his stage as if he's the god of getting
stoned, which I guess he really is. He sits on the wooden
chair with the broken back and leans against the wall.
The stoner disciples all do the same on their plastic lawn
chairs. No one says a thing. It must be some stoner thing
that I don't get, so I stoop back under the garage, mix
another freshy, and then go back inside. The teenage
idiots have climbed on their skateboards and Coby hits
the garage door button to raise it a few feet.

Good luck, dude," the skinny idiot yells as the door
swings up. "You'll need it." They all laugh as they duck
under the door and skate down the driveway and into the
night.

I walk past Coby and start to punch the Musashi
heavy bag in the middle of the garage. "Man, I can't wait
to jack up those fucking jokers in that crazy show in a
couple of months," I grunt between hits. "All these little
punks won't be laughing then. They'll know who Walter
Foxx is."

"Walt," Coby laughs, "they won't even remember
who you are."

"You, too?" I say. "I don't care. I'll show everyone."

"That isn't what I meant," Coby says. "Everyone will
just know you as Krazy when you destroy those fuckers
in the cage."

"No way," I say. "That name is just a gimmick. No
one will remember it."

"Oh, yes they will," Coby insists. "You'll see, Walt."

"Well, I don't care what they know me as just as long as they know me," I say. "Coby, I've been good. I haven't come close to getting in a fight in months. I don't want to fuck this up. All I do is go to the grocery store, get booze and cruise with Adolf. I'm just chilling. The show is going to change my life. I just know it. I just have to figure out what I'm going to do afterwards. I can't keep selling garage doors."

"Let's not worry about that now," Coby says. "I've got something else I need to focus on."

"Like what?" I ask.

"Like breaking the record for the world's biggest bong hit," Coby says. He puts his lips to the monster bong and inhales for at least 30 seconds. He finishes and holds his breath, his face starting to turn red.

"Alright, man," I say. "Good luck with that. I'm outta here."

Coby nods and waves, still holding his breath, as I walk under the garage door and get into my truck. I drive away but start feeling that I need to hang out with someone who isn't stoned. I decide to go over to Linda's house, a late-night standby that I haven't seen since I went to jail. She lives 20 minutes away in a big apartment complex in Wong Beach.

I park in front and walk through the broken apartment gate and down a hallway to her door. I listen outside for a few minutes to make sure she doesn't have company but only hear the TV going. I finally ring the doorbell and see an eye appear in the security hole and then the sound of a deadbolt being thrown.

Linda pops her head out and breaks into a smile. "Hey, Walt. What's up?"

"Just cruising around," I say. Got out of jail a little bit ago and just wanted to see how you are."

"I wondered what happened to you," Linda laughs. "Guess that explains it. Come in for a while. Nobody's here but me."

I walk into her apartment and see that nothing has changed in nearly a year. The living room is off to the left with an overstuffed brown sectional couch in the corner and the kitchen is on the right. There's a glass coffee table in front of the couch with ten lighted candles of various sizes, casting flickering shadows on the paintings of flowers hanging on the walls.

"I haven't seen you in ages," Linda says. "How are you?"

"I 'm doing pretty well," I say. "I got jammed up on a bullshit assault charge and did some halfway house time. Now I'm doing a couple of bids a week at the garage door shop."

Linda shakes her head. "A guy with a college degree should be doing more than that."

"Yeah, I know," I say. "I actually have a fight coming up that will be on pay-per-view TV."

"You're kidding me!" She says with delight.

"Nope," I say. "It's that NHB fighting show that everyone is all up in arms about. It's real fighting with no rules."

"That's perfect for you, Walt," Linda says. "You're going to do really well."

"Yeah, I'm going to kick some serious ass," I say. "But I think I'm the only one in the world that thinks I have a chance."

"Tell me all about it," Linda says.

We start to talk and I end up going out to my truck and bringing in my rooster supplies and mixing drinks for us. We catch up and laugh and party until nearly 3:00 AM and I finally leave and drive home and fall into my king-sized bed in the middle of my parent's garage. I go to sleep thinking that maybe one day I'll have my own place that I can actually invite a girl to. I fall asleep in a drunken stupor and awake to the sound of Adolf snoring in my ear.

"Quiet, fucker," I say, pushing him away.

I roll over and look at the clock and see the red LED numbers shining out 11:03 AM. I lie in bed for a while and contemplate going to sleep again but then am jerked to full wakefulness by the sound of my pager going off. I reach across the bed and fish it out of my pants pocket and see that Coby is calling. *What the fuck does he want?* I drag myself into the shower, get my workout gear together, and then head to the weight room. I do a couple of warm-up sets on the bench press and my pager goes off again in my gym bag. I ignore it and it buzzes again a couple of minutes later. I finally dig it out of my bag and see Coby's number again with "911" behind it. *What the fuck?*

I go over across the weight room, grab the office phone that is in the coaches' corner cubicle, and punch in Coby's number.

"What the hell do you want?" I say. "I'm in the middle of a workout."

"Forget the workout," Coby says. "We have an emergency. Get over to my office now!"

23. Shady Business

I tell Coby I'll meet him as soon as I finish my workout and hang up the phone. As I go back to the bench, past the neck machine, I wonder what the fuck he wants. As I power through the rest of my workout, I run possible scenarios through my head. Maybe he's come up with another great sponsor like Baton. That would be sweet as sugar if he did. I have a great lift and am feeling as strong as the elephant on my leg. I can't wait to work out tonight and get in some more practice crushing the jiu-jitsu guard.

Still feeling fresh after my training, I leave the gym and walk out to my Interceptor in the parking lot, slapping my weight belt on the asphalt as I go, warning all my enemies to beware. I climb on my bike, push the start button, and rev the engine to the steady roar that I never tire of. I flip up the kickstand and settle into the duct-taped seat that fits my form perfectly after years of riding.

I pull out slowly as I wind through the parking lot then drop my body next to the red, white and blue gas tank and twist the throttle harder when I get to the two-lane road. The wind blasts through my hair as I speed by the tennis courts, the green mesh plastic strips tied to the chain link fence fluttering from my tornado wake. I zip onto the freeway, and blast towards Decisions, weaving in and out of traffic at high speed and getting to the office off-ramp in no time. As I idle down the cul-de-sac and shut off the bike in the parking lot, I keep wondering what the fuck is going on.

I go through the glass doors, wave at the receptionist, and go inside and up the stairs to Coby's office. Coby is sitting in his chair with his head in his hands and then looks up at me as I enter.

"Dude," he says. "We have serious trouble. Shady says you're out."

"What?" I scream. "I knew it! I fucking knew this wouldn't work!"

"Calm down, dude," Coby says. "Getting mad won't help. Let's call him on the speaker."

He punches buttons on the phone and pushes down the speaker switch. Coby leans back in his chair and I move closer to his desk as the phone rings and then a woman answers.

"Hello," she says. "No-Holds-Barred Championship."

"Hi," Coby says. "This is Coby Swapper and Walter Foxx. Is Bart there?"

"Hold on, please," she says.

There's a few seconds of silence then the phone clicks back on. "Bart Shady speaking."

"Hey, Bart, it's Coby. I'm here with Walter."

Shady's voice comes back, as cold as ice. "It won't do you any good to keep calling me. I've already told you that Foxx is out."

"Why, Bart?" Coby says. "He agreed to let you call him Krazy. Is it because he went to jail for street fighting?"

"No," Shady answers. "It's because he's a raving lunatic. He ran around the event for two days totally out of control. He crashed parties he wasn't invited to, made a spectacle out of himself, got in my face at the show, took an NFL Hall-of-Famer's beret off his head, threatened fighters and announcers, and basically scared the hell out of everyone."

"Come on, Bart," Coby says. "I'm sure he was just having a little fun."

"I wouldn't describe screaming all night in a hotel room and keeping the owner of the show and his wife awake all night in the room next door, fun," Shady says.

"It was just a little misunderstanding," Coby says.

"Lanny Meyer, the owner of the NHB show, understood his screaming quite well," Shady continues. "Lanny called the front desk multiple times to complain about the noise and they were ready to call the cops before he finally shut up. Then he stalked Lanny in the parking lot the next morning and nearly scared his wife to death. He's totally out of control."

"What about the letter?" Coby asks. "He's been training like crazy and really wants to fight."

"He'll never fight in the NHB," Shady says. "It's never going to happen. The decision has been made and it's not up to me anymore. He's definitely out for good. There's nothing more to talk about."

There is total silence for several seconds and I feel like a dagger has just stabbed my heart. Shady doesn't care that he has totally fucked up my life. It's all about his hurt feelings and getting even with the people he can't push around.

"Well, keep him in mind," Coby says. "He's ready to go."

"It's over," Shady says. "Don't call me again."

Shady hangs up and Coby pushes the speaker phone button. The office is as quiet as a cemetery as he hangs up the receiver. The silence is deafening and the only

noise is the buzz from the fluorescent light overhead. It's
like someone just died.

Coby looks at me with his eyes bulging. "Walt, what
did you do?"

"I told you already," I say. "I was just myself. I get up
from the chair and walk towards the door. "Forget about
it, Coby. I'm outta here. It always seemed to be too good
to be true. Fuck it."

"Don't give up, Walt," Coby says as I walk out. "I'll
get you in."

I don't answer as I walk out the door to where I was
before. I walk down the same hallway I used when I was
going back to the halfway house and walk to my
Interceptor in the parking lot. I'm too numb to even be
angry. It's like I have no emotions left inside at all. I start
the engine and drive down the cul-de-sac at five miles
per hour. I'm down and out and feel like I'm going back
to the halfway house. *Fuck the world*. I don't want to go
home so I cruise over to Fred's office and go inside.

"Hey, man," I say. "I need some bids to do."

Fred sees that I'm upset and answers me carefully.
"What happened to the fighting thing?"

"Fuck that," I say. "They blackballed me. They say
I'm too scary to let into the show."

"Fuck 'em, then," Fred says. "Their loss. I'll get you
some bids. I'll call you in a day or two and get you going
again. Call me anytime you want."

"Thanks, bro," I say.

I go outside and climb back onto my bike. I can't help
but think that selling garage doors is going to be my life.
I drive home and see that nobody is there. When I open
the front door, Adolf comes running.

"Come on, boy," I say, walking out to the garage. I jump on the bed and stare up at the empty rafters. They seem emptier than ever before. "Adolf, what am I going to do with my life?" I lay there for an hour and finally hear my mom pull into the driveway and walk in the front door. Adolf jumps off the bed and runs out to greet her. I get up and sheepishly follow, feeling like a schoolboy who got sent home early from school.

"I thought you would be training?" my mom asks as I walk into the kitchen.

"I don't have anything to train for," I say glumly.

"Oh, no," my mom says. "What happened?"

"They banned me," I say. "They don't want a real fighter. They're all posers. They saw a little bit of me and got scared. I feel bad about Ted from Baton and all the people who were helping me train. They're going to think this was a fake. I feel like I'm one of those phonies who try to rip people off by saying they're fighters just to make money. I always knew these NHB guys weren't real. They spent too much time with stupid gimmicks trying to promote morons who aren't fighters. I knew Bart Shady was a lying thief from the beginning. It's a personality trait that will get you killed around me."

I leave the house and go to meet up with Poppa Chulo and Rolando at the wrestling room. I climb the cement stairs to the shoddy gym in my street clothes and see them standing outside the door.

"What's up, Walt?" Rolando says. "Are we going to roll?"

"No, Rolando," I say.

"We only have a couple of months till you fight," Rolando says.

No, Rolando," I say. "We don't have anything."

"What?" he says in confusion.

"There's no days, no weeks, no months, no nothing," I say. "Bart Shady fucked me and kicked me out of the show."

Rolando's face shows shock and Poppa Chulo's mouth drops open.

"What about the letter?" Poppa Chulo says.

"It doesn't mean shit," I say. "Shady doesn't have anything to do with the show. He's just an errand boy. He's a big, goofy no-nothing matchmaker with no pull at all. Calling yourself a matchmaker is the biggest joke of all. He's all mouth. He told Coby I was crazy and said they didn't want me in the show anymore."

"What the fuck do they know?" Poppa Chulo spits out.

"Exactly," I say. "They don't know who the real fighters are. They're posers choosing posers. Fuck it. I'm going out by myself to get drunk."

I walk away from the wrestling room and go back down the cement stairs. I drive to the grocery store and walk my paces with my eyes nearly closed. I head out into the night and mix a rooster and cruise the residential highway till I reach a good buzz. I mix another and decide to drive to the Café Pistol. When I get there and walk in, I see how things have changed. The Dead Grunion has closed down for good so there's no spillover into the cafe. It's slow and I have no problem getting a seat at the bar where I order a double Stoli with a cran back.

As the bartender makes my drink I stare into the mirror behind the bar. What am I going to do now? I finally had a purpose in life; no-rules fighting was perfect for me and now it has all been taken away. My drink comes and I throw it back in a single motion.

"You want another one?" the bartender asks.

"Yeah," I say. "Another double Stoli."

He brings it to me and I drop some straws of cranberry into the clear liquid. It makes me wonder what life is about as it turns a perfect shade of light pink. One small event can change your whole universe just like a tiny dab of cranberry can color an entire glass of vodka.

"That looks like a girl's drink," a voice says beside me.

I look over at the stool to my left and see a big guy sitting there with glass of whiskey in front of him.

"What's up with you, dude?" I say as our eyes meet.

"What's up with the cranberry, Alice?" he says.

I shrug and look away. I'm big, I'm strong, I'm in shape and I can tear anybody's head off with my bare hands. I look at this moron sitting next to me staring at me and just begging for a beating. I don't know him from Adam but I know the look. It isn't the right time for him right now. He has no idea he's in the crosshairs of death at the wrong place and wrong time. I'm in a very dark place. With just one sentence I could make this guy think he could take me and get him to go outside, where I have no doubt I would beat him to death. I weigh the consequences.

This could be bad. As mad as I am I have no doubt that I would kill this beggar. My life is spinning out of control and this could be the final act that pushes me over the edge. I can't let myself fall down that slippery slope. Being incarcerated is not how I want to spend the rest of my life. I stare at my own reflection in the mirror behind the bar and smile. I can't give into this thing that keeps pulling me. I want to fight in a cage but not spend my life in one. I think of an alternative life and my thoughts go back towards taking the LSAT, getting into law school, and living the boring life of a lawyer.

I take a big swig off my rooster and start to laugh. I'm in my late twenties and living the same life as when I got out of high school. Up to the point where that cop's son lied on the witness stand, I was one happy motherfucker. I was a late twenties teenager still going to college and beating up people that begged for it while working at a liquor store. Now I need a life and a direction. All my friends that I went to school with are now cops, firemen, or work for the county. I'm living in my parent's garage and looking for my passion to come find me.

I love to brawl but now I have no one to fight. One slip-up and I'm going away to prison for years. Bart Shady has pulled the carpet out from under my bar stool at the very moment I felt my life was turning around. I take a big swig off my rooster. But even if I got into the NHB what would it mean? They offered me $2,000 to fight. What was I thinking? That I was going to beat up the world and make $60,000? Inside I knew all the time that it wasn't going to happen that way. It would have been fun but it wasn't going to be a life. I wanted to do it for fun and not for money. You just can't make a living doing no-rules fighting.

I glance over at the beggar next to me and he's still mad-dogging me, giving me a hard stare. I swirl my glass in counter clockwise circles on the bar and keep my head down, ignoring the temptation to fuck up this fool. More drinks go down and I get increasingly frustrated. The feeling goes deep into my core and I feel like I want to kill the world. I have a moron begging for a beating sitting next to me, but Johnny Law has caught up with me. If I give into my instincts I'll go to prison and my destiny will turn out like all the people who think they're better than me have predicted.

"What are you trying to do?" the beggar asks. "Dig a hole with your drink all the way to China?"

I look over and stare at him. "No. I'm digging a hole six feet deep for you. You want something, you fuck?"

The beggar's mouth closes and I look in the mirror, grab a penny, and throw it on the bar. I turn my glass upside down over my mouth, drain the last of the liquid, put the glass on the bar and turn to look at this beggar who is sitting two stools down from me. He's in his mid-thirties, weighs around 240 lbs. and is wearing a tee-shirt with a blue marlin on it. He's in white shorts with tan Topsiders and no socks. His hair is unkempt and he's unshaven, meaning he probably lives on a boat in the Happening Harbor marina.

I walk towards the exit which is on the other side of his bar stool and stop momentarily ready to pull the trigger. Oh, I want to blast him. In my head I can picture his blood splattering on his shirt as he falls down unconscious to the floor with a broken nose. I'm known here, though, and when the cops arrive, I'd be easy to identify. I force myself to turn away and hurry down the hallway to the front door and go outside. The little man inside my head is telling me, *Don't look back! If he comes out, you'll have to fuck him up.*

As the door closes, I break into a jog towards my truck with sweat running down my face. It's like the days of old except now I'm running away from a fight instead of running away from the cops because I trashed a big mouth beggar. I get behind the wheel of my truck, shut the door, and stare out the window. I need to go back in and fuck that guy up. I'm shaking in excitement and getting fired up.

I hear the little man speak again: *Get out of here. Don't look back.* I reach out to the ignition, insert my key and turn on the engine. I back out of the parking space and drive out of the lot. There are no fire trucks with paramedics coming to treat my victim and no cop cars rushing to arrest me. There's just silence and emptiness. I drive home and go to sleep in my bed in the garage.

24. Down and Out

I get up in the morning feeling drained of all emotions but I've got to go to Fred's to sell garage doors now that my NHB dream has been crushed by Bart Shady. I decide to stop training just to say *fuck-off* to the world. I squeeze Adolf and am glad to notice that our walks are paying off. He's finally back in shape and isn't fat anymore. Now he's skinny and I'm big. I grab a quick shower and head over to Fred's office and walk in the door where Fred is sitting at his desk.

"Hey, Fred," I say. "Any bids?"

"Got some for you tomorrow," Fred answers.

I walk up to my old desk and sit down. Fred hesitates a little then gets up and walks over to me.

"I wasn't going to say anything," he says. "But it really sucks what they did to you. What happened?"

"Fuck, Fred," I say. "I don't know. They just told me I'm out."

"What about the letter?" Fred asks.

"It meant nothing," I say. "It turns out that Big Bart Shady is just a matchmaker. Just a goofy fool in a wannabe position trying to pretend he's somebody he's not. He said I was crazy but that's only because he isn't a warrior. He doesn't kick ass and tell."

"Well, Walt," Fred laughs. "You are a little crazy."

"That's what they say," I answer. "I'm outta here. I'll see you tomorrow."

I head out, stop off at the grocery store, and load up with vodka and cranberry juice. I pick-up Adolf and I cruise around as the sun sets over the ocean. I drive down

Warner Blvd. then go home for a quiet night. The next day I go to Fred's place, get some bids, drink at night, and go home. This quickly turns into a routine over the next few weeks and before I know it, I find myself selling garage doors full time, working in the afternoon and partying at night.

Even though I'm making enough money to party, an undercurrent of anger is growing steadily inside me. I'm living in my parents' garage and have no future prospects. In the back of my mind I have this constant nagging thought about what I'm going to do with my life. I thought I had some sort of direction but in truth it was just a diversion that was quickly taken away. I can only think it was not meant to be. There is just no place in the modern world for a true warrior.

For several weeks I go into a funk, getting drunk and going to strip clubs every night. One night I get wasted at home and head out to a club in LA County that I've been going to regularly for the past couple of years. When I walk in the front door all the workers know who I am and I take a seat at the stage and order my first drink. I'm in luck as my favorite dancer appears.

Her name is Nashua and she's a bronze Sade lookalike with curvaceous hips, natural double Ds, and a small waist that you could put your hands around and touch your fingers. She wiggles on the pole as I sip my drink. When the song comes to an end, I put five dollars in front of me and she gets it first, with a big smile, before going around to pick up the singles that the riff-raff have left her. I leave my front row seat and walk to the entrance where the doorman is.

"Hey, Jimmy," I say. "What's up?"

Jimmy, the doorman, who I've partied with over the years, is wearing his usual plaid buttoned-down, short-sleeve shirt with gray polyester slacks. His cheater glasses and nearly bald head make him look like Woodsy the Owl. He's a calm guy who has given me a lot of wisdom over the years.

"Damn, Jimmy," I say. "I'm pissed and in a rut. I've got nothing going on. I was going to fight in that NHB show on TV but now I've got nothing to look forward to."

"What happened?" Jimmy asks.

"They gave me a letter that said I was in their summer show," I say, "but then they kicked me out. I went to their last show in North Carolina and had a little fun and now they're telling me I'm crazy."

"Isn't being crazy what that show is all about?" Jimmy says.

"Not really," I say. "It's all about martial arts bullshit. It's fucked up. Now all I've got to look forward to is a life in the garage door business; what a fucking joke. I have no direction. I'm just floundering."

I pound my drink and go back into the bar and order another rooster. When I go back to the door Jimmy is taking money so I take a swig and chill as the patrons go through the turnstile.

When it's clear, Jimmy comes over and stands by me. "If this fighting thing doesn't pan out, at least you've got garage doors to fall back on," he says.

"Fuck, Jimmy," I say. "That's for high school dropouts and dumb fucks. I've got a college degree. Selling garage doors just pays my party bills."

"You're smart," Jimmy says. "You'll figure it out. Just don't get desperate. Things have a way of evening out over time."

"I'm lost right now. I just want to fight. I don't even care about the money. Get your cocktail waitress over here, I need another rooster."

We sit and power drinks silently until we're rip-roaring drunk, but I'm still brooding inside.

"Fighting is my passion," I finally say. "I just can't live without it."

"Things will get better," Jimmy says. "Look at me, I get paid to watch half-naked girls dance all night and get free drinks. I've got money. I just do this to keep from getting bored. The only reason I'm telling you this is that over the years I've seen people give up on their dreams because of bad choices and end up where they don't want to be."

I'm quiet for a moment, thinking about the choices I made to end up where I'm at now. At the time they all seemed good. *Is it too late to change? Should I even try?*

"What I'm saying," Jimmy continues, as if reading my mind, "is that you have to be yourself and not worry about what happens next. If you don't succeed at least you'll still be able to look in the mirror and know you tried."

"Maybe so," I say. "I'm just tired of being fucked around. I'm ready to kill someone."

"Just be yourself," Jimmy says. "You'll be okay."

Some more customers walk in and Jimmy goes over to collect their cover charge. I walk to my truck and slide into the driver's seat with my head against the back window. I close my eyes for a minute then survey the half-empty parking lot. It's a seedy area but I'm looking out for cops, not bad guys.

I turn the key in the ignition and the thin layer of frost on the windshield begins to flake off as heat begins to warm the cab on the cold and foggy night. I push the stick shift into first gear and inch out of the parking and drive towards the freeway. I get on the 405 going north towards LA County, heading towards South Bay and Bart Shady's office. That big doofus is going to get a visit. It's late, but in our talks, he told me that he stays late at his office a lot.

I already have the entire scenario in my head. I'm going bash that big fucker in the head a few times and wait a while for the shock to wear off and to let him suffer. Then I'm going to look him in the eyes, put my face an inch away from his and say, "Remember me?"

The Smiths are playing on the stereo as I exit the freeway and drive towards Shady's with my fists ready to go. *You don't play with me, you big fuck.* I know in my head I'm going to bash this big oaf. My hands are vibrating eagerly on the steering wheel from the rough road. I haven't delivered justice to anyone in a long time, by my standards, and I would never give someone the business unless they really deserved it. I like to get up close and personal with beggars but Bart Shady won't be a challenge and won't give me the honor of putting up much of a fight. He has fucked with my life and I'm going to squash him like the worm he is.

I open the door of the chariot that has taken me down this paved highway of suburbia into the shithole of LA County. No wonder my parents escaped behind the Orange Curtain that keeps out the slugs of biologic trash which fill this petri dish of life these people call home. It was a short journey in my truck to get where I need to be, but it seems like a lifetime.

I finally arrive and stare out the windshield for a quick second. A smile from my reflection in the glass wavers from the shifting fog outside as I feel my heart pound harder. Delivering justice is what I'm supposed to do in life. *Nobody fucks with Walter Foxx.* I hope I'll be able to stop once I start punching Bart Shady's lying face. A warrior has to maintain self-control but I feel it slipping away in my righteous anger. *This is not my first BBQ*, I remind myself. *I can't let emotions cloud my actions.*

I open the door, get out, and slam it behind me. The thud of the door against the frame delivers a burst of heated air that brushes my being. I slip my fists into my pants pockets forcing the instruments of justice tight against my thigh. My smile gets bigger in anticipation as I look over the top of my little white truck. I take a deep breath and the cold air burns my lungs.

At the end of the strip mall is a *Come-and-Go* convenience store. Inside the brightly lighted hub of cheap essentials I can see the master chefs preparing their fine dining of microwaved hotdogs and nacho cheese chips. A true late-night culinary delight. I might be tempted to join them after I take care of Shady.

I scan my surroundings and take in what I need to do. I have my plan of attack firmly in my head. If anything goes wrong, I'll have an unimpeded path back to my getaway truck. The outdoor mall is a bit of a dump but from where Big Bart was before it looks like the *Taj Mahal*. I move closer so I can read the signs on the doors and see that his office is upstairs but is completely dark. But that doesn't mean he isn't there. I bet he's inside watching Mexican Jiu-Jitsu tapes and *Kung-Fu Theater* reruns. I envision him with his flattop widows peak and his fat doughboy body that is all that's left of his steroid-taking days. I'm sure visions of being a badass are running rampant inside the fantasy land of his own thoughts. I can imagine him pointing into a mirror and pretending he is Little Winchell Duncan refereeing a fight: "Let's go! Let's get down!"

My smile gets bigger and I clinch my hand into a tight fist as I walk towards the stairs that will lead me to this big fat blob who has ruined my life-long dream. A bright flashing light revolving in clear plastic on top of a moving vehicle that I've seen many times before shoots into my peripheral vision. *The cops? How did they...?*

"Freeze, scumbag!" a voice blares out over a loudspeaker. "Hands up!"

I raise my hands over my head so I don't get shot by mistake and slowly turn towards the voice, blinded by the bright light. I squint my eyes and gradually adjust to the glare. Instead of the black-and-white four-door cop car I'm expecting, I see a golf cart with *MALL SECURITY* written across the front. There's movement behind the plastic windshield and I see a tiny man slide off the seat. I've got six inches and 50 pounds on him. I roll my eyes and drop my hands.

"Hands up!" the rent-a-cop yells out.

I cover my eyes with my left hand against the glare and raise up my right in a middle-finger salute.

"Uh, okay," the rent-a-cop says, obviously used to having his commands ignored. "I guess one hand will do." He reaches inside the golf cart and turns off the spotlight. "If I leave it on too long the *Come-and-Go* complains that I'm driving away business. Ungrateful bastards."

He swaggers towards me in his cheap blue uniform that is two sizes too big. As he gets closer and sees my size the swagger turns into a slow saunter and now this wannabe is unsure about exercising his non-existent authority like he has a thousand times in his dreams. There's a yellow sticky taped to his chest with *"Partrol Oficer"* misspelled in Magic Marker. For some reason, I feel like I've seen him before.

He stops six feet away and rests his hand on a Radio Shack walkie-talkie as if it's a gun. "No loitering allowed unless you're looking for the *Come-and-Go*, in which case..."

The golf cart comes alive and a female voice erupts over the golf cart's CB speaker. "Winchell! Come in! This is Eclair! Pick up now or you're in big trouble!"

I know this moron, it's Little Winchell Duncan, the referee from the NHB show. Bart Shady must have hired him to save money and to have someone below him he knew he could boss around.

Little Winchell stops cold and looks at me with what I'm sure he thinks is a menacing glare, but which just makes him look constipated. "Hold on, I gotta take this in the cart. My walkie-talkie doesn't work. It's just for show."

He walks over to the golf cart and picks up the CB handset. "Copy that, Eclair. This is Winchell. Golf cart is A-OK. 11-7, over."

"That's 10-4, genius. Don't forget to pick up dinner from the *Come-and-Go* on your way home. Unless you pissed them off again. In which case you're sleeping on the couch tonight."

No, dear," Winchell says, "Uh, I mean commander." He throws a sideways glance at me, evidently hoping I didn't pick up on the fact he is talking to his wife. "Dinner is a go. Over and out!"

He hangs up quickly, apparently before she can issue any further orders. As he walks back to me the swagger is completely gone and he looks like a whipped dog. I almost feel sorry for him.

"Hey," I say. "Aren't you Little Winchell, the referee from the NHB?"

The stoop goes out of his back and he straightens up out of his slump. I can tell I just made his day by recognizing him.

"Yes, I am," he says, his voice artificially dropping an octave lower to a baritone. "You want an autograph?"

"No, man. I'll pass," I say, watching his face drop. "But I heard you were an L.A. Sheriff's Deputy. You moonlighting or something?"

"Uh, well, I'm working on becoming a deputy," he says. "But I haven't been able to pass the written test. Some of those questions are hard and I can't remember all the codes. But I study Mexican Jiu-Jitsu with Big Bart. That's why he hired me. I'm a lethal weapon."

"I can tell from hearing you talk to your wife," I say, my irony totally lost on him. "But that's why I'm here. I came to see Big Bart."

"You missed him," Winchell says, "He left a while ago. But I still gotta finish my shift. Should I tell him who came by?

"Just tell him that Walter Foxx was here," I say.

Little Winchell flashes me a thumbs-up sign, "Will do. Are you sure you don't want an autograph? Let's go! Let's get down!"

"You know, Winchell, I was wondering. Isn't that the same thing that boxing referee Miller Blame says before a fight?"

Winchell shrugs sheepishly. "I kind of borrowed it from him. I couldn't think of one of my own. You got any ideas?"

"Sorry, man," I say. "I'll catch up with Big Bart later."

He nods and the CB radio in the golf cart comes alive again. "Winchell!" A deep female voice says. "When you get dinner make sure you pick up a dozen donuts, too. I'm hungry!"

Winchell scoots back to his golf cart and picks up the handset. "13-9 baby doll. Uh, I mean commander."

"That's 10-4, you little bitch!" Éclair yells. "How do you ever expect to get a real badge if you can't remember the codes!"

"Over and out," Winchell says. He looks up at me with a beaten-dog expression and a light comes on in his eyes. "Hey, I remember you now. You're Krazy Foxx, the bar brawler. Man, I'd like to see you in the cage."

"I'm working on it," I reply. "I hope you make into the Sheriff's Department, Winchell. You have all the makings of a good cop. Keep studying. I can tell you're smart enough."

Little Winchell's chest puffs out and he throws me a sharp salute. I turn and walk back to my truck and get in. I look into my rear-view mirror and think about Little Winchell and all of a sudden, my life doesn't seem that bad anymore. As I drive back to the sanity of Happening Beach, the smile on my face is as big as its been in weeks.

Morning comes quickly in the unheated garage and I can see my breath as I open my eyes. I climb out of bed and put my feet on the floor and the cold vibrates up my legs, through my spine, and into my brain. I remember last night and start to laugh. Thank God Big Bart wasn't in his office or I wouldn't be here right now. I think about it and laugh some more. *No, Shady wouldn't be here but neither would I.*

Even though I don't have my fight to look forward to I need to work out. I haven't done anything in two weeks and I need to start in again for the beggars of the world. I would hate to let them down when they come pleading for a beating. Instead of taking a shower I put on my Baton shorts and shirt and my rubber support belt with my Walkman inside and head out for a run. I run my normal course through the neighborhood. I grew up in this housing tract and know the area well and people know me, even if most of them don't like me.

I start out slowly on the two-mile path and then push hard when I get to the long stretch that leads to my house. I was burning down this route when I was a freshman in high school on the wrestling team. Now a bunch of time has passed and nothing has changed except for the date. The only thing different is that I'm now the ruler of this town when it comes to ass kicking. I'm the motherfucking bad ass that will tear you apart with my bare hands but only if you beg for it. As I speed up my heart races along with my rage.

The two-story houses with green grass lawns become fuzzy pictures as I blur by them. My heart pounds inside my chest but I ignore it and push harder and harder, only quitting when I get to the finish line of my house. I gasp for air and then sit on the front of the curb in the late morning sun, letting the sweat pour over my face from the river of pain I just created.

My heart beats in my chest like a bass drum as I stare down at the curb. The water running down the street in the gutter flows by like the sweat from my body. I love to train. It's the fluid of my passion and of my pain. The sweat falls off my forehead into the cement gutter and mixes with the water that carries the neighbors' dirt away.

I reach up and take off the rubber band that holds the headphones to my ears. They won't stay on because of all my years of wrestling. I don't scar and my ears are only slightly cauliflowered but they have been damaged just enough to keep the left headphone from going all the way into my left ear.

I walk into the house, wipe the sweat off my face and grab Adolf, wrestling with him in the living room. He is strong and struggles for top position, making me laugh as he growls louder. I finish with him and grab a quick shower and then get into my truck and head to Fred's office. Skip is there and looks up at me with a weird vibe. Before I can really say anything, Fred comes out of his office.

"Hey, Walt," he says. "What's up?"

"Not much," I say. "Just wanted to know if you had any bids."

"Yeah," Fred says. "I need to talk to you about that."

Fred turns and walks into his office, motioning me to follow. Fred has always been a rip off so I know something is up. He would sell his own mother for a dollar so I know he doesn't have my best interests at heart. He sits behind his desk and I take a seat facing him. He leans forward and puts his elbows on the oak desk.

"Walt," Fred says. "I'm going to cut your pay. From now on you're going to get eight percent commission instead of ten."

I look at him silently for a moment. "Whatever, Fred," I say.

His eyebrows lift as if he's a little surprised I didn't argue. "Okay, Walt. I guess that's it then."

I get up silently and walk out to my desk in the small showroom. With each step I think back over the past year. First, I went to jail, then I got kicked out of the NHB, and now my low paying job just became even lower paying. I keep getting kicked when I'm down with no end in sight. I'm a college graduate with some jail time and nothing going on. What am I going to do in life? Be a garage door salesman? All I want to do is beat up big dumb goofs who push their weight around and beg for a beating. But I can't even do that anymore because if I get arrested again, I'll go to prison. Everything has been taken away from me.

Skip doesn't have any bids until tomorrow so I leave the office, drive to the grocery store, do my loop, and then make a rooster in the parking lot. I head home and pick up Adolf and just cruise around the residential highway, hoping to not see anyone. I'm so frustrated with my position in life that I don't trust what I might do if someone really pisses me off. After cruising for a while, I go back to my garage where it's safe for me and also safe for the world and pass out with Adolf.

25. Jam at the Joint

I get up in the late morning and feel like keeping my drinking run going. I have nothing to look forward to so why the hell not? I see a box of doughnuts on the kitchen counter that my dad left and eat a chocolate bar, cinnamon roll, and a couple of glazed doughnuts. Fortified with sugar and grease, I take a shower, mix up a traveler, and head to Poppa Chulo's and Rolando's apartment. I walk up the skinny sidewalk and notice that the grass is turning yellow and needs watering. I pour some of my rooster onto the grass as an offering to the lawn gods and walk in the unlocked double doors of their bottom apartment in the white fourplex. Poppa Chulo and Rolando barely look up as I come in. They were as excited as school kids on a field trip when we had the NHB to look forward to, but now there's no life left in them.

The cheap cloth living room sofas are in their proper places, meaning there was no takedown party last night. I sit at the cheap secondhand thrift store bar that was probably nice twenty years ago. Now the brown vinyl wallpaper in front is ripped to shreds and the Formica top is faded from years of use and abuse from its present and previous owners. The four bucket bar stools are made of the same ripped vinyl as the bar. I spin around on the stool to face Poppa Chulo and Rolando.

"Let's party, guys," I say. "I'm more depressed about the NHB than you but we've got to get our heads on straight."

They shrug and stare at their old 19-inch black-and-white TV that is the same vintage as the bar. It sits on stained reddish-brown shag carpet, supported by a three-foot square wooden stand with a diamond criss-cross design cut into the wood in front. For some reason the top of the stand has avoided being trashed and still has a nice finish and shine. Their three couches are circled around it and they're watching golf in a near catatonic state.

"You guys need to wake up," I say, stepping in front of the screen and blocking their view.

"Yeah, fuck this bullshit," Rolando says, looking up. "Life goes on. Let's go to Champions around the corner and play pool."

"But they don't have hard alcohol," I say.

"Don't worry," Rolando says. "We go there all the time. They won't bother you if you're with us."

"We'll get you in with your pink cup," Poppa Chulo says.

As we exit the apartment Poppa Chulo leaves the front doors wide open.

"Hey, aren't you going to close the doors?" I ask.

"Nah,' Poppa Chulo says. The neighbors know to not mess with the apartment. Besides what are they gonna steal?"

I can't argue with Chulo logic so we pile into Rolando's old light blue Camaro that has faded almost to gray. Poppa Chulo climbs in the back seat and I grab shotgun on the torn-up seats and we head to Champions around the corner in a strip mall next to a pizza joint. I make a big rooster in the parking lot and follow Rolando and Poppa Chulo to the front door.

"What's in the cup?" a big, fortyish brown-haired bouncer says.

"Just Gatorade," I say.

"Don't worry about it, Daryl," Rolando says, "He's with us."

The door man shrugs and motions me in and I follow Rolando and Poppa Chulo to a bar in the back and sit down on a stool. It's against a wooden wall that goes halfway up to the ceiling with windows the rest of the way up. You can see the neighborhood through the glass and it gives the place a homey feel. The regulars are sitting around smoking and guzzling beer in their Dickies pants and blue-collar shirts with their names embroidered on their front pockets. They sip their beers with bored looks on their faces, staring off into oblivion and talking about their wives and fucked-up lives.

Rolando and Poppa Chulo start a pool game while I sit on my stool and take in the surroundings. As the pool balls drop and my drink gets lower the plastic cup gets colder as there is less liquid to insulate my hand from the ice cubes. I look at the unshaven drinkers around me, sipping slowly and trying to hold onto their buzzes as long as possible. They're here to get numb. They never pay attention to their surroundings but I always watch for trouble around me.

Several of them flap their gums to each other non-stop even though they're drinking, which means they're on a roll. They talk about nothing as if it's the most important thing in the world. It's early afternoon when I get there but I keep drinking and mixing roosters in the parking lot as the sun goes down. Soon, I've been there for a few hours watching Rolando and Poppa Chulo shoot pool.

My buzz is as bright as a heavily decorated Christmas tree and with no presents to open I've finally had enough.

"Let's go," I say to them.

They shrug and give up the table and we leave the familiarity of the corner bar and go outside. I'm hungry so we go to the pizza place next door and get a couple of slices each. I power mine down after heaping on the parmesan cheese and get some hot oil on my face, which pisses me off.

"Let's get the fuck outta here," I say, wiping my face."

We walk out the glass doors, across the strip mall parking lot, and pile into Rolando's beaten-up Camaro, the chariot that brought us to Champions. As I refresh my rooster Rolando turns the key and the gray ghost fires up, sending evil snorting out of the exhaust. My buzz is full and strong and I take a long sip then remove the top of my cup. My nectar is now down to three-fourths of the cup so it won't spill.

"Let's go to The Joint," Rolando says, backing out of the parking space.

"No way, man," I say. "That is not a place I want to go to."

"No, Walt," Rolando says. "It's cool. I know everyone there."

"I'm not going there," I say. "Some hippie guy is the owner. His brother races offshore powerboats with Coby. I don't like the guys Coby hangs around with."

"Relax, Walt," Coby insists. "It's the closest place to get drinks. It'll be okay."

I shrug and the Camaro rumbles across town the short distance to The Joint. I'm down to a quarter cup as Rolando pulls into a shithole parking lot in front of an old single-story tilt-up building filled with closed single-bay auto repair shops. The steel roll-up garage doors rattle back and forth from the wind gusts of the cars that pass by. They all have dirty paint, covered in grease, with catchy business names stenciled on in peeling letters. We pass the Grease Monkey garage with a hand-drawn picture of an ape on the industrial roll-up garage door and park in front of the plain wall at the end with "The Joint" written on it.

"Rolando," I say, as he turns off the engine, "I really don't want to go in there."

"Don't worry," Rolando replies. "It's just a few drinks. I'll take care of anyone who messes with you. You'll be okay."

We get out of the car and walk towards the double steel doors at the entrance. I take hit a from my pink cup and there is nearly no ice or mixer, just pure Stoli. The dark entrance looks like church doors to me, inviting me inside to atone for my sins, or perhaps to deliver judgment on others for theirs. I'm keyed up as I walk through the doors. I've been watching low-life scumbags at Champions all day and know that I'm overdue for the trouble that always seems to find me.

I pass between the doors, take a big swig, and walk into the dim light. As the scumbags inside come into focus an uncontrollable smile comes over my face. One of these idiots just might want to play. I hold onto my pink cup like a little kid holding onto his float when he goes swimming. As I walk deeper into the bar, the rods and cones in my eyes adjust and it brightens. I've seen this place many times before even though I've never been here. There are no windows and bricks fill up the recess where the old service doors used to be. I hide my pink cup behind me and walk to the bar. It's in the shape of an L and made of dirty butcher-block wood. The stools have black vinyl tops with stainless steel legs. Rolando, Poppa Chulo and I settle into stools next to each other and I take a shot from my pink cup. The bar maid is on a raised platform so you can look at her bikini-clad body. The cheesy bitch dances around the beer spigots then walks up to us.

"You studs want a beer?" she asks.

Rolando and Poppa Chulo each order one and she looks at me expectantly.

"I'm fine," I say. "I'm just drinking Gatorade." I flash my pink cup and take a swig, which is enough to make her turn away.

I look down the front of the 40-foot-long bar and see a bunch of regulars at the end, leaning over the top as if they owned the place. They look my way like they know who I am. This is a real shithole; the kind of bar in Happening Beach where scumbags like these would know beggars who have received justice at my hands.

As we sit at the short L section of the bar it reminds me of the hotel hallway in North Carolina where I stayed for the NHB. At the far end of the room there's a long-haired hippie sitting next to a fat barfly bitch. Behind them are two pool tables in the darkest part of this dive bar. The eight locals across from them all have faces that I can read like the morning newspaper. Every time I look their way they quickly stare down at their drinks.

The hippie with the barfly bitch is dressed in dirty board shorts, a ragged yellow surfing tee-shirt, and flip flops. The skank with him is wearing blue jeans with a tight, white tank top that shows the fat flowing over her waistband. She's got big breasts and a belly to match from spending too much time in dives like this, sucking drinks. The jukebox beside the hippie and the fat barfly is playing a Social Distortion song.

Rolando and Poppa Chulo get about half their beers down when Poppa Chulo's brother, Pedro, walks in. We started college at Wong Beach State the same time but he's not a true street warrior so I rarely see him. He orders a beer for himself and we all decide to play some pool. The tables are empty so we grab some seats around them and start playing. The locals at the far end are still looking away every time I glance at them and the hippie and the fat barfly are in their own world. Even though they seem to know who I am there are no danger signs and the surroundings seem to be safe.

"What happened to that fight show?" Pedro asks me while he is racking up the balls.

"I scared them and they canned me," I say. "I guess they don't want real warriors."

"What are you going to do now?" Pedro asks.

"I don't know," I say. "I've got to figure my next move. I got my degree, now I have to use it."

"That's awesome you graduated," Pedro says. "I dropped out and I'm working at a grocery store now. It's union so it pays pretty well."

"Yeah, but you have to love what you do and not just do something for money," I say. "My life has caught up with me. I have to grow up and man up. I just don't know what direction to take."

"Yeah, dude," Pedro says. "Life is fucking hard."

We play cutthroat and all the balls drop out of the pay-to-play pool table with Poppa Chulo winning, and we walk back to our stools at the bar. The other three order more beers and I go outside, make a freshy, and return. The locals are still chatting it up and the hippie and the fat barfly are making out in the corner. The deserted pool tables look like dark, empty coffins with their black felt sucking in all available light like a black hole. With no balls dropping and no music now playing the bar is a quiet as a desert ghost town at high noon.

When I first got there the bar seemed to be full of a bunch or hardworking guys talking shop. But as time passes, I can see the mood change as they start to get drunk. They are looking over at me now with harder expressions on their faces. But my looks at them are getting harder also. They still aren't man enough to hold my gaze for longer than a second or two, though, before looking away. They're just a bunch of nobodies. One of the locals says something to the hippie and the fat barfly and they break their embrace and both look over at me.

I'm the only one who has noticed what is going on, though. Poppa Chulo and Pedro are sitting by the pool tables, clueless, and Rolando is beside me sipping his drink as if he didn't have a care in the world. I slide behind Rolando's stool and put him in a chokehold, sliding my left arm under his chin, grabbing the top of my elbow with my right arm, and squeezing. As he starts to laugh, I glance down the bar at the locals who are looking over with scowls. I release the hold and put my mouth next to Rolando's ear.

"Watch yourself, man," I say. "There's some shit about to go down."

26. Swing and a Hit

The mood has changed and the hippie has had enough to drink that he now has that look in his eyes that I know all too well. It's like a cold breeze you first feel when you're a child without a jacket. It's almost like he doesn't know it, but I do and I'm waiting.

"Don't look at my girl, asshole," the hippie finally says loudly.

I wondered what the locals were saying to him and now I know. I'm not in the mood to be bullied over something I didn't do and he's in danger of paying the price. His eyes are heavy and half-closed from too much to drink but I have heavy and dark thoughts.

"Hey!" he yells out. "Did you hear me, asshole?"

The silence is heavy in the bar as I stare straight ahead. "What the fuck are you talking about," I say. "Why would I look at a fat skank like her?"

It can't be the first time that Miss Nightmare has heard those words but nevertheless she gasps at the insult like she was the Virgin Mary. The hippie gets halfway out of his chair and I have a good look at him. He looks about the same age as me and his hair is straight and hangs to the middle of his back, brown and ready to be pulled off his head. A pencil neck holds up a head that is mounted above bird shoulders. I'm a primed fighting machine while this hippie with a big mouth and ugly girlfriend is a wooden toothpick. I'm the sharpest knife in the drawer and he's going to be carved up and put into the wood chipper if he keeps it up. The bar maid turns around and looks at me and I start laughing. Poppa Chulo and Rolando trade glances as if they can smell what's coming.

"Shut your mouth, you fucking redneck," the hippie says. "I know the guy who owns this place. I'll get your ass kicked out."

"Maybe I'll just kick your ass instead," I yell, getting off my stool. "I hate fucking hippies. I was punk rock when it meant something, you Motley Crue wannabe fuckwad. I will fuck you up with interest. You don't have any fucking idea. I never forget and I always get even. Fuck with me when I was a little kid and I'll pay you back 20 years later. Just because your hair is long you think that makes you a badass? I'll cut it all off with a pair of toenail clippers. I'm Walter Foxx and you can tell the owner right now that I hate loudmouthed hippies!"

"The owner actually isn't here now," the bar maid says to me.

"Good," I yell. "Because I'd cut his hair off, too."

Poppa Chulo is getting tense in his chair, ready to jump in if the shit hits the fan, while Pedro has a look of sheer terror on his face and is backing towards the door. He's such a pussy that it's hard to believe that he and Poppa Chulo have the same parents. Rolando is sitting at the bar staring at his beer, as if this was an everyday occurrence that doesn't merit his attention. Finally, his head pops up and he looks over.

"What's up, Walt?" Rolando asks.

"Nothing," I say. "Just having a little fun with a beggar."

The rat ass hippie is looking at me hard, staring his way into a beating. I see him clearly as he tries to show off for the fat barfly. But I definitely don't like to be stared at. It's a form of intimidation and I will not let anyone punk me.

"Keep staring at me, fucker," I yell across the bar. "I've given you a warning and I'll bash your long-haired head in."

The bar is like a fire pit, and the more I stir the logs the brighter the embers will get. The hippie hasn't taken his eyes off me for a couple of minutes and his face is just begging to be hit. I can't go off on him because I don't want to go to jail but my patience is wearing thin.

"What the fuck is that hippie looking at, Rolando?" I ask.

Rolando just shrugs and stares into his beer but I'm extremely pissed. My neck feels like I've done a set of bridges on the mat. The muscles on the back of my neck are as tight as a drum. It's like all these Motley Crue hippies forgot how punk rock made them obsolete. He's just another dumb fuck who thinks song lyrics are true and having long hair gives you some kind of mystical power. As I continue my stare down with this guy who looks like a girl my blood pressure climbs higher and my heart races. He doesn't know that he's in my crosshairs and on my radar screen. My internal sensible self is telling me: *Don't do it. You'll go to State Prison.* But my ass-kicking self is telling me: *Be yourself and let the chips fall where they may.*

"You want some?" the stupid hippie says. "I'll give you some."

"Step over here," I say. "I hope that skank is worth a beating."

He's on the end of the L-shaped bar with his fat barfly girlfriend. The pool table area behind them is as empty as his eyes, only illuminated by the dim overhead lights and the flashing jukebox.

"Come get some, fatso," he says.

We look at each other, neither one of us making the first move. This guy is giving me the key to a prison cell for a long time. My eyes lower as I envision the spring on a rat trap closing over me. Sound echoes as the steel rips into the wood and crushes the rat. But there will be no furry rat to throw away, only me. I want to crush this fucker but instead I look away. *It's your lucky day you stringy-haired hippie. I never swing first.* I look at him like a nice juicy fruit that I want to take a bite from. And the more I look at him the harder he stares back at me. I can't let him off the hook. Justice demands retribution. I turn and look at Rolando next to me.

"I need you to kill this hippie fucker," I say.

"Just calm down," Rolando says. "He's all talk."

"I can't be good anymore," I say, "but you have to do it for me. If I get another assault conviction I'm going to prison. I want to rip this long-haired fucker apart with my bare hands but if I do, I will fuck up my life worse than it already is. I can't do ten years behind bars. Once I go in, I'll never get out."

"Forget it, Walt," Rolando says.

I take a swig off my pink cup as the jukebox comes to life and plays "Brown Sugar" by the Stones. I look over at the hippie and he sticks his middle finger in the air and flips me off. The locals in the bar behind him all laugh. *Fuck it.* I start to move towards him but Rolando grabs my arm.

"Don't do it, Walt," Rolando says.

"You have to protect your boyfriend?" the hippie sneers at Rolando, staring at him hard and giving him the finger now.

Rolando instantly forgets me and releases my arm and looks at this fuck. "Don't start in on me, motherfucker," he says. "I was just trying to save your sorry ass."

"How about you kiss my ass instead," the hippie tells him.

The hippie's mouth has worked on Rolando far better than my words. Rolando gets off his stool and walks towards him. The hippie is a skinny 6'2" tall and thinks he can easily beat Rolando at 5'10". But he doesn't know that Rolando was an all-American wrestler at Husker A&M. Rolando stops in front of the hippie and sizes him up.

"What the fuck is your problem?" Rolando says. "Quit mad-dogging us. Nobody wants your fat skank girlfriend."

A nervous look comes over his face as Rolando stares him down. He looks down and puts his hands to his side. It looks like this stand-off has come to an end. Pedro and I are sitting on our stools with Poppa Chulo standing. It looks like he wanted to take things to the last second before backing down. The locals are watching but don't seem to care about backing him up.

"Fuck you, asshole!" a high-pitched voice screeches out over the jukebox music.

From out of nowhere the fat barfly girl flies in from behind her boyfriend and gets in Rolando's face, waving her arms like a madwoman. The hippie is so surprised that he actually takes a step backwards away from Rolando. As she squares up in front of Rolando, Poppa Chulo and I move forward and Pedro moves back towards the door. Rolando tries to turn away from her but the fat bitch moves with him, keeping in his face.

"I'm not a skank," she screams. "But you're a low-life scum!"

She raises her hand to slap Rolando but he grabs her wrist with his left hand, puts his right palm on her face, slips his foot behind her ankle, and pushes her face backwards, sweeping her feet from under her. She spins like a propeller to the bar floor and hits with a loud crash in front of the pool tables. The hippie steps back and bends over to check on her. I turn to check on the locals just as a black flash races between me and Poppa Chulo and spears Rolando in the back with his shoulder.

A black guy has made it through the barrier that Poppa Chulo and I set up to shield Rolando from the locals and tackled Rolando. They land on the pool table and then tumble to the floor.

"Let it go!" I scream out, spreading my arms wide.

I'm not worried about Rolando. He's an All-American wrestler from Husker A&M and can handle himself. The black guy is on top of him as they drop to the bar floor as the locals look on, afraid to do anything. Besides, it looks like the Black Flash is winning because he's on top. I know the situation will change quickly, though, because Rolando has been training with me on top of him for the last couple of months and knows all the reversals.

The hippie and the fat barfly move behind the pool table and after a few seconds the black guy goes flying off Rolando into the air. He falls to Rolando's side and Rolando swishers his hips, goes on top with his legs straddling the guy's chest, and lets the dogs loose on the Black Flash. He's now getting paid back for his sucker maneuver as Rolando lands shot after shot to his face.

His local bar buddies are too afraid to get involved with me and Poppa Chulo watching intently. The Black Flash goes limp as Rolando puts him on Queer Street and I know it's time to stop him. I don't want Rolando to hurt this guy seriously and get into trouble so I grab him from behind and pull him off.

"Rolando," I yell. "It's me. You got him good. Let's go!"

I've got my arms under Rolando's armpits, pulling him backwards towards the front door. We have to leave. I can't do this anymore and get into trouble. Rolando has his arms up to protect himself in case we get jumped. I have my arms under Rolando's armpits and I'm watching everyone in front of us. If they make one wrong move, I'll let him go and start to blast. It looks like we're going to get out without any more trouble.

A loud crack suddenly echoes through my head and a bright light flashes in my eyes. My arms go numb and then limp as I drop Rolando to the floor and stagger down to one knee. *What the fuck was that?* I fight to remain conscious as darkness swirls around me. I glance behind me and through a fog see the end of a broken pool cue lying on the floor. Beside it is a pair of low-cut leather boots with dark, blue, work slacks hanging over them.

My eyes travel upwards past the pants to a blue-collared shirt draped over a 5'10" 200 lb. muscular young guy. He has short brown hair and is clean shaven but his face is dirty and he's wearing a goofy corduroy baseball cap that seems out of place on him. His right hand is squeezing the small end of a broken pool cue.

My pain-shocked brain fights to make sense of these inputs and I think back to the light flash. I focus on his eyes and they look familiar. They're the same eyes from the back of the church when the cop's son sucker punched me and started me on my downward spiral. These are the eyes that all the posers and scumbags have. As my head spins and I try to stay conscious, I realize what happened: this fucker cracked me from behind with a pool cue when my back was turned. I try to get to my feet but his hand raises up again with the pool cue. I know that if this blow lands it just might be the end for me. I tuck my chin in and brace myself for the killing blow.

27. Parking Lot Payback

As his hand starts to come down with the pool cue, I lunge forward and wrap my arms around him, causing the blow to glance off my shoulder and miss my head. Now that my arms are around him, I'm too close for him to swing the cue with any force. Now he's in my world and will pay for his cowardice. Justice is mine and I will repay. I squeeze him like a polar bear squashing a seal in the arctic. He is helplessly wrapped up with no way to escape. His feet leave the floor as I lift him up and consider his punishment. His legs are dangling beneath me and moving in the air as he searches for traction.

I head towards the front doors keeping him firmly in my grasp. This coward has to pay for his blatant disrespect. He tried to kill me by hitting me with a pool cue from behind but I will pay him back man-to-man. I know there are security cameras inside; I spotted them when we first walked in. I decide to take him outside with me where no one can see the polar bear eat the seal for dinner. I'm back out of the front doors that I came in; the same doors I didn't want to enter in the first place for fear of becoming the Walter of old.

As I back out with this beggar wrapped up tight to execute his sentence, his arms wriggle and move, grasping and reaching out for anything to hold onto to stop where he is going. His fingers latch onto the edge of the door near the hinges. I back through it and he holds on for dear life. His eyes look like they did when he stood in front of me swinging the pool cue and are the same ones I saw at the church when my life started going downhill. I loosen my bear hug and begin to shake him, sliding my arms from his chest to his knees

His arms are fully extended now and his body is parallel to the floor. I pull with all my might to pry him loose and my hands go from his knees to his ankles, just below the bottom of his blue work pants. I'm pulling so hard that I think the door frame will pop out but he still won't budge. I trap his boots with my biceps and begin to him whip back and forth, letting his body go slack like a rope and then pulling it tight like a guitar string. I'm having no luck breaking his grip so I release my biceps lock on his ankles.

I put my left palm on top of his left boot, and grab his left heel with my right hand, leaving his left foot jitterbugging on the ground. I take a deep breath and begin to twist his foot. A smile comes over my face as he screams loudly. The first three inches twist easily but then I meet resistance as his knee joint locks. I put some muscle into it, twisting counterclockwise harder and winding the clock back in time. His hands are still holding onto the door frame as his body goes up and down like a wave as I simultaneously twist and pull his leg. No matter how hard I pull, though, he won't let go. I put my weight on my left foot, lift my right foot up, and kick the steel-toe of my Doc Martens boot onto the knee joint of the leg I've been pulling on.

With a loud scream his body goes limp, his fingers release the door frame, and his body drops to the floor. The seal knows that he's going to get eaten by the polar bear. I drag this guy who just tried to kill me out the door by his dirty work boots to his date with justice. This is a place that I didn't want to go but fate has forced this situation on me and told me this is who I am. As his

300

screams get louder my smile gets bigger, I drag this head-bashing-from-behind coward across the asphalt parking lot.

It's time to pay you back for trying to kill me from behind for no reason. The song of justice sings in my head as his screams of fear and agony sing through the cold night air. The chrome grills of the old cars reflect light from The Joint sign into his face. I pull him down two parking spaces into an empty spot that fate has reserved for me. I sandwich him between the curb and the cement parking bumper that sticks out of the asphalt like a tombstone. His screams stop as he pretends to be unconscious or dead, not knowing that he might not need to pretend soon.

The cement curb and bumper have formed a frame for this fuck. He is going to be a piece of art inside the frame and I am going to be the artist of this trash-filled, motor-oil stained parking lot. When I let go of his boot he rolls over onto his stomach and presses his face into the filthy asphalt. As I get ready to bounce his head into a million pieces Rolando runs up with the fat end of the broken pool cue in his hand.

"This fucker broke the cue over your head," Rolando says breathlessly.

"I know," I say. "And for no fucking reason."

He is laying belly down with his elbows in tight, covering his upper torso. His forearms and hands are next to his face and ears as he covers up like a turtle. I think for a second about how I'm going to crack this nut.

"You shouldn't have beat me over the head," I say.

I nod curtly at Rolando and then start to jump up and down on this fucker's legs while Rolando takes the pool cue that was broken over my head and beats the guy's

301

back. The sound reverberates like a pneumatic jackhammer at a construction site. The soles of my Doc Martens dig deep into the flesh of his legs, tearing the skin under his pants. Rolando pauses after a minute and makes eye contact with me, raising an eyebrow in a questioning look.

"Hit this motherfucker harder!" I yell.

We start in again and this idiot gives up his silence and starts squealing like a rabbit being attacked by coyotes in the Malibu hills. After a minute he can't take the pain he begged for and rolls over, trying to block the pool cue with his arms. Rolando pauses to take aim, feints once to move his arms out of the way, and then whistles the pool cue down directly on his face, breaking his nose and sending blood exploding in all directions. His head bounces off the cement bumper and settles motionless to the asphalt.

"He'll have a headache tomorrow," Rolando says.

"Yeah, you knocked him out," I say. "He got what he deserved. Get your car and get the fuck outta here. I'll get Poppa Chulo and Pedro."

Rolando runs across the parking lot to his Camaro and flips the license plate down like he is getting gas, hiding the numbers and leaving the gas cap exposed. He jumps into the driver's seat, burns his tires in reverse then shifts into first and races away from the scene. I run back through the front doors of The Joint and see Poppa Chulo just inside the entryway, keeping back the locals who are staring curiously through the door. Pedro is standing off to the side with a terrified look on his face.

"Let's get out of here!" I yell.

Pedro makes a break for the door and scurries away like a rat while Poppa Chulo holds his position at the door, jostling with the locals, who don't seem to know what they want to do. I grab the back of Poppa Chulo's shirt and yank him towards me. I know the cops have to be on their way.

"Let's go!" I order.

Poppa Chulo backs towards the door while I keep watch to make sure no more evil comes out of the shadows. In the back of my mind I know the demon that tried to kill me from behind has been taken care of and is lying in the parking lot. The black double steel door rattles as it shuts behind us. As we hurry through the parking lot the masterpiece of my payback is now conscious, framed by the parking lot bumpers and black asphalt canvas with blood red as the primary color.

His arms are pulled underneath him and he is resting on his elbows with his forearms flat on the asphalt. His head and upper body are propped up and his head is on a swivel, moving back and forth, trying to shake the blood off his face and understand what happened. I slow from my hurried pace as I come upon him. *What happened is that you tried to kill me from behind with a pool cue across the back of my head.* As the blood falls from his face he looks to be fucked up good.

"What did you do to him?" Poppa Chulo asks.

"This is the guy who tried to kill me," I say. "He deserved everything he begged for." We start to walk away but the guy's voice stops me.

"Fuck you, motherfucker," he says.

I stop, take a step back and look at him, and have a flashback to that fateful night when the cop's son hit me at the church.

The guy has a smart-ass grin on his bloody face and rolls to his side, going for his back pocket where I can see the outline of a folded knife.

I raise my heavy Doc Marten boot off the asphalt and kick him in the face, the weight of my boot impacting his sensory window to the world. His eyes go blank and blood flies from his nostrils, spraying across the parking lot. My Doc Marten has found its mark and this fuck has been kissed by the metal eyelets. I punt his face again and his teeth fly out of his mouth like popcorn from the machine at the movie theater. I can finally relax. My life is not threatened anymore. These drunk morons were actually trying to murder me. We spin away to get into Pedro's jeep but only see his tail lights as he drives away from us into the night, leaving us to fend for ourselves in order to save his own ass. Poppa Chulo stands there open-mouthed as if he can't process what his brother just did but I grab and shake him.

"We're on our own," I say. "We're in shape. Let's run to your apartment."

Poppa Chulo and I leave the parking lot in full stride, running at a hard pace away from the commercial buildings to the apartment area that Poppa Chulo lives in. As we clear the area around The Joint I start to laugh.

"Poppa," I say. That fucking guy got just what he begged for." With each stride to Poppa Chulo's apartment the side of my head hurts more and more. "Did you see that guy's teeth fly everywhere?" I ask.

"Yeah, Walt, that was crazy," Poppa Chulo says.

"I hope the cops aren't at your apartment," I say. "You know they're probably looking for us by now."

We increase the pace and run the two miles back to the apartment in short order. Pedro's Jeep is out front. He could have given us a ride but he took off and left us. He's not like us; he's a frightened coward. Poppa Chulo and I walk in the door and see Rolando standing by the window, looking out the curtains. Pedro is nowhere to be seen.

"Fuck," Rolando says. "I thought the cops would be here by now. You think they know who we are?"

"Fuck, yeah," I say. "You go there all the time."

Rolando turns away from the windows and comes over and looks at my head. "You're all fucked up," he says.

"What?" I say.

"You have a bump the size of an egg on the side of your head," Rolando says. "Right above your ear. It's fucking huge."

I walk across the living room and look in the mirror behind the cheap bar and see a giant bulge on the right side of my head from where that idiot hit me from behind with the pool cue. As my buzz wears off, I realize that I can't go on living like this anymore. It's just a matter of time until I get pushed into a situation that I can't walk away from. If that moron had gotten to his knife I wouldn't be standing here now. As my buzz dies down the pain gets sharper and I realize my head is killing me.

"Walt, that was crazy!" Poppa Chulo says, coming over to me.

"Why do you say that?" I ask.

"When that guy broke the pool cue over your head it sounded like a stick of dynamite going off. It was so fucking loud the whole bar echoed."

"I didn't even know what happened until I saw the guy standing over me with the broken pool cue in his hand," I say. "That was evil. That guy came out of nowhere. I've got to get home while I can still drive."

I half-stagger out to my truck and drive slowly towards my parents' garage where it's dark and cool. As I pull onto their street after getting off the freeway, I look for any black-and-whites waiting for me. I'm surprised and relieved to see that the street is quiet and empty. I park out front and make my way into the dark garage. Adolf follows me in and jumps up and his tail starts to beat on the bed. I can always depend on him being happy to see me.

I get undressed and gingerly roll into bed. Every little motion makes my head throb. I reach up to the right side of my head and touch the lump that has grown from golf-sized to softball-sized. I turn onto my left side and close my eyes, surprised that I can drift off to sleep with my head throbbing badly.

28. Shakedown Street

Beep! Beep! Beep!

"Ah, fuck," I say groggily. "Not today."

Adolf looks up to make sure I'm not talking to him then lays his head down and closes his eyes. I slam down the snooze button and nine minutes go by before the alarm clock starts beeping again. I smash the button down and roll out of bed, eliciting an unhappy growl from Adolf. I've got to get up and go to work. This everyday bullshit is driving me crazy. I walk into the kitchen and my mom is there, spreading peanut butter on toasted bread.

"Morning, Mom," I say.

She looks up and starts to smile at me and then sees my head and frowns. "What happened to you?"

"Nothing, Mom," I say. "Just a little accident. But if the cops come looking for me tell them that I don't live here."

I walk down the hallway to the shower wondering why they haven't shown up yet. There were so many people at The Joint that I can't believe no one identified me. I take a long hot shower and the water feels like rocks when it falls on my head. I get out and dry off and take a long, hard look in the mirror. It takes me a while to focus my blurry vision but the softball-sized swollen bump finally comes into view, as does my memory of last night's events.

The bump on my head is bright red and huge. That fuck really did try to kill me. I have a knot in my stomach as I think about the cops showing up at my door at any

minute. *Is this where my life is finally taking me?* My
passion has steered me in the wrong direction and I know
I'm going to prison. I fucked that guy up good; there's no
way he didn't go to the hospital. But that fucker tried to
kill me so it's a clear case of self-defense. I had to drag
him out of the bar and into the parking lot to save my
own life.

I dress quickly, get into my truck, and start driving to
the garage door office. As I make my way there, I can't
help but think how much I hate waking up to an alarm
clock. I can't live a normal life. I pull into the office
parking lot and walk down the hallway to Skip's desk.

"Hey, man," I say. "Any bids?"

"Nothing," Skip says. "Maybe in a day or two...holy
fuck! What happened to your head?"

I smile and shrug. "Slipped in the bathtub."

Skip smiles back. "Yeah. Got ya."

"Okay," I say. "I'm outta here. If Fred asks tell him
I'm hurt."

I leave the office and cruise home where I pick up
Adolf and go to the store for a supply run. I make a
traveler in the parking lot, take the top off, and head out
to Rolando's and Poppa Chulo's street. I'm half
expecting the cops to be there but as I turn the corner all
is quiet. It's almost eerie how peaceful it is. That guy got
fucked up bad but yet I haven't seen one cop. It's really
weird. I walk in the unlocked front door and Rolando and
Poppa Chulo are in the same positions I left them in last
night, each lying on their own couch.

"Where are the cops?" I ask. "They didn't come by
my house last night."

"Not here, either," Poppa Chulo says. "It's strange."

"You guys hang here," I say. "I'll be back in a few minutes."

"Where you going?" Rolando asks.

"To 7-11 to get a disposable camera for you guys to take pictures of my head," I say.

I get the camera and another twelver and Rolando takes a couple of shots when I get back and then we all sit around and crack soldiers.

"Fuck," Poppa Chulo says. "What are we going to do?

"Yeah, it's only a matter of time before the cops show," Rolando adds.

"Look," I say. "The guy hit me with a pool cue from behind and tried to kill me. That's what everybody saw. Nobody knows what happened outside. That's why I dragged him out there. The only people who can fuck this up for us is us. If the cops show up, you guys know the drill. Do not talk to them, period. We do all our talking through lawyers. I learned my lesson."

"It's just weird they haven't been here yet," Rolando says.

"Trust me," I say. "They're coming. But we can't do anything about it so let's party."

We drink till dark and then go to this shithole bar across town. Rolando goes in first and Poppa Chulo tags along with me to a 7-11 next door to get some cranberry juice.

"Rolando is scared about last night," Poppa Chulo says as we wait in the checkout line. "He wants to go to the cops."

"Listen, Poppa," I say. "Tell Rolando to keep his mouth shut and everything will be okay. Nobody saw anything but us."

We go back to the bar and they get beers while I sip on roosters. As the night goes on a big Mexican steroid guy who works the door of this dirt bag bar pops off. He starts telling us that he was a kick-ass wrestler at Bakersfield College. I've known him for years and he always tries to scare everybody with his bullshit and his size. Even though Poppa Chulo is only the size of one of his legs he gets in his face.

"Fuck you, dumb fuck," Poppa Chulo says. "You ain't shit."

The big bullshit artist laughs and looks the other way. This big steroid goof has been banging around the wrestling rooms for years. He never wants to do takedowns even though I've asked him a hundred times. He's just a wrestling poser and I would love to tear his head off. As he starts to fire back, Rolando and I come into view and the poser realizes he'd better behave or be exposed for the phony that he is.

"Hey, guys," he says. "Everything cool? You need anything?"

"Yeah," I say, walking past him towards the door, "for you to shut up."

We leave and climb into Rolando's Camaro and stop at the Del Taco drive-through across the street where we order a bunch of bean and cheese burritos. When we get our food and head out, I tell Rolando it's going to get hot but to not talk to cops when they come around.

"Walt's right," Poppa Chulo says. "Nobody in The Joint saw anything. I was blocking the door."

We get to their apartment and I grab some burritos. I give Rolando one more warning to keep his mouth shut and then cruise across town in my truck towards home. As I drive, I run through different scenarios in my head. I know nobody saw anything besides that fucker hitting me in the head inside the bar. No one can testify regardless of what the guy whose ass I kicked says. As long as we don't talk everyone will be okay.

I move through the streets cautiously, the way I've been living the past few days, looking each way at every intersection for the cops. I go to the street my parents' house is on, taking the long route and driving slowly down the long road. It's so foggy my headlights barely reach the houses on either side. I strain to look to the end, where my parents' house is and my heart is pumping. This time it's not beating fast because I'm sprinting but because I'm running from the law. My thoughts are racing a mile a minute.

Are there any black-and-whites out front? I'm not even sure they're looking for me. But they can't arrest me because I didn't do anything wrong. I just reacted in self-defense. That guy tried to kill me and got what he begged for. Oh, thank god. The cops are not here.

I pull into the driveway and slip into my king-sized bed in the garage. Adolf lies on his side and happily serves as my pillow. I squeeze him to let him know that I'm not going anywhere and he groans contently as I drift into sleep with my troubled thoughts. As soon as my eyes close the alarm goes off. At first, I think I set it wrong but then I see shafts of sunlight coming through the garage door and realize it's morning.

I get up over Adolf's complaining groans and walk to the shower. As I'm going back into the garage, I hear the chain on the front door rattle and I freeze. *Oh, fuck. It's the cops.* I slowly creep around the corner and look through the green glass on top of the door. There's nothing. It's just the wind. The cops must not be looking

311

for me or they'd be here by now. The wind really starts to whip around and I can hear it loudly in the garage as I get dressed. I put on a Spooner and white jeans and head to Fred's office.

I finally have some work, which I'm glad about, because I need the money. Skip gives me the addresses for two bids and I head out on the road. I had almost expected the cops to be at the office looking for me. It's crazy that they haven't shown up with a warrant or at least to question me. Where are they? I'm sure they know who I am. I have a good day and sell both doors, which will keep me in drinking money for the next week or two. I go back and tell Skip and he's glad because that will keep Fred off my ass. I sit down at one of the desks and stare straight ahead.

"What are you thinking about, Walt?" Skip asks.

"Nothing," I say. "I just fucking can't believe my life. This guy hit me with a pool cue from behind the other night and tried to kill me. I got him back good and now I'm afraid the cops are after me and I'll go to prison."

"Fuck, Walt," Skip says. "You have a huge lump on the side of your head. It's obvious that it was self-defense."

"Yeah," I say. "But he got fucked up bad."

"If you were in trouble, the cops would be here by now," Skip reasons.

"You don't understand," I say. "It doesn't have to happen right away. It took the DA and that cop's son six months to come up with the lies to get me. If they want to get me in trouble they can. Justice in a court is a fucking joke."

My pager goes off and I stop talking to Skip and dig it out of my pocket. I look at the number and see that Coby is calling. After the fuck-up with Bart Shady he's the last person I want to talk to but I call him back anyway from the office phone.

"What's up, stoner?" I say.

"Walt, we need to talk," Coby says breathlessly. "You know the bar you were at the other night? The Joint?"

"Yeah," I say, getting a sinking feeling in the pit of my stomach.

"Well, it's owned by my boat racing buddy's brother," Coby explains.

"I know who he is," I say.

"He called me to get in touch with you," Coby continues. "He said the cops were all over his bar and they know it was you who fucked some guy up. He says that you're fucked."

"I figured that out on my own," I say. "Fuck that hippie scumbag. I don't care about him."

"Wrong," Coby says. "He says he has a video of what you did."

"I didn't hit anybody inside the bar," I say.

"Just call him," Coby insists. "He sounds serious."

Coby gives me the scumbag's number and I hang up. I have to clear my head to think. I lean back in the fabric swivel chair which creaks as the springs compress. Thoughts race in my head as my feet leave the blue carpeted floor. As they dangle in the air, I start to circle my feet endlessly as if I'm running in place and can't get any traction. I'm close to the floor but yet I can't touch it. It seems like everything in life is just beyond my reach.

"I am so fucked, Skip," I say finally. "Coby says the jackass who owns the bar is the brother of his boat racing friend. He says the cops are all over and he has a video of me beating this fuck up but I didn't do anything. But if I just get accused and arrested that could be enough to send me to prison. He wants me to call him. This is getting crazy."

There's nothing for Skip to say so I take the number and walk out of the office. It seems that I'm going to find my destiny after all. As hard as I try to hide from it, I just can't escape. I fire up my truck and drive over to Coby's office, feeling like I did when I was at the halfway house. I make it down the cul-de-sac and go in the front door and back to his office. Coby is sitting in his usual state: legs crossed on his desk, eyelids closed, and stoned out of his mind. His eyes open and his legs go off his desk when I walk in.

"What the fuck is that little fucker saying?" I ask angrily.

"Dude," Coby says. 'He says he has you on video tape."

"Fuck him!" I say, my temper exploding. "Listen up good. You tell him that I'm not playing games. I'll hurt that wannabe boat racing star so bad he won't be able to steer a rowboat."

"Calm down, Walt," Coby says. "He's not a boat racer. He's the brother of a friend I race with."

"Well, he doesn't know who he's fucking with," I say.

"I told him," Coby says. "But he says he has you on video tape and he wants you to call him. He has cameras everywhere."

"Fuck it," I say. "Dial this fuck's number. If he gets me in serious trouble, I've got a right cross with his name on it."

Coby dials and then presses a button to activate the speakerphone. A thin voice answers on the other end and says hello.

"Hey, Brad," Coby says. "It's me. I've got Walt here on speakerphone."

"Tell that punk to listen good," Brad whines over the speaker. "Can he hear me?"

"Yeah," Coby answers.

Just from his voice I can tell he's a typical little dog, trying to bark and make noises like a pit bull. He's a tough guy over the phone or behind a desk but a coward face-to-face. I raise my eyes at Coby but his eyes are glazed and there's nothing behind them but pot smoke.

"I've got you on video, punk," Brad continues. "But lucky for you I don't like pigs. Never have. Do you know what you did? You dragged a guy out of my bar kicking and screaming and beat him within one inch of his life. Lucky for you I took down the camera outside before the cops came, otherwise you'd already be in jail. But I have the tape. If you don't want to go to prison you need to give me one thousand dollars to keep it out of the hands of the cops."

"All I did was defend myself after a scumbag hit me from behind with a pool cue. I didn't start anything," I say.

"I don't know how you remember it but the video says otherwise," Brad continues. "I can tell the cops what was on it. You'll get eaten alive in court. When you're in Chino all the gangs in there will have your ass on a platter. I'm giving you a chance to make it all go away."

I roll my eyes at Coby. This fuck definitely doesn't know who I am. If I go to prison, I will own the place but I definitely don't want to be there.

"Okay," I say. "I'll see you tomorrow around noon at The Joint."

"Alright, punk," Brad says in his best Clint Eastwood wannabe voice that he figures will make me quiver in fear. "Don't forget the cash."

Coby pushes the hang-up button and the speaker falls silent as he falls back into his chair.

"Coby," I say. "Who the fuck is this moron?"

"I do some gardening business with him," Coby says vaguely.

I say nothing but it figures. I can tell by his voice on the phone that he's a little bitch with drug connections; someone that Coby would definitely hang with.

"Are you mad at me, Walt?" Coby says.

"Not you," I reply. "I'll get this poser in the end like everyone else. Eventually I get all the scumbags. It's up to him how bad he gets it. But I can tell you right now that I wouldn't want to be him."

"What are you going to do?" Coby asks.

"I don't think he has a tape," I reply, "but he has me by the balls. I don't care if he doesn't have it because if I give him the grand then I'll have the bar employees on my side. Fuck! I've got to find someplace to think."

As I leave the office I look back over my shoulder and see Coby return to the same position he was in when I first came in: legs crossed on top of the desk, eyelids down, and face frozen and glazed over. As I close his office door, I'm mad as hell but I can't help but laugh about how fucked up my life is.

First, I go to jail for something I didn't do, then I get kicked out of the NHB for no reason, and now I'm being extorted in order to stay out of prison. Around every corner, things just seem to pile up on me. I might show up tomorrow with the money, or I might show up with bad intentions. Either way, I know that I'm not going to prison and will do whatever it takes to stay out. I may be going down, but it'll be in a blaze of glory that the whole world will remember.

The adventures of no-holds-barred fighter Walter Foxx that began in book one, *Bar Brawler*, are continued in book three, *Cage Fighter*, of the *Befor There Were Rules* trilogy.

Visit Tank.Abbott on www.instagram for the latest *Befor There Were Rules* news and information.

available at www.amazon.com

Made in the USA
Columbia, SC
06 April 2023

14910608R00193